SUNBURN

"A delight from page one with its perfect-pitch dialogue, memorable characters and flashy, funny story line ... from first page to last *Sunburn* charms."

Miami Herald

" 'I got regrets like Heinz got beans' says Vincente Delgatto, an aging Mafia Godfather, at the opening of Laurence Shames's engaging new novel. The results are arresting and ... the Florida scenery comes to life"

New York Times

"The continually entertaining Laurence Shames reintroduces the dysfunctional Delgatto crime family in Key West. Well imagined and extremely enjoyable. Delightful."

Chicago Tribune

"Mix sharp humour, compulsive tight plots and the heat of Florida together and think of Laurence Shames ... here is an American crime writer with style, wit and suspense."

Today

"Shames makes funny with Mafia phonetics and the vanities of old *Capos* grown frail. Despite a cast of so many aged, the plot starts jumping like it's on speed when a Godfather, holidaying in Key West, decides to dump a lifetime's secrets onto a ghost writer, to the consternation of the FBI and mobsters."

Guardian

Laurence Shames is the author of *Florida Straits, Scavenger Reef* and *Sunburn*. He divides his time between home in Key West, Florida, and Shelter Island, New York.

LAURENCE SHAMES

SUNBURN

PAN BOOKS

First published 1995 by Hyperion, New York

First published in Great Britian 1995 by Macmillan

This edition published 1996 by Pan Books
an imprint of Macmillan General Books
25 Eccleston Place, London SW1W 9NF
and Basingstoke

Associated companies throughout the world

ISBN 0 330 34356 4

1 3 5 7 9 8 6 4 2

A CIP catalogue record for this book is available from
the British Library.

Phototypeset by Intype London Ltd
Printed and bound in Great Britain

To my mother, for making me romantic
To my father, for teaching me how to tell a joke

ACKNOWLEDGMENTS

Deep thanks to Brian DeFiore, an editor of such uncanny instincts that his letters to authors should be gathered as a text. Gratitude to my friend and agent, Stuart Krichevsky, for taking the enlightened position that just because I'm doing exactly what I want to do, that doesn't mean I shouldn't get paid for it. And love to my life's true ally, Marilyn Staruch, who said one night at dinner, as the wine was moving sadly toward the bottom of the bottle, *What if Bert goes to New York?* . . .

PART ONE

CHAPTER ONE

"REGRETS?" SAID Vincente Delgatto. "Shit yeah, I got regrets. I got regrets like Heinz got beans."

The old man pushed some air past his pale gums and espresso-stained teeth. The sound that came out wasn't a sigh exactly, wasn't a laugh, was more like a half-resigned grunt that had kept an edge to it, a hiss. He reached up to straighten his tie. This was an old habit, a gesture that helped his composure and helped the transition from one thought to the next; his hands were almost to his throat before he remembered he wasn't wearing a tie.

He was sitting poolside in Key West, at the home of his bastard son, Joey Goldman. It was January, twilight, 77 degrees. A breeze was moving the palms, the fronds made a dry rattle, like maracas. It was not an American sound, this rhythmic scratching, it was an island sound, Caribbean, it made Vincente think of Havana in the old days, of smoky New York nightclubs back when Latin was the modern thing and women wore pointy brassieres and hats with fruit. For a moment he saw himself as a young man, dapper, limber, doing the rhumba with his long-dead favorite mistress, Joey's mother.

"Shit yeah," he repeated, "I got regrets."

He took a sip of wine, looked off at the green sky to the west. Back home in Queens, the sky never looked like that—green, yellow, with pink spikes sticking up like the crown of the Statue of Liberty.

"But ya know," he resumed, "it's funny: in songs, inna movies, there's always some old guy, he's washed up, a has-been, he's got no hair, no teeth, he's wearing rubber underpants, and he's bragging about how he doesn't regret nothing, if he had it all to do over, he'd do it exactly the same. It's like . . . like a whaddyacallit—"

"A cliché?" put in Sandra Dugan, Joey's wife.

"Yeah, Sandra, thank you. A cliché. Like this is what an old fart automatically says. But come on. Ya live to be seventy, eighty years old, and wit' all the millions a chances ya get to fuck things up—'scuse my language, Sandra—you'd do it all the same?"

"Some people," Joey said, "maybe they would."

"Bullshit," said his father. "There's only two reasons why a person would say that. One, he's so pigheaded he can't admit he made a mistake. Or two, he's so feeble inna head, his memory is so shot, he really can't remember what he did or shoulda did. Me, I remember. For better or worse, I remember."

"Right, Pop," Joey Goldman said. "And this is why I'm telling ya: Write it down."

The old man was shaking his head almost before his son had started to speak. He had a long face, Vincente did, with a big bridgeless nose and full lips that looked even fleshier against his sunken cheeks. His black eyes had always been deep-set but in recent years they seemed to have burrowed even farther into their bony sockets: they nestled in the shadows of brows and lids and wrinkles, it took a certain effort to reach them.

"Fuhget about it, Joey," he said. "No offense, but it's

4

like the worst fuckin' idea I ever heard. People like us, we don't write things down. Do we, Bert?"

"Hm?" said Bert the Shirt d'Ambrosia. He wasn't much older than Vincente, three, four years, but he'd lived in Key West for a decade or so and the easy life of Florida had somewhat melted his alertness. Also, he'd died some years before. Not for long, but he'd had a severe upset on the Eastern District courthouse steps, and in the hospital his heart had stopped for maybe half a minute; he'd used the flat place on his EKG as an argument for being excused from a profession that usually did not allow retirement.

"Write stuff down," Vincente repeated. "People like us, we don't do it, right?"

"People like us," said Bert, "a lotta guys can hardly read. How they gonna write?" He underscored the question with upturned palms, which then came to rest on an ancient chihuahua curled in his lap.

"OK, OK," Vincente said, a little bit impatiently. "But aside from that, we don't write things down because we don't write things down."

"That's true," said Bert, and he petted the dog. The dog had been gray to begin with and now, at age thirteen, was turning ghastly white. It was white at the tips of its outsized ears and white around its bulbous eyes, which in turn were going milky with cataracts. The dog was always shedding white hairs the length of eyelashes, and Bert, unconsciously, was always plucking them off his gorgeous silk and linen shirts of mint green, lavender, and midnight blue.

"Besides," Vincente said, "ya write something down, right away people can see it—"

"That *is* the idea," Sandra put in.

"Whose idea?" Vincente said. He had one of those rumbling voices that didn't get louder as he got worked up, it got deeper, it moved the air in a way that was felt more than heard.

"And about this regrets thing," said Bert the Shirt. Having been dead and then alive, he didn't always see things in the same order as other people, he didn't believe that time and thought and conversation went in one direction only. "What is there really to say about it? This guy, maybe I shouldn'ta clipped 'im? That guy, maybe I shoulda clipped 'im sooner?"

Vincente silenced his colleague with a lifted eyebrow. Certain things you didn't talk about, not even kiddingly, not even among family. Discretion—this was something no one seemed to understand anymore. Keeping secrets—when did this come to be seen as a bad thing? It used to be a sacred obligation to keep secrets; it was like guarding a treasure. It took courage, discipline. There was a soldierly pain that went with holding things inside, and the bearing of that pain became a source of pride, of dignity. Didn't people realize this? You kept secrets not for pleasure but because it was a duty. Keeping secrets had cost Vincente pain and anguish all his life; it cost him pain and anguish still. He thought about the pain and the hard pride it engendered, and he did a slow burn within himself.

"Nah, Joey," he said at last, "fuhget about it. Writing stuff down." He made that hissing grunt again. "Just fuhget about it."

Joey Goldman pursed his lips, looked down at his fingernails. This, he thought, was the story of his life where family was concerned. You try to do the right thing, you try to help; it ends up being the wrong thing, it ends up in a squabble. He got up just enough to reach across the patio table and pour more wine for everyone. He knew the question that needed to come next: Pop, then what *are* you gonna do? And he knew he couldn't ask it, it was too raw, too sharp. So he got up and strolled over the damp tiles around the swimming pool to light the propane grill.

After three years in the Keys, Joey was a regular Floridian. He cooked outside, he ate outside, he lived in sunglasses, he'd almost learned to swim. And, unlike when he'd lived up north, he hardly ever got knots in his stomach, except where his family was concerned.

CHAPTER TWO

"Everyone's got a book in 'im," said Joey Goldman. "I read that somewhere, maybe I heard it on TV, who remembers? But I think it's true. Don't you?"

"A decent book?" said Arty Magnus. "No, it isn't true. It's one of those lame and stupid democratic lies."

It was around five-thirty the next day and they were sitting at the Eclipse Saloon, their elbows deep in the vinyl-covered padding that edged the U-shaped bar. The place was filling up around them, starting to smell of smoke and suntan lotion. Tourists who felt more authentically schnockered if they drank near locals were rubbing shoulders with the stuffed fish hanging on the walls.

"Come on," said Joey. "Wit' the crazy things that happen to people, the wild thoughts they have?"

"Joey," Magnus said, "lemme ask you something. In kindergarten you finger-painted, right?"

Joey nodded.

"You squeezed the paint out on your fingers, you shmeared it around. It felt nice, right? You expressed yourself—"

"I see where you're goin'," Joey cut in. "But it's not the same."

"Joey, was your painting any good? Did anybody but your mother wanna look at it?"

"But a grown person," Joey pressed. "Someone who's seen a lotta life. It's different."

"Is it?" Magnus said. "I'm not so sure. This town, every jerk in every bar thinks he has a great story, a goddam saga. I've never seen a place where there's so many basically dull people who think they must be great eccentrics, real characters, just because they live here."

Joey sipped his rum and orange juice, fiddled with the earpiece of his shades, which dangled from the pocket of his shirt, and considered whether he would push the question or let it drop. He decided the hell with it, he'd let it drop, but his mouth carried on without him. "The person I'm thinking about, he isn't from here, he's from New York."

"Ah," said Magnus, "another place that people think makes them automatically interesting."

"It's my father," Joey said. He said it softly. The words were almost lost in the buzz of the bar.

Arty Magnus frowned, took a hand that was cold from holding his bottle of beer, ran it over his tall forehead and through his frizzy hair. Magnus was city editor of the Key West *Sentinel* and, like most journalists, he reveled in the confidence that he could really cream someone with a few well-chosen words, but it shamed him, seemed a failure of attention and a sloppy piece of work, to give offense without meaning to. "Shit," he said. "Sorry."

Joey shook it off. "Hey, I'm just thinkin' out loud heah. No big deal. I'm a little worried about the old man, is all."

Magnus kept a safe and sympathetic silence, and after a moment Joey went on.

"His wife died a couple weeks ago."

"Your mother? Jesus, Joey—"

"Nah, not my mother."

"Stepmother then."

"Nah. Just his wife. It's a long story. But inna mean-time, after forty-seven years, he's got nobody at home. He leaves here, he goes back north to an empty house."

"That's gotta be hard," said Magnus. He lived alone, Arty did; he knew the faintly thrumming silence one hears after the click of the key, the squeak of the knob on a front door with no one waiting behind it. "He work? Retired?"

"Anything but retired," Joey said. "But he's had some . . . I guess you'd call 'em professional setbacks. My old man, he's used to having authority. Lot of authority. Now . . . it's just all going sour for 'im."

Arty Magnus took a sip of beer, blinked his hazel eyes, then splayed his long thin fingers on the bar. Several thoughts occurred to him, the first of which was how little he really knew about Joey Goldman, much less his family. Who was this guy, whose widowed father had apparently not been married to his mother, who'd arrived in town with nothing, got a dumb job hawking time shares on the street, and within a few short years, at the green age of thirty, had set himself up as something of a big shot in local real estate? They had friends in common, Arty and Joey did; they got together now and then for drinks. But they weren't close, and life-before-Key-West wasn't something that casual Key West friends often talked about; they'd come to Key West to wash away the life before.

The second thing that occurred to Arty Magnus was what a maddening and undodgeable pain it was to see one's parents get old and slow and grouchy and alone, to see them insulted by sickness and abandoned by time, useless in the world's eyes and eventually their own. He made bold to put a hand on Joey's forearm. "It's tough," he said. "It's really tough. But there's only so much you can do."

"Yeah," said Joey, "I know, I know. That's why I was thinking, a book maybe . . ."

"Joey, listen," the editor said. "I don't want to sound discouraging. Your father wants to think through his memories, write them down—hey, I think that's great. If he thinks of it as a book, what's the harm? But between us, Joey, a book is a different kind of thing. It isn't finger painting. It isn't just somebody remembering."

Joey put a couple of fingers around his glass, helped the streams of condensation run down to the bottom. "Yeah, I'm sure you're right," he said. "I mean, you've done it, right?"

It was an innocent question, it wasn't meant to needle, but it found Arty Magnus's sorest spot as sure as a blast of dentist's air finds the hole in a tooth. No, he hadn't written a book, though he'd meant to for as long as he could remember. He'd meant to write one in college, he'd meant to write one in grad school; he'd filled several dozen spiral notebooks with ideas, sketches, observations. He'd meant to write a book while living in New York, and six years ago, when he'd moved to Key West, part of his reason had been the hackneyed and half-ironic belief that *that* would be a good place to write a book. But he hadn't.

He'd done a lot of things instead, been impressively resourceful at finding things to do instead.

He'd helped elevate the *Sentinel* from a fifth-rate paper to a third-rate one. He'd learned to sail a boat. He'd become a fair fisherman and, to his own surprise, an impassioned gardener. But he was forty-one years old, a few silver wires were beginning to wind like tinsel through the brown corkscrews of his hair; it had lately dawned on him that all those ingenious *insteads* had so far used up half his life, give or take a few years.

Joey looked sideways at him and knew he'd said the wrong thing. "Hey." He backpedaled. "Doesn't matter."

They drank. Behind the busy bar, Cliff the bartender was in his glory. He had a cocktail shaker in either hand, was taking an order from a fat guy in a lime-green tank top and carrying on a conversation with a plastered redhead. Arty Magnus looked straight ahead and waited for the sting of this book thing to subside. Then he figured it would subside faster if he distracted himself by playing journalist.

"But Joey, your old man: you really think he has a story?"

"Yeah," said Joey. "I really do."

Arty gave a noncommittal nod and tried to picture what Joey Goldman's father must be like. What would his name be? Abe Goldman? Sol Goldman? A little old Jewish guy not unlike Arty's own father, a retired CPA, warm, decent, unfascinating, a man of lengthy anecdotes and jokes with forgotten punch lines, who at that moment was either playing rummy, striving for a bowel movement, or watching the market final up in Vero Beach.

"Why?" said Arty. "What makes you think he has a story?"

But now Joey got shy. He had dark blue eyes that were a little surprising against his jet-black hair, and when he got to feeling bashful they narrowed down; the long lashes shaded them like awnings. "I dunno. Maybe he doesn't."

Arty Magnus, reluctant newspaperman, had done a one-eighty, had come to feel that maybe he did. "His background? War experience? Wha'?"

"I dunno, Arty. Let it go, it's probably a dumb idea."

"Nah, come on, Joey," the editor coaxed. "If there's really something there—"

Joey Goldman sighed. He leaned a little lower across the padded bar, twined his fingers, and cast wary upward glances over both his shoulders. He pursed his lips, then gave an instant's worth of nervous smile that was erased almost before it could be glimpsed. "Arty, are we whaddyacallit, off the record heah?"

"Of course we are," said Arty Magnus, but he said it a little too blithely for Joey's taste. Joey raised a single finger, and his face took on a look that Arty had never seen before. It was a look not of threat, exactly, but of purpose and of a solemn pride that carried with it a burden and a sadness. The slight cleft in Joey's chin grew suddenly deeper, his skin appeared suddenly more shadowed with the full day's growth of beard.

"No shit now," he said. "Off the record?"

Magnus, slightly chastened, slightly rattled, said, "Yeah, Joey. Yeah."

Joey Goldman sat up straight, gently tugged the placket of his shirt, gave his neck a rearranging twist. He put his palms flat on the bar, leaned close to Arty Magnus, and softly said, "My old man, he's the Godfather."

The blender was slushing up a batch of frozen daiquiris. The air conditioner was whirring. There were

conversations all around them, and here and there cigarette lighters were rasping into flame.

"Excuse me?"

"You heard me."

"Cut it out."

But Joey just looked at Arty, and Arty understood he
wasn't kidding. He drained his beer, held the empty
bottle against his lips an extra second, and tried to think.
Then he said, "Goldman?"

"Try Delgatto," Joey said. "Vincente Delgatto."

"Holy shit," said Magnus.

Joey lifted an eyebrow. The momentary hardness had
gone out of his face, was replaced by a wry look, a little
bit self-mocking but tempered by years of settling into
the oddness of his beginnings and making a life that by
now felt hardly odd at all. "So whaddya think?" he said.
"'Zere a book there?"

"Jesus Christ," said Magnus.

"Well, do me a favor," Joey said. "Fuhget we talked
about it. It's a very dumb idea."

"It isn't dumb—"

"It's impossible. It's against everything the old guy
thinks is right. He'd never do it. It's just tavern talk."

"But—"

"Nah, I shouldn'ta brought it up. I guess I figured,
Hey, you work for the paper, you probably know guys
who write books."

Magnus put his bottle down and twisted it against his
soggy coaster. The noise of the bar flooded in on him,
surrounded him like puffs of cotton, both buffered him
and kept him pinned. "Guys who write books," he said.
"Yeah, I know a few."

14

CHAPTER THREE

"OK, YA don't want religious, fine, it don't have to be religious. But I'm tellin' ya, really, somethin's gotta go there. A birdbath, a Cupid, a fountain, somethin'. The way it is, it's like . . . naked."

Sandra Dugan nodded, smiled politely, and let her father-in-law continue with his decorating advice. They were standing out on the patio, which was, in fact, somewhat radically austere. An expanse of chalky flagstone gave onto an apron of pale blue tile around the pool; on the far side were clustered a few simple lounges. A modest iron table and chairs hunkered under a broad umbrella. Beyond the flagstones, there was no lawn, just white gravel; palms sprouted wherever there was earth for them to root. Aralia and oleander hedges framed the property, and here and there herbs and flowers sprouted in clay pots that reminded Sandra of the French Riviera, a place she had never been.

"And ovah heah," the Godfather was saying, "this empty corner, look, ya put a little love seat, ya have a guy build a trellis for ya, better still an arbor, like. Ya put grapes. Beautiful. Ya sit inna love seat, ya look up at grapes. Fabulous."

Sandra nodded. She wondered if she could possibly explain to Vincente that what she really enjoyed looking at was air. This, for a girl who'd grown up in cramped and cluttered Queens apartments, was the great novelty, the design breakthrough. Air. Not hassocks, drapes, or doilies. Not torch lamps, end tables, or souvenir ashtrays stuffed with crumpled butts. Not weird-shaped glasses with pink spiral stems, not decanters filled with colored water, not radiator covers with little octagons. . . .

"Or even, like, heah," Vincente said, "when you first come out the house. There's no drama to it, it's *boom*, all of a sudden you're onna patio. But maybe, some kinda archway like—"

They heard the front door open.

"Joey's home," said Sandra.

"Yeah," said his father, "you'll talk to Joey, you'll decide what kinda statues."

Later, in bed, Sandra said, "Joey, I hate to complain, but it's getting to me, it's been almost two weeks, your father is driving me a little bit bananas."

Joey swallowed his first impulse, which was to stand up for blood no matter what. Married just short of three years, he still sometimes had to remind himself who his life's true ally was. He exhaled slowly, stroked his wife's short blond hair.

"I know he means well," she went on, "but he's got this way about him. Like he knows what you want better than you know what you want. He's sweet but he's bossy."

"Force a habit," Joey said. "He's the Boss."

"Not in my house, he isn't," Sandra said.

Joey leaned back on his pillow and pondered this. He knew his wife was right, and it was a breathtaking notion:

They were the grown-ups here, this was their place; they owned it and they ran it. True, the old man might occasionally conduct his coded business on their phone, might now and then commandeer the study to receive an emissary from New York or Miami, but it was still *their* house, it lay beyond his father's power like an embassy lay beyond the power of the country it was standing in.

"Joey, try to understand. I just don't like someone telling me I need more furniture. I don't like someone telling me I need a carpet. It's my dining room, I don't want a stupid chandelier—"

"Sandra," Joey interrupted. "Coupla days, Gino'll be down. It'll take some a the pressure off."

Her green eyes glinted a faint silver in the dimness. "Gino? Take the pressure off? That'd be a first."

Sandra, on a roll, was right again. Had Gino Delgatto, Joey's older, legitimate half-brother, ever in his life made anything easier for anybody? Not that Joey could remember. Gino was a schemer, and not bright enough to keep his scheming simple. He pulled other people in, used them. Last time he'd been in Key West, he'd almost gotten Joey whacked. True, that misbegotten caper had bank-rolled Joey in his new, civilian, perfectly legal career—but that hadn't been any thanks to his big brother.

"I just mean," Joey said, "Pop'll have someone else around, other things to talk about."

Outside, a light breeze made the palm fronds rattle, moved the thin curtains around the open bedroom windows. Moonlight filtered in. The air smelled of jasmine and cool sand.

"What kind of other things?" asked Sandra.

17

"Hm?"

"Gino. Why's he really coming down? He's doing business in Florida again?"

"Sandra, hey, his mother just died. He wants ta spend some time wit' his father. 'Zat so hard t'understand?"

Joey didn't say it loudly, didn't get up on an elbow, but there was enough of a rasp in his voice to let Sandra know he shared her qualms about Gino's visit. It let her know, as well, that his restraint was about exhausted, that the reflex to stand up for blood might now be triggered by a single syllable. Sandra simply snuggled up against her husband's shoulder. When a marriage works, it is in no small part because a woman and a man have come to recognize in precise measure when enough has been said.

But while Sandra had griped and was now serene, Joey was less so. He blinked up at the ceiling, took a deep breath, let it out so it puffed his cheeks. "Sandra," he said, "don'cha know why Pop is askin' ya these things? About carpets, statues, furniture?"

"He isn't *asking* me, Joey. He's telling me what—"

"He wants to buy us something. A housewarming, like. He's tryin'a figure out what you want ... I know him, Sandra. Innee old days, he woulda took me aside and handed me cash. But money, ya gotta understand, money is a gift but it's also control, a way ta remind ya who ya gotta go to ta get it. Now he's tryin' ta do somethin' different. Somethin' for both of us. For the house. It's like his way a sayin', OK, ya got your own life now."

There was a silence. Shadows of palm trees played on the bedroom curtains.

"Now I feel like an ungrateful bitch."

"Nah, there's no reason for you to feel like that. Pop,

18

he doesn't make it easy. I mean, someone else, he'd just say, 'Hey, I'd like ta get ya somethin',' you'd say 'Thank you,' and that'd be it. Wit' my old man, it's more complicated. His way, I guess he thinks it's more elegant, more dignified. More somethin'. It's like he's talkin' a different language. A language from a different time. T'understand it, I guess ya gotta know 'im a lotta years."

He paused. He pursed his lips, considered what he'd just explained to Sandra, and realized that he'd also just explained it to himself, but incompletely. He worked his arm under his wife's blond head, then added, "An' ya gotta give 'im the benefit a the doubt. I guess what I'm sayin', ya gotta love 'im."

CHAPTER FOUR

THE OFFICES of the Key West *Sentinel*, like everything else about the paper, were shabby, cheap, and disheveled.

They were located on the second floor of an unhistoric building on a cheesy block of obnoxious Duval Street. To get to them, you squeezed into a corridor between a T-shirt shop and another T-shirt shop, then went up a narrow stairway that not infrequently smelled of urine or of barf. Behind a frosted glass door with flaking letters on it, a suite of tiny rooms snaked away. Dampness lived in the ancient wooden floor, it felt unwholesomely spongy underfoot; light came from egg-box fluorescents that made eyes nervous. Certain privileged cubbyholes had windows, certain privileged windows were equipped with archaic air conditioners. These air conditioners no longer refrigerated; they only dribbled condensation on the rotting floor and threw the same air back at you. Their real value lay in their pulsing, rumbling whine, a strangely restful noise that muted the bad amplified music, unmuffered motorcycles, and drunken cackles from the street.

It was around eight when Arty Magnus returned from the Eclipse Saloon. No one was working late, because at a paper like the *Sentinel* no one ever did. He went to his desk, switched on the AC and his obsolete computer, and opened up the bag of pretzels he'd brought for dinner. He hooked into the database, typed in the name DELGATTO, VINCENTE, and started eating.

The database went back ten years, and the oldest reference to Delgatto was from *The New York Times* of December 20, 1985.

Frankie Scalera, aged boss of the Pugliese family and for a decade the head of the New York Mafia, had recently been rubbed out, and organized crime experts were analyzing the likely shape of the post-Scalera Mob. The new Godfather, it was broadly agreed, was Nino Carti, a preening thug of violent charisma. Carti lacked finesse, but he was young, broad-shouldered, and cocky; he represented, in the words of one FBI source, "the Mob's last best hope to rejuvenate itself." Carti's underboss would be Tommy Mondello, regarded by Mob watchers as an uninspired choice. Mondello wasn't bright, nor was he showy. One state attorney dismissed him as "a glorified bodyguard" whose main qualification was that he would be no threat to Carti's leadership.

More interesting, in the experts' view, was the promotion to consigliere of Vincente Delgatto.

Delgatto was sixty-three at the time—almost two decades older than his new bosses—and there was much conjecture about the meaning of this wide disparity. One investigator saw Delgatto's selection merely as "a sop to the old men" and claimed he would be a figurehead with no real power. Another expert said, however, that while Delgatto's position might indeed be a symbolic one, the symbol was significant; it indicated that the "Sicilian Mob was not ready to abandon altogether its traditions of respect and relative restraint, to sink wholly into the depths of random violence and dog-eat-dog."

This discussion, in the short term, turned out to be academic, because the Mafia, for the next three years or so, was Nino Carti, period.

Arty Magnus, his back to the dribbling air conditioner, munched pretzels, skimmed through hundreds of Carti cites, and remembered the cult of personality that had pertained through the late eighties. Carti made all the decisions; Carti hogged all the headlines. Carti was a one-man show.

But the flamboyant Godfather's fame was also his undoing. By 1989, the Feds and New York State had put together a blue-ribbon task force whose single mandate was to make an airtight case against this brazen gangster whose continued freedom was a needling embarrassment. "We want him badly," said an unnamed prosecutor, when the 116-count indictment was finally announced. "He's made it so the machine can hardly run without him, and if we put him away, that's our best chance to destroy the entire enterprise."

Carti told the press, "I wish the suits good luck."

Then, in early 1991, as the still-cocky Godfather was waiting to go on trial, the unthinkable occurred. The *Daily News*, with its great gift for succinctness, put it best in a front-page headline: MONDELLO RATS OUT CARTI. The nearly invisible underboss, picked solely for his dumb and doglike loyalty, had contemplated those counts of murder and extortion in which he was also an accused and cut himself a deal.

Over the next months, the gambits of prosecutors and defense attorneys dominated the New York local news, but when it became clear that Nino Carti was going away, probably for life, the journalists' attention returned to the

Mafia's battered state and uncertain future. The database showed a steeply rising number of references to DELGATTO, VINCENTE. Arty Magnus ate his pretzels, rubbed his itchy eyes, and delved.

WHO'S NEXT? asked the *Post* on September 18, 1991, the day after Nino Carti's sentencing. The gist of the article was that there now existed an unprecedented power vacuum at the top of the Mob. Vincente Delgatto, sixty-nine, was the highest-ranking member of the Pugliese family not in custody, but sources quoted in the article doubted that he would ever see the solemn inter-family ceremony that signaled the coronation of a God-father. "He's a competent administrator," said one Mob watcher, "but an old man with old ideas who no longer inspires fear. His moment has passed." Warned another expert, "There are four other Mafia families in New York, and if they see this as an opportunity to wrest power from the Puglieses, it won't be pretty."

But the gang war hinted at in the *Post* didn't happen— at least not right away—and an article in the *Times* a couple of weeks later suggested why. Prosecutors were crowing about the broader applications of the RICO case they had built against Carti. Having firmly established the Mafia as "an ongoing criminal enterprise," authorities could now bring charges against anyone who headed that enterprise. Boasted one FBI source, "The way it is now, it's like a shooting gallery. The first duck that pops up is the first duck that gets nailed."

Given this situation, it became ever clearer that the Mob was floundering. Hierarchies were breaking down; lines of jurisdiction were blurring. And the Mafia's lack of leadership was costing it. SICILIANS LOSING GROUND TO

CHINESE GANGS IN GARMENT DISTRICT, reported the *Times* in March of '92. IRISH TOUGHS FLEX MUSCLES ON THE DOCKS, said the *Post* in April.

Then, in May, *Newsday* scooped the competition and surprised the experts by reporting that, at a subdued and formal sit-down at a social club in Queens, Vincente Delgatto, seventy, had in fact been ratified as *capo di tutti capi*.

Details of the ceremony were lacking, of course. But the reporter's unnamed source did offer the following analysis: "The Mob needs a boss. Delgatto knows that, everybody knows it. What's unusual, though, is that, typically, bosses have been driven by greed, blood lust, ego. Delgatto seems to be accepting the crown out of duty. It's become a lousy job."

Taking his cue from this remark, the reporter dubbed the new leader "The Reluctant Godfather."

Arty Magnus looked up from the screen and said the phrase aloud. His voice sounded a little strange in the empty office. That's good newspaper work, he thought: Get the story first and be the first to put a spin on it. Reluctant Godfather. Smart.

He blinked, his eyelids felt rough as they ground together and almost stuck, and he realized quite suddenly that he was fried. He looked at his watch; it was nearly midnight.

He felt suddenly jittery and suddenly depleted: midnight under fluorescent lights with a green computer screen in front of him and nothing but three beers and a bag of pretzels in his skinny gut. He yawned, got up from his desk, and stretched. He switched things off, headed for the door, and on the way downstairs he was laughing at himself for the wise, well-meaning, patronizing way he'd been trying to tell Joey Goldman there was a snowball's chance in hell that his old man had a story.

The editor unchained his ancient fat-tire bicycle and climbed aboard.

The Reluctant Godfather. The nickname was still rattling around inside his head, and he added to it another phrase, a private joke, a distorted echo: The Reluctant Writer. He tried to chuckle over that one, but nothing resembling a laugh came out. He pedaled off down Duval Street. Slurred and whiny music still spilled out of mostly empty bars; here and there couples strolled, leaned against each other, purred and giggled. Being tourists, they were trying much too hard to have a good time, there was something bleak about the effort, but Arty Magnus grudgingly acknowledged that maybe, just maybe, they were succeeding. The word reluctant would not let go of him. He rode home tiredly, wondering all the way if maybe he was just a reluctant sort of guy.

CHAPTER FIVE

Two DAYS later, a gorgeous Saturday, Gino Delgatto showed up in Joey Goldman's driveway with a bimbo on his arm.

This should not have been surprising; Gino always traveled with a bimbo, sported one like a Brit carries an umbrella, would have felt as at sea without one as a musician on the road without the comfort of his cello. Certain things about Gino's bimbos varied, others always stayed the same. Hair color might be blond or red or black, but it was always the kind of hair that looked immaculate on beauty parlor day and then got wilder and spikier through the week. Eyes might be any shape and any hue but were always graced with unlikely lashes and surmounted by brows plucked slenderer than anchovies. Chests were always prominent, the rest of the torso seeming to fall back from the boobs as in some trick of exaggerated perspective; hips tended to be slim, buttocks flat, the whole tail section suggesting something of the mermaid.

Of this particular bimbo, not much could at first be seen. She was wearing big round sunglasses that covered her from the middle of the forehead to below the cheek-bone, and a vast sun hat that carried its own eclipse as she moved toward the front door.

As for Gino, he'd gained some weight he didn't need. His sheeny pants were creased between his beefy thighs from sitting on the plane, he walked like the material was crawling up his ass. He squinted in the sun, or maybe he was smiling; pads of fat crinkled at the corners of his flat black eyes, his full lips spread and the flesh stacked up in his pudgy cheeks.

It shouldn't have been surprising that he brought a bimbo, but he hadn't said anything about it, and as Joey, Sandra, and Vincente stood there in the doorway, a slight strain on their faces hinted that maybe they were a little bit surprised.

Sandra thought: His mother just died; he's here to see his father; he's such a jerk.

Vincente thought: Gino, he's my firstborn; I love him, but he reminds me of the worst and saddest things about myself when I was young.

Joey thought: My big brother; it kills him that I have a house big enough for him to have a room in; he worked it out so there's no way he can stay here.

They all met on the lawn, under the frangipani tree. Gino kissed his father on both cheeks, shook hands with Joey, gave Sandra a hug she didn't want. Then he stood back, glanced up at the sky, and spread his arms in a mock-hearty gesture, the gesture of a lounge comedian telling his audience that life is wonderful now that he's onstage. "Florida," he said. "Beautiful."

He dropped his hands, folded up the smile. So much for Florida. "Come on, let's go in. I gotta pee like a racehorse."

He started for the house, then noticed that slightly awkward glances and attempts at greetings were passing

27

between his family and his traveling companion. "Oh yeah," he said, "this is Debbi. You'll like 'er, she's a good kid."

Inside, Gino trundled off to the bathroom, seeming to make a point of seeing nothing on the way. But Debbi took everything in; she turned her head this direction, that direction, her enormous hat tracking like a radar dish. "This is so nice," she said, looking at the louvered windows, the ceiling fans, the white wicker furniture sparsely arrayed along the pale bare wooden floor. "So airy."

Sandra decided she liked her.

"Can I get ya something?" Joey asked. "You guys had lunch?"

Gino, coming back up the corridor, one hand still fussing with his fly, answered for her. "Nah, nothin', Joey. We just stopped by ta say hello. We gotta go get checked in, have a shower."

"Where you staying?" Sandra asked.

Gino welcomed the question, the chance to make it clear that for him there could only be one place. "Flagler House. Oceanfront. The best."

Sandra and Joey shared a look. The last time Gino had been in Key West, he'd misplaced a fraudulently rented Thunderbird, run up an eleven-thousand dollar tab at Flagler House on someone else's Gold Card, then bolted by water in the middle of the night. But there was a lot of turnover in the hotel business, it was a universe of forgotten faces, and Gino would no doubt have a different piece of plastic and a different name this time.

"So you'll come have dinner later," the older brother said. "You'll be my guests."

"We thought we'd all have dinner heah," said Joey.

"Nah," said Gino, "come on, let Sandra outa the kitchen for a change."

"We don't cook inna kitchen," Joey said. "I grill out onna patio."

But Gino hadn't waited for an answer. He was heading for the door. A jolt and a breeze pulsed out behind him, like when a truck slams past on the highway. He blew by Debbi and she started to follow; then she stopped and walked up to Vincente. For the first time she removed her sunglasses. Her eyes were a green that was almost blue, and even though her hair was all up in her hat the old man knew she was a redhead. Joey's mother had been a redhead.

"Mr. Delgatto," Debbi said, "I just want to tell you I was very sorry to hear about your wife."

The Godfather took her hand in both of his and shook it warmly. "Thank you, dear, that's nice a ya ta say."

Gino started up the rented T-Bird. Joey, standing in the doorway, said, "Nice car. The license and the credit card—they match this time?"

The visitor gave a serene thumbs-up. As soon as the bimbo had got in he floored it in reverse and spit some gravel onto Joey's lawn.

"Kids," said Vincente. "You never had any, didja, Bert?"

"Nah," said Bert the Shirt. "My wife. Her insides. Nah."

"And the girlfriends? No slips wit' the girlfriends?"

They were on the beach across the road from the Paradiso condo, where Bert lived. They sat in folding chairs and looked out at the ocean. If you had to talk about the past this was the place to do it because the ocean was a wide flat bath of forgiveness and forgetfulness, it took the sharp edges off memories like it did off stones. Here an old man could recall things with acceptance, with affection, and with less pain than he feared would be there.

"A million years ago," Bert said, "yeah, I had a slip or two wit' girlfriends. But ya know, it wasn't like wit' you and Thelma. I wasn't in love wit' them, they weren't in love wit' me. No one wanted a kid. But ya know somethin', Vincente? Those years, OK, I did what guys did, but the truth is I was much happier home wit' my wife."

"I wasn't," said the Godfather. "I guess that's a shitty thing to say, Rosa barely cold. Not her fault. She was a good soul, she tried. But happy at home? Nah. Bored stiff at home. The saints, the candles, the sewing kit always out. I envy you, Bert."

Envy was a hard thing to answer, so Bert the Shirt just looked out at the ocean. The sun was very low, there was just enough haze so you could bear to glance at it, and a gleam like grayish-green aluminum was coming off the water. Absently, Bert stroked the geriatric chihuahua curled up in his lap; short white dog hairs came off on his blue silk shirt shot through with silver threads.

"Fuckin' dog," he said at last. "Fuckin' Don Giovanni is the closest thing I got ta kids. Just as well. Two-pound piece a crap is so much aggravation, I can't imagine—"

"Yeah," Vincente cut in. "Wit' kids there's a lotta aggravation. But more'n 'at, there's mystery. Lotta mystery."

He paused. A skinny cloud slid across the sun, the sun seemed to be dropping through it like a shiny quarter going through a slot.

"Like my two boys, go figure. Joey—you're right, Bert, I really loved his mother. She's the woman I shoulda spent my life with. But fuck me, I didn't. So Joey wants ta be everything different from what I am. This thing of ours, he wants no part of it—and I don't blame him, it's turned to shit. He's got a terrific wife, he's true to her, it makes him happy. What I'm sayin', everything I've done, everything I am, he wants ta be the opposite."

Bert petted the dog that weakly quivered in his lap. Vincente had his black shoes on and he was nuzzling the beach with them, like he was secretly wiggling his toes in the coarse coral sand.

"Then there's Gino," he went on. "Gino thinks he's doin' exactly what I want 'im to, probably thinks he's just like me. But Bert, I gotta tell ya: I look at Gino, I get a pain in my gut. I look inna mirror, wha' do I see? I'm a old man. My skin don't fit, my ears hang down. I'm ugly. *Brutto*. It don't bother me. I done a lot, I felt a lot, I know how I got to this. I look at Gino, I don't know what I'm lookin' at. He don't think, he don't feel, he took the life that was handed to 'im and never for a second looked outside it. Either he ain't really like me, or I been kiddin' myself a lotta years. Ya see what I'm sayin'?"

"Yeah, Vincente, yeah," said Bert. "It's like a whaddya-callit, one a them things that cuts both ways, paragram, paragon, somethin' like that. Joey, he ain't like you onna surface, but inna bones, he is. He's got some spine, some independence to 'im. Gino, the surface is there, but you go below it—and wha'? Ya fall tru' the bottom, ya slip out his asshole, I dunno."

"Bert, hey, he's still my son."

"Sorry, Vincente. On'y—"

"And the bitch of it?" the Godfather went on. "It's my fault. My fault, I mean, that my two boys, they gotta turn themselves inside out, go through contortions like, either to be like me or not be like me. If they understood better why I did the things I did—"

"Vincente," said Bert. "Hey, fuck do I know? But sons, I'm not sure sons ever understand."

The Godfather chose not to be soothed. "Like wit' Joey," he went on. "Deep down, probably he thinks I'm a skirt-chaser and a bully. OK, old days, he ain't far wrong. But God as my witness, Bert, that ain't the whole story. Things we did, we had reasons. Joey don't know the reasons. Gino don't know the reasons."

Bert didn't say anything for a while, he was watching the sun go down. This was a thing with him. He cherished the moment when the flattened orange ball would squeeze onto the horizon, it always struck him as a kind of victory, an omen, though of nothing in particular, when the sky was clear and he was in the right place to confirm that the day had ended, the sun had sunk into the ocean. He watched it settle halfway in, a fat man wading belly deep; then he said, "So Vincente, tell 'em the reasons."

The Godfather made a hissing grunt. Except for a dubiously lifted eyebrow he was motionless in his beach chair, but it seemed to Bert the Shirt that he was wriggling, writhing, like fingers, fists, were poking at him from within.

Bert's dog had fallen asleep, was making a soft wheezing snore in his lap. "Ya wanna do it," the family friend said gently, "there's gotta be a way ta do it, Vincente. A way ta say what's on your mind but still keep the secrets secret."

CHAPTER SIX

BEN HAWKINS, the only black agent working organized crime in the New York office of the FBI, was wearing a neat conservative business suit because he always wore a neat conservative business suit to the office, but that didn't mean he was happy to be there. It was a January Sunday, 9 A.M., 12 degrees outside. There was dirty frost on the windows. Lavender steam poured out of the Con Ed smoke-stacks and blew flat away on an arctic wind whooshing down from Canada. Hawkins had been with this squad for sixteen years, the coarse hair on his temples had grown gray in service to this squad, and he knew there was no damn reason this meeting had to be held on Sunday morning, except that the supervisor, Harvey Manheim, was getting grief from the higher-ups and thought it his duty to spread the grief around.

Now Manheim strolled into the conference room, nodded, sprayed hellos among the fifteen, eighteen agents there assembled. He had slightly bulging eyes and the deep-hinged mouth of a ventriloquist's dummy; he wore a tweed jacket and corduroy pants and carried, as always, his unlit pipe. He took up his position at a small lectern at the front of the room, between two big easels that held organizational charts of the five New York Mob families. "Gentlemen," he said, "thanks for coming. We're here for an update."

Outside, a gust of polar air rattled the windows. An agent named Frank Padrino could not help muttering, "What's to update, Harvey?"

He shouldn't have said it. It played right into the supervisor's hand.

"What's to update?" Manheim parroted. "Nothing's to update. That's the point. How long's Vincente Delgatto been in place now? Coming up on three years. And what do we have on him? Nothing."

"He hasn't made a wrong move," came a voice from the back of the room.

"He hasn't made *any* moves," another agent said. "It's like some kind of Mafia gridlock out there."

Manheim ignored the comments. "And do you recall," he went on, "the confident line we gave the press when Carti was put away—that we could now prosecute any leader?"

Ben Hawkins shifted in his chair. He was tall, not fat but ample in his flesh, ambiguous in his features, with a narrow-bridged nose and almond eyes that nearly wrapped around his head. "We didn't say that, Harvey," he ventured. "You did."

The supervisor raised a professorial finger. "The Bureau said it. And now the Bureau has to make good on it."

He paused a moment to let the institutional weight of this sink in. Then he pointed to Padrino, who had the thick neck and squashed nose of an aging fullback and who knew the Mob better than the Mob knew itself.

"Frank, what's going on right now—this gridlock, if you will—what do you make of it?"

Padrino pursed his lips, put a finger on his chin. "No one really knows how strong Delgatto is," he said. "He's the Godfather, yeah, but what does that mean these days? The only other family with a legitimate boss is the Fabrettis, with Emilio Carbone. The official bosses, Delgatto's contemporaries, are mostly in jail. Some of them have figured out they're gonna die there. So why should the younger hoods accept this old man that's been forced on them?"

Manheim liked what he was hearing; it was taking the discussion where he wanted it to go. "So you're saying they'll move against him—"

"I'm saying they might," Padrino corrected. "In the meantime, Delgatto is probably too weak to really lead, too strong to topple. So everybody's waiting."

"Not the other gangs," said Manheim. "The Asians. The Latins. They're already sniffing weakness."

"Yeah," Padrino conceded, "that's already happening."

The supervisor hugged the lectern, caressed his unlit pipe. "All the more reason we should intervene now," he said, "before there's a full-scale bloodbath."

Ben Hawkins had small ears, ears that, like the rest of him, were as gray as they were brown, a color like that of tree bark. Those ears had become acutely tuned to political nuance in meetings such as this. He could generally tell when a conclusion had been rehearsed, had existed in advance of the evidence that supposedly led to it. "Intervene how, Harvey?"

"Preempt a power play," the supervisor said, "by taking Delgatto off the street ourselves. We give the prosecutors a week, ten days, to cross the *t*'s and dot the *i*'s; we can arrest him anytime. Probably get bail set around six million."

"Arrest him for what?" asked another agent.

"RICO conspiracy," said Manheim.

He said it with an attempt at granite certitude, but the slightest hint of apology still came through, and the words were met with the sort of embarrassed silence that follows an all too public fart. A long moment passed; a draft went through the room like shaved ice blown across the windowsills.

" 'Zat all?" asked Ben Hawkins. "RICO conspiracy? Aka guilt by association? Was I absent that day, or do I seem to remember that was kicked out of the Constitution?"

Manheim said nothing.

Frank Padrino said, "Jesus, Harvey, those cases are such bullshit. Lawyers' delight."

Manheim crossed his ankles; his hinged mouth chewed out words. "Gentlemen, we're here to enforce laws, not have opinions. You don't have to like RICO—"

"But juries have to," Hawkins interrupted. "And they don't."

"Shit," said Padrino. "Without Mondello turning, even Carti might've walked on RICO, and Carti was guilty as sin. Now you've got Delgatto. He's a little old man, he looks like a guy who alters pants. You'd have a very tough time proving he's personally committed a crime in forty years. The jury won't go for it. We'll look ridiculous."

Manheim ran a hand through his thinning hair and called up the pale and tentative candor allowed to the middle manager. "Guys," he said, "listen. Strictly between ourselves, I don't like this either. But I got the DA on my ass. He hasn't had a lot of headlines lately, he's suffering withdrawal. He wants us to come up with a way to grab the Godfather. It's that simple. And let me tell you something: For the guys who find a way to do it and to make it stick, it's going to be a career-maker."

A hush descended. Career-maker. The word had magic in it, it warmed the room like the red coils of a toaster. The younger agents squirmed in their chairs as though with thoughts of sex. One of them, a square-jawed fellow named Mark Sutton, with all of six months on the squad, didn't so much speak as ooze forth words from the simmering bubbling well of his ambition. "There's gotta be a way," he said.

"You bet there is," Manheim said approvingly.

"It isn't RICO," said Ben Hawkins. "RICO won't stick."

"So we'll find a better way," said Sutton. He said it with the shrill annoying confidence of the young, and Hawkins, his own face caught in an involuntary wince, took a moment to study him. The young agent's hair was too perfect; it looked sprayed, like the hair of a sports-caster. His face had the neat and regular features of a recruiting poster and exuded about as much humanity. He wasn't big—in fact, he looked like he'd barely made the height requirement—but he worked out hard; you could see the telltale bulges between his shoulders and his neck.

"A better way," said Harvey Manheim. He leaned across the lectern and zeroed in on Sutton. He'd found his boy. "Yes. Let's get right on it."

"Small detail you ought to know," Frank Padrino put in dryly. "Delgatto's down in Florida. Miami agents made him at the airport a couple weeks ago."

A suspicious, worried look flashed across Harvey Manheim's face. Was he the last to know? Would it count against him that he was? "What the hell's he down there for?"

Padrino shrugged. "His wife died a few weeks ago. Maybe he's just resting."

Manheim frowned. You couldn't indict a man for resting or for mourning. He struggled to stay on the offensive. "Listen—Florida, Flushing, I don't care. Let's get the background going, be ready to jump on him when he comes north. Frank, you work with Sutton—"

"Jeez, Harvey," said Padrino, "I'm finally getting some penetration into the Fabrettis—"

"OK, OK," the supervisor said. "Then Ben, you and Mark, you're partners on this."

It happened so fast that Hawkins could do nothing but blink. He was fifty-three years old, easing toward retirement with a lot of distinguished work in his file; he had no one to impress. Still, it was hard, probably impossible, to be the second guy to beg off. He scowled at Frank Padrino, then looked with dim distaste at the gung-ho and irritating Sutton. A case I don't believe in, the veteran agent thought, with a pushy child for a partner. For this I put on a fresh suit on a Sunday morning?

CHAPTER SEVEN

As THE meeting was breaking up in Queens, the God-father was planting impatiens in Key West.

On his knees on the white gravel, he leaned into the narrow flower bed and his skinny slack haunches in their baggy pants stuck up in the air. He didn't wear gloves. A lot of people, he thought, they said they liked to garden, but what they really liked was to look at flowers while sipping a gin with clean hands. How could you garden with gloves on? How could you feel things in detail? How could you know how firm a stem was, how much dirt to shake off where the root ball ended?

Vincente dug a little hole, scratched it out like a terrier, and decided that the problem was that nowadays, what with the price of real estate, gardening was only for the wealthy, the refined. Didn't used to be that way. In Sicily everybody gardened. Hell, in Queens in the old days everybody gardened. Who gardened now? Wetback gardeners mostly, digging without gusto in other people's dirt, being badly paid by clean-handed bankers and brokers in Westchester. The same bankers and brokers who looked down on people like Vincente. Why? Not because they were outlaws. Hell no, there was brotherhood and grudging admiration about that. No, they looked down on the Sicilians because the Sicilians got their hands dirty and made their money on things with strong aromas. Fish. Garbage. Could you imagine a WASP banker showing up at Fulton Street at 4 A.M. to put on slimy rubber boots and get into the freezer with twenty tons of cod? Could you picture a Jew broker climbing a mountain of table scraps, Kotex, and gull shit to bring his coffee grounds and lamb chop bones to the dump? No. Those were jobs for wops, for dagos. Those were jobs for people who didn't go to twenty years of school and weren't afraid to get some honest stink up their nostrils and kind of liked the idea of getting elbow deep in smelly, gritty, wormy life, elbow deep in dirt.

Not, Vincente thought, that this Key West stuff could really be called dirt. Key West had no dirt, only coral limestone, nubbly gray rock that didn't weigh much and had holes in it. You wanted dirt, you went to the store and bought it in a bag. Imported. A luxury item. Hell, even in Queens there was dirt . . . Gently, the Godfather turned over a cluster of blood-red flowers and squeezed them out of their tiny plastic pot. He placed them in the hole he had dug, snugged them in with the flat of his hand. Then he took stock. He had about a dozen pots of impatiens to go, maybe eight more feet of border, and only a quarter bag of topsoil.

Still on his knees, he looked back over his shoulder and yelled across the pool. "Dirt, Joey. We're gonna need more dirt."

His son was sitting under the patio umbrella, eating cantaloupe and looking at the Sunday *Sentinel*, making sure the Paradise Properties listings had not been garbled beyond all recognition. "Have some breakfast, Pop," he said. "Dirt, later on, we'll get more dirt."

Vincente considered. He didn't like to stop in the middle of a job, it went against him. But the prospect of resting let him realize that his knees were hurting from the gravel, the hinge at the bottom of his back was complaining. So OK, he would take a break. He started to stand up, then realized with shame and some surprise that it wasn't going to be a simple or a graceful process. He pretended to be puttering, stacking up the empty pots; he didn't want his son to realize that his head was swimming or to see how long it took him to regain his feet. He stalled; at length he rose. Then he dusted himself off and strolled around the pool to have a cup of coffee.

At first glance, the Godfather was unimpressed with the Key West nursery.

"Up north," he said, "the nurseries up north, they have more stuff. Ornaments like, trellises. Fountains, ya know, like comin' outa fishes' mouths, angels peeing, that kinda thing."

"Here it's mostly plants," said Joey. "Baby trees, sometimes ya see 'em comin' right outa the coconut. And flamingoes maybe. Ya know, their feet are metal rods, ya stick 'em inna ground."

"Flamingoes?" said the Godfather. "Sandra want flamingoes?"

Joey thought it best to let the question slide, he just led his father through the ranks of encroaching palms and ferns. Hibiscus flowers tickled their forearms as they passed; miniature oranges scented the air with citrus. There was no roof at the nursery, just a fine black netting that kept the birds away and muffled the ferocious sunshine. Nor was there a floor. The bare ground was covered with chips of wood and bark that felt moist and cozy underfoot, it made you realize why bugs and mice and lice liked to live in rotted logs.

At the end of the aisle, between the palm food and the snail bait, they ran into Arty Magnus.

He was wearing olive-drab shorts and torn sneakers with no socks. His legs were long and bandy, a little bit like frogs' legs; his knees turned out just slightly and were rubbed red from kneeling in his yard. He had pieces of leaf in his frizzy hair.

"Joey," he said. He tried to put some heartiness in it, but he was thoroughly distracted. Something was eating his jasmine leaves, and he was in the grip of that dismay known to every gardener, less an anxiety than a fatalistic dread, the sure knowledge that at that very moment one's beloved exotics were being reduced to naked scaly twigs by malicious vermin of infinite appetite and implacable will.

"Arty, how ya doin'?" Joey said.

The editor was going to say something breezy and move on, but then he noticed the old man half hidden by Joey's shoulders. The Godfather. The Reluctant Godfather. Standing in a Florida nursery on a Sunday morning like any other *alte cocker*, a little stooped, a little bored maybe, surrounded by tagged foliage and big bags of things that would rupture him if he tried to lift them. Arty Magnus suddenly felt that he was staring. He tried to pull his gaze away, he turned his head but his eyes stayed steady like the needle on a compass. It was getting uncomfortable, then Joey shuffled his feet in the mulch and said, "Arty, I'd like you to meet my father. Pop, this is Arty Magnus."

No mention of a name, the editor noted. Incognito. Even in Key West, where in theory there was no Mafia and in fact no one read the papers. He extended his hand, and now it was Vincente who was looking harder and longer than might be thought polite. He was examining Arty's hand before he shook it, noticing the fine dark lines of embedded soil that marked out creases and wrinkles the way ink marked out fingerprints.

"Nice ta meet ya," Vincente said.

"Nice to meet you, sir," said Arty.

Feet wriggled in the tree bark.

"We're here for dirt," said the Godfather. "How 'bout you?"

"Poison," said the editor.

The old man stood with his back to a ficus. He folded his hands as at a funeral and nodded sadly. "Sometimes ya gotta kill the little bastuhds. Sometimes there's just no other answer."

On the way back to Joey's, Vincente said, "Your friend, his hands—he digs inna dirt."

"'Course he does, he works for the paper."

"Nah, I'm serious," said the Godfather. "A man who gardens, I like that. Life, death, ya take responsibility. What ta take away, what ta leave. He knows somethin' . . . What's he do for the paper?"

"City editor, his title is," said Joey. "Assigns things to the reporters. Covers some things himself. City commission, politics."

"Ah."

In Joey's neighborhood the blocks were short and

there were stop signs on every corner. It was hard to get going more than fifteen miles an hour, and on those lazy streets Joey's refurbished 1973 El Dorado convertible got about eight blocks to the gallon. But nice light filtered through the mahogany trees; there was time to check the progress of the poincianas and time to mull things over.

"But ya know what he really wants ta do," said Joey, two blocks later.

"Who?"

"Arty. The gardener . . . What he really wants ta do is write books."

The Godfather looked out the open passenger-side window.

"Yeah," Joey went on. "And I bet he'd be good at it. Not afraid ta dig in wit' his hands, ya know what I'm sayin'?"

Some people were playing badminton on one of Key West's rare large lawns. Vincente watched the slow and idiotic flight of the shuttlecock against the flawless sky.

"Tell ya what," said Joey. "Why don't we have him to the house for dinner? Shoot the shit, talk about gardening. How would that be, Pop?"

There is a moment when an idea either puts on flesh or is forgotten, squirms into possibility with the red stretch of any birth or vanishes without a trace. Vincente propped his wizened elbow on the hot frame of his window. A deep breath whistled in his nose as he slowly turned toward his bastard son. In his face was relief and a tentative capitulation, a half acceptance that maybe he had reached the age when sometimes, on certain things, maybe certain other people knew better than himself. "OK," he said. "That'd be OK."

CHAPTER EIGHT

It was just noon when Gino rolled off of the bimbo.

He blinked up at the ceiling of his deluxe room at the Flagler House, mopped his damp chest on the sheet, then turned his hairy back to her as he reached for the phone to call room service. "Whaddya want for breakfast?" he asked.

"You're so romantic," Debbi said. "So tender."

"Eggs, omelet, wha'?"

She didn't answer right away. Her body felt numb, her head was heavy on the pillow, she was faintly nauseous. It had started to dawn on her that maybe she shouldn't have come to Florida, that maybe she was less blithe than she thought she was, that Gino in small doses was OK, a nice dinner, an evening out, but traveling with Gino was much too much and much too little.

"Come on," he said. "They're onna line." Into the phone he added, "Hol' on a minute, the duchess can't make up her mind."

Debbi was looking at the bright wand of sunshine that squeezed through the place where the blackout curtains overlapped. It was spectacular, that slash of light, it hurt the eyes. She imagined the grainy heat of the beach, the green sparkle of the water, the sudden coolness of a passing cloud. It should have been a day of clean enjoyment.

45

"I'll have the family cocktail," she said.

Her last name was Martini. Family cocktail was her little joke.

"Little early, ain't it?" Gino said.

"And a bran muffin," Debbi said. It was hard to make bran muffin sound defiant, but she tried.

Over breakfast, Gino announced that they were driving to Miami.

"But we just got here," said Debbi.

"Right," said Gino, puncturing an egg yolk. "And now we're goin' there. What of it?"

Debbi had put on a hotel bathrobe. The neckline of it showed some pretty freckles at her throat. Her red hair was flat on one side and wild on the other. "I thought we came here so you could visit with your father."

Gino chomped a triangle of toast. When he talked, the melted butter put a greasy yellow shine at the corners of his mouth. "We're comin' right back. But I gotta see a guy. I'll leave ya at a mall, you'll like it."

Debbi sipped her drink. The gin tasted weird but it was more the toothpaste than the hour of the day. "I don't wanna go to a mall. A mall I can go ta anytime. I'll stay here, I'll go ta the beach."

"The beach, you'll get sunburn."

"I like sunburn. I came here for sunburn. Sunburn, Gino—not ta go to a freakin' mall."

"Nah, I want y'along."

"Wha' for?" she said. She toyed with her bran muffin; brown crumbs spilled off it like tiny dislodged rocks bouncing down a hillside. "Ya don't talk ta me. Ya don't talk t'anyone."

"Shut up, Debbi. Half a drink, you're soused already."

46

But she wasn't soused and she stuck to her opinion. Gino didn't talk to people, he just made noises with his face. Even last night, at the bigshot fancy dinner he'd hosted for his family, was there anything that might be called a conversation? *How's the shrimp, Pop? More champagne?* Was there anything about Joey, about Sandra, about their life here in this town? Was there anything, one word of fond remembrance, about the dear departed mother? No. Nothing. She, Debbi, hardly got to talk; Gino always cut her off. Sandra was nice, showed some interest, asked her if she worked. Debbi had barely mentioned the pet salon when Gino barged in to call for more wine. That was classic Gino. With him a dinner was all grunts and sucking noises and grand gestures to the waiter. Everyone was uncomfortable and only Gino didn't seem to notice. Gino, you put a lobster bib on him, he was happy. The strange part, the only thing she could hang on to to persuade herself she wasn't shacked up with a total heartless louse, was that Gino meant it in his way when he said he wanted people around. He just didn't know how to be with them when they were.

She nibbled some bran muffin, washed it down with gin, and spoke without really meaning to. "Gino," she said, "I just don't understand you."

He was mopping up the last of his egg yolk with the last of his toast. His face was turned up to catch the runny orange paste before it dripped in his chest hair; it wasn't a moment to try to explain things to a half-soused broad. "There's nothin' t'understand," he said.

Debbi Martini smiled for the first time that day. It was not a happy smile, but there was in it the quiet pleasure of bedrock comprehension. Gino saw the smile and

47

mistrusted it, understood somehow that it came at his expense, though it didn't dawn on him that, against all habit and inclination, he'd just said something wise and true.

CHAPTER NINE

"ARTY, MORE pasta?" Joey Goldman asked.

He held forth the huge ceramic bowl, the last of the steam wafted upward and was sliced by the slowly spinning blades of the ceiling fan. After a moment's hesitation, Arty Magnus took up the challenge, seized the dish in his big dirt-digging hands.

"Good eater," Vincente murmured approvingly. "Guy's a good eater."

"Don't look like he is," said Gino grudgingly. "But OK, give credit. These skinny guys, sometimes—"

"He isn't skinny," Debbi said. "He's lean."

"Let 'im eat," said Sandra. "Joey, fill his glass."

The editor said nothing, but as he dug into the unending mound of linguine and clams, it vaguely struck him that here he was, in a houseful of strangers, never mind Mafia, who were analyzing his dining habits and his physique, talking about him as if he weren't there—and it didn't even seem especially odd. With the first forkful of his third helping, he realized why. It reminded him of his own family, his Jewish family, who, when they paused long enough in their devouring to talk at table, generally restricted their remarks to observations on the stomach capacity and metabolism of the others present. Jews and

Italians: the world's referees of intake, the arbiters of appetites.

The guest stabbed a clam, raveled it in pasta, and sucked it down with a somewhat theatrical zest. On the issue of food, at least, he knew what was expected of him at this table.

In other ways, he had no idea what was expected.

He understood there were a lot of things he shouldn't ask, he shouldn't say. But what *should* he say? And why had he really been invited in the first place? To talk about gardening, Joey had said when he'd called. To let the old man hear about the real Key West. Reasonable enough. But in the meantime there'd been antipasto, there'd been grilled eggplant, there'd been several bottles of Valpolicella, and so far gardening had not been talked about, the town mentioned only in passing. Now the main-course dishes were being cleared, Joey and Sandra working their way around the table, clattering and clinking. Arty made a move to rise and help; Joey pushed him by the shoulders back into his chair.

So he sat and sipped his wine. He took the liberty of pouring more for Debbi, whose glass did not seem to stay full for long. Gino unwrapped a cigar, put it in his mouth unlit; he leaned back in his chair so that his shirt stretched open between the buttons and revealed little ovals of belly hair. The Godfather slowly and grandly wiped his lips on a corner of his napkin, reached up to straighten a tie he wasn't wearing. Then he said to Arty, "Newspaper business—ya like it?"

After the small talk and the mumbling, the editor was a little nonplussed to be asked a real question, and a touchy one. "Not much," he fumbled. "No."

The Godfather nodded, considered. At his back was a sweep of bare white wall broken up by louvered windows. Early moonlight filtered in, threw dim stripes on the floor. "Why ya do it then?"

Arty could not hold back a quick nervous laugh. He heard it from the wrong side of his ears and realized he was a little drunker than he'd thought. He realized something else as well: He was looking at Vincente, past the folds and wrinkles that, depending on how hard you dared to look, either hid his eyes or lured you farther into them, and all at once he understood that the man's power, his leadership, lay in the fact that he could not be fibbed to, or not for long; he would draw out truth like salt drew water out of fruit. Arty felt fear and reassurance together, a sort of jumpy freedom. "It's my living," he said.

"You're educated," said Vincente. "Bright. Ya don't like it, ya could do other things."

Arty drank some wine. He hazily remembered being told as a child that he had to tell the truth, and as long as he did so he would not be punished. This was one of the disastrous childhood lessons that adults had to unlearn, and in unlearning it grow sad and dead at heart; in the Godfather's rumbling voice and unflinching tunnel eyes was a brutal reassertion of that lesson, a defiant claim that in his small world the rule still held. "Yeah," the guest admitted. "I could."

"It's not that easy to switch," Debbi Martini put in. "Even with my job—"

"Your job." Gino cut her off. "Dogs' toenails. Besides, you ain't educated."

She reddened. It was hard to tell if it was pique, or alcoholic flush, or sunburn growing ripe.

"Secrets," Vincente said to Arty. "Newspaper business, I'd think you'd have ta keep a lotta secrets."

"Sometimes," Arty said.

"Like someone tells ya somethin', confidential like. It's a whaddyacallit, an ethical thing, ya can't tell nobody, right?"

"That's right," said the editor.

The Godfather nodded, considered. Slowly he leaned forward, picked up the wine bottle, and refilled Arty's glass. He poured a splash into his own and raised it in a silent toast. It took him a long time to settle back against his seat, and when he'd done so he fixed the guest from under the ledge of his eyebrows. "So Ahty," he rumbled. "Y'ever tell?"

The editor felt pinned in his chair, felt as though leather straps had suddenly bound his wrists and ankles. He stared down the chute of the Godfather's eyes. He knew absolutely that he was being judged, and yet he had no difficulty with his answer. "No," he said. "Never."

Vincente held the stare a moment longer, seemed to be harboring Arty's words in the deep whorls of his old man's ears, testing them for an echo that might yet prove false. Satisfied, he did not relax his vigilance but redoubled it. There then came one of those dizzying moments that changes everything, that cleaves time once and for all into before and after. The Godfather had been introduced only as Vincente, Gino only as Gino; the weighty name Delgatto had never yet been spoken. The evening had been a charade of innocence, of not saying what was known. Now the Godfather was calling off the farce, bestowing on Arty the flattering and perilous gift of candor.

"My business too," he rasped. "Lotta secrets. All secrets, my business. Lotta things ya don't wanna tell. Lotta things ya wanna tell and can't."

"Must be difficult," Arty said.

Vincente looked at him hard, decided that he understood.

"Me, I can't keep a secret worth beans," said Debbi.

"Which is why nobody tells you nothin'," Gino said.

Joey and Sandra came out of the kitchen. Joey carried a tray with an espresso pot and cups and a plate of pignolia cookies. Sandra held an enormous bowl of fruit salad: pineapple, papaya, mango, tangerine. But the little dinner party had got away from them somehow, words and glances had been rerouted; their own dining room seemed strange, as if in their brief absence someone had rearranged the furniture. Coffee was sipped, dessert nibbled, but conversation sputtered, chairs no longer felt comfortable, and it came as a relief when Gino slapped down his cup and said abruptly, "Who wants a cigar?"

Arty Magnus had not smoked a cigar since college. The last one had inflamed his sinuses and given him a two-day case of heartburn. But now he bravely rose with the other men and passed through the wide unadorned doorway to the patio. The moon was bright, you couldn't quite see colors but you could tell the red impatiens from the pink; the air was still, a second moon was floating in the pool.

Gino held a lighter in his fat cupped hands. There was something ancient in the act of sharing the offered flame.

Through the kitchen window, Sandra saw four red points shining through the silver moonlight, the cigar tips of the Godfather, his two unmatching sons, and the nice new fellow who was being drawn into their circle.

CHAPTER TEN

"Dog's constipated," said Bert the Shirt.

"Who isn't?" said the Godfather.

They were standing on Smathers Beach in the half hour before the sun went down. Vincente's black shoes and Bert's white sneakers scratched against the nubbly limestone that passed for sand. In the green water, three or four miles from shore, a couple of sailboats were scudding by; farther out, beyond the reef, a shadowy freighter was riding up the Gulf Stream.

But Bert wasn't looking at the water, he was watching his straining chihuahua squatting in the knobby coral. The dog was hunkered down on its hind legs, its back was arched, it was trying so hard to pass a stool that it was quivering all over. Its little white rat's tail was pumping hopefully, the tiny pink button of its asshole was pressing outward like a flower about to open. But nothing happened, and the clogged dog stared up through its milky eyes at its master, seemed to implore an assistance that no mortal being could provide.

"Fuckin' age," said Bert the Shirt. He gave his head a slow shake; his white hair with its glints of bronze and pink caught the sunlight different ways. "Poor dog don't even jerk off no more. Used to be he'd lick 'is balls. Once, twice a week he'd hump a table leg, try ta fuck a squeak toy. Ya know, he showed some zip. Now? Two fuckin' bites a dog food, a heart pill, drops in 'is eyes. His big thrill? He can pee onna rug, I don't yell at him no more. Some fuckin' life, huh?"

Vincente didn't answer. He was looking out at the ghostly freighter, at the tired sun suspended in its slow plunge to the sea. "*Omertà*, Bert," he said. "The honorable silence. Ya think it counts for anything? Ya think it means shit anymore?"

Bert didn't miss a beat. Since his brief death he had trouble staying on track, but making transitions had never been easier for him. "Since that mizzable fuck Valachi spilled his guts? On TV no less? Remember those little black-and-white sets, big box, little picture, by the time they warmed up the show was over? Ya think about it, what's left to be silent about? Like there's someone out there, he's been in a coma forty years, he don't know there's a Mafia? The movies, the books. Now I read where they're sayin' Edgar Hoover was some kinda nutcase Nazi faggot. Liked ta put a helmet on, have people tie 'im up and call 'im Edna. So who ya gonna believe?"

"Ain't a question a who ya believe," the Godfather said. "It's a question a doin' the right thing."

"Who's arguin'? But Vincente, can we talk heah? You and me, we're old, I mean, speakin' whaddyacallit, figurative, the dog can't shit and we can't lick our balls no more. Least I can't. But hey, one good thing about gettin' old, ya don't have to pretend no more; there's no reason ya can't just lay things out, say, Here it is, take it or leave it, kiss my ass. So like even with this code of honor bullshit—hey, I believed in it, you believe in it, but how many guys really believed in it? It just gave them an excuse—"

"It don't matter," said Vincente, "what the other guys believe."

Bert fell silent. Don Giovanni gave up on a bowel movement. The dog lifted slowly out of its arthritic crouch, kicked weakly at the coral knobs, and was again defeated, failing now to cover a mess it had failed to make. Its pale whiskers hung dejected, its expression was chagrined. "Nah," the Shirt said finally, "I guess it don't."

The sun hit the horizon; its reflection joined with it and gave it the shape of a stubby candle, a squat pillar of flame. The air was the same temperature as skin, if it wasn't for light salty puffs coming off the water, you could forget that it was there. "'S'pleasant here, ain't it?" said the Godfather. He said it as though he'd just that moment noticed.

"Very."

"Peaceful like. Simple. Makes ya feel like, hey, what's the big deal if an old man says some things, eases his mind?"

Bert the Shirt said nothing, just watched the sun slip into the Straits, savored the small victory of being alive and in that place to see it.

The Godfather said, "So why can't I do it? Why do I feel like there's some nasty fuck out there"—he paused and tapped his scrawny chest—"or maybe inside here, that isn't gonna let me?"

The next morning Arty Magnus was sitting at his desk, his back to the dribbling, droning air conditioner, his feet propped comfortably between his telephone and his computer terminal. He was reading that day's *Sentinel*, counting typos, mismatched pronouns, yawning in his soul at the flat gray dullness of the merely factual, the smothering monotony of what was called the news. How was it possible that, in a world so full of nuance, nuance in the paper was as rare as cats that swam, that in a town so full of humor, the paper's occasional attempts at levity fell flat as pounded veal?

Thinking about it made Arty groggy. He got up to fetch another cup of coffee.

On the way back from the dispenser, he decided to hang out awhile by the AP teletype. It was an old machine, archaic, a clunky-looking workhorse on a graceless pedestal, but Arty liked the way it chattered, how it filled up endless rolls of yellow paper with its untiring monologue. For an outfit like the *Sentinel*, the wire was the only pipeline from the drear world north of mile marker twenty; it carried epochal dispatches from places like the UN, Tokyo, and Washington, D.C., portentous accounts of coups, disasters, the fall of the West, which would then be reduced to four-line items that ran next to the police blotter in the column OTHER NEWS.

Arty sipped his coffee and watched the yellow paper fill up with ink.

DATELINE PARIS: ECONOMIC SUMMIT FLOUNDERS.
DATELINE MOSCOW: RUSSIANS TALK OF ETHNIC CLEANSING.
DATELINE NEW YORK: MAFIA BIG SLAIN IN BROOKLYN.

This one Arty read.

The gist of it was that Emilio Carbone, fifty-nine, boss of the Fabretti family, was midway through a plate of calamari rings at a seafood joint in Sheepshead Bay when three gunmen walked calmly through the swinging kitchen doors and shot him eleven times in the liver and the lungs. Also killed was fifty-six-year-old underboss Rudy Catini. The restaurant was full but no one seemed to get a good look at the shooters. An FBI expert said that the very public nature of the killings meant one of two things: Either the hit was sanctioned by the other families or it was carried out by a renegade faction whose clear aim was to intimidate. The rubout, stated the source, was "a sign of weakness, not strength, further evidence of the Mafia's desperate condition."

Arty sipped his coffee and wondered if Vincente yet knew. Or if Vincente, for that matter, between planting flowers and pruning shrubbery, between strolling on the beach and eating with his family, had pronounced sentence on Carbone. Who knew what strings the old man pulled, how ruthless he might be, how he really operated? What would it be like, Arty wondered, to pick up the phone like you were ordering a pizza, but instead you ordered someone killed?

He was back in his office when, three quarters of an hour later, Marge Fogarty, the silver-haired copy editor and keeper of the three-button switchboard, called to tell him a man was on the line for him but wouldn't give a name.

Arty put his pencil down. He knew it was the Godfather, knew it with the placid certainty that sometimes tells a batter when a curve is coming, a gambler when an ace is going to fall. He picked up the receiver, saying nothing till he heard the inquisitive Marge drop out of the circuit.

"Hello?"

"Ahty, I wanna talk ta ya. Can ya meet me for a little while?"

The editor, a reluctant sort of person, didn't answer for a moment. He was playing a game with himself. He knew he would say yes, but it dawned on him that he should take the time to wonder if he would say yes of his own free will or if he was already slipping into some sort of nameless perilous thrall. It was important, he felt, to be clear about that now, because the thrall could only deepen with involvement, become an atmosphere, a fact of nature, a gravity you forgot about but that was always tugging. He persuaded himself that he could say no, then said, "Sure."

"The nursery," said the Godfather. "Plants, we both like plants. Whaddya say, we meet at the nursery, have a little talk?"

CHAPTER ELEVEN

ARTY MAGNUS locked his old fat-tire bicycle, wiped some sweat off his neck, ran a hand through his damp and frizzy hair.

It was a weekday morning and the nursery wasn't crowded, it had the brisk backstage atmosphere that pertained when only the professionals were around. Here and there workers went by with shears, with trowels, with atomizer bottles. People carried trees, it looked bizarre when all you saw was feet beneath a walking poinciana. Under the bird netting, the light was soft and cool. One quadrant of the yard was being misted; a lavender fog hung over it.

Midway down an aisle of buttonwood and bougainvillea, the Godfather was sitting on a slatted bench. He was wearing a gray suit that was much too warm for the weather; you could see the texture of the wool. Cinched tightly around his shrunken neck was a wide tie of burgundy silk. He sat with great stillness, his veiny spotted hands resting on an ebony walking stick with a scalloped silver knob on top. He saw Arty and lightly patted the bench next to him, a grandfatherly gesture, beckoning a child to sit down, to pass some time with him.

Arty sat. The Godfather slowly waved a hand across the greenery, breathed deeply of the flowers and the peat.

"I love this," he said. "Florida changes ya, don't it? I first saw this place, it was too plain for me. Now it's perfect."

Then there was a silence, a long one. A workman walked past with a shovel, it made Arty think of Emilio Carbone.

Finally Vincente said, "Ya know who I am."

It was not a question, and Arty just nodded.

"Ya know why I wanna talk to ya?"

Arty shook his head.

The Godfather stared at him and seemed to be deciding whether he had just been fibbed to. "I think ya do," he rasped, "but OK, it all makes sense. Ya wanna write books, you're scared ta write books, the chance ta write a book jumps up and bites ya innee ass, y'act like ya don't notice. This is why ya still work for a newspaper."

Arty said nothing. If he felt insulted, he'd missed the one clean moment to hit back; after that it would just be whining. He looked off toward the baby palms, felt a sudden ludicrous compassion for their struggle up toward daylight, their wispy nakedness before the wind, their helpless patience with the whims of rain.

"I'm askin' ya to work with me," the Godfather resumed. "Tell my story. Be my whaddyacallit, my ghost-writer."

Arty's feet shuffled in the mulch. A mushroom smell came up from the scratched-at earth. His mouth fell open, but all that came out was a strangled *aah*, a doctor's office sound.

"Ya scared?"

Arty nodded.

"Of me? Or the book?"

"Both."

62

"Fair enough," said the Godfather, and he reached up toward his tie. It could not have been any straighter or any snugger, but he toyed with it anyway, smoothed it down inside his buttoned jacket. He turned a few inches toward the younger man, laid his ebony walking stick across his lap. "Ahty, lemme tell ya a coupla things about how I do business. I don't pressure nobody, I don't get nobody involved that doesn't want to be involved. Ya wanna say no ta me, ya can. No hard feelings. That's the God's honest truth."

Arty looked past the web of brows and wrinkles into the sockets of Vincente's eyes. "I believe it," he said.

Vincente raised a finger. "Believe this too: If we do make a deal, the deal is sacred; it lives as long as we do. Know that. It isn't something you walk away from, some lawyer gets you out of. Any doubts at all, be safe, say no."

Arty's hands were damp, he rubbed them on his pants legs. A man came down the aisle with a hand truck full of poison. The mist went off in one section of the nursery and came on in another; a fresh green smell wafted over from where the watering had started.

"So here's what I'm thinkin'," the Godfather went on. "Five thousan' a month, for as long as it takes. Ya keep your job, it's better that way. The thing is, nobody can know we're doin' this—nobody. 'Cept my sons, I think they got a right ta know. And my friend Bert, he'll figure it out. But no one else. Our secret, Ahty. Y'unnerstand?"

"But a book isn't—"

Vincente fiddled with his tie again. "Nothin' comes out till I'm dead. Which, let's face it, doesn't figure ta be that long. After that, Ahty, y'own it, ya do what ya want."

He paused, gave a hissing grunt. "'Course, if it's like everything else I done in my fuckin' life, it'll turn out no good innee end. But you, maybe you'll make it good, maybe you'll make a fuckin' fortune on it."

A cloud crossed the sun. Under the black mesh net the dappled light went gray and flat, a cool breeze made the baby palm fronds scrape and rattle in their pots.

"Coupla hours," the Godfather said, "I'm flyin' a New Yawk, a week, a month, I don't know for how long. Think it over while I'm gone, will ya do that for me?"

Arty nodded. He reminded himself he could still say no.

Vincente slowly swiveled on the slatted bench to face him, you could see the knobby thinness of his bent leg underneath his woolen pants. "Ahty," he said softly, "I'm like stranglin' inside, I'm like chokin' on shit and bile and secrets and things I think are wrong. What I'm askin' ya, I'm askin' ya ta help me get ridda that shit, y'unnerstand?"

The ghostwriter nodded, swallowed. The sun came back, picked out twenty different kinds of green: waxy, dusty, bluish, silver.

The Godfather turned away, sat facing straight ahead, his hands propped on his walking stick. "Go now," he said. "I wanna sit here a few minutes, smell things, look at people work." He lifted a hand just enough to make a small embracing gesture toward the foliage, the burlap bags, the clay pots stained with wet. "I love it here," he said. "I had my way, I'd spend a lotta time, this is where I'd sit."

PART TWO

CHAPTER TWELVE

THE GODFATHER recoiled.

He waved his hands in a fending gesture, leaned far back, and pulled his face away as if shrinking from a bad smell. "Ahty, no," he said. "No tape recorder."

"But Vincente," said Arty Magnus, "it'd make things so much—"

"Ahty, fuhget about it. A tape recorder, believe me, it's like a loaded gun."

Arty Magnus looked down at his switched-off Panasonic. Tiny, cheap, held together with duct tape and powered by batteries no bigger than suppositories, to him it did not look like a deadly weapon. But, he reminded himself, it didn't matter how it looked to him: He was a ghostwriter now; it was his job to see with different eyes, to learn to speak in another person's voice, to describe the contours and the rules and the terrors of someone else's world. "OK, Vincente, no tape recorder."

It was early February. The Godfather had returned to Key West the day before. He'd been in New York about two weeks, during which time the FBI had monitored his movements. But the Bureau's top priority had become the rubout of Emilio Carbone, and nothing had been found to link Vincente to that murder, or to anything else that might make the careers of prosecutors or of agents.

Unharassed, he'd chartered himself a plane and flown back down to Florida.

He'd called Arty at his office and just said, Well?

Arty had decided to answer terseness with terseness; he'd made no mention of the hell of ambivalence he'd been living in, no mention of the insomnia, the death of appetite and flight of concentration, the weak-kneed giddiness as of the stroll to the end of the diving board when you know there are two ways down but one of them has come to seem impossibly wimpy. He'd just said, When do we start?

So now it was dusk and they were sitting on Joey Goldman's patio, glasses of wine at their elbows, a plate of olives and celery between them. The smell of chlorine came up from the pool, giving a perky tang to the sweet depleted smells of flowers closing for the night. A dragonfly flew past, its wings glinted a dull silver and in the stillness you could faintly hear their papery buzz.

Arty put his tape recorder back into his canvas bag, spirited it away with a slight embarrassment, as if it were a rejected sex toy. "OK," he said again, producing instead a water-stained notebook with a blue cardboard cover and a ninety-nine-cent pen snugged into the spirals of its binding. "So I'll take notes."

But the Godfather wasn't crazy about that idea either. He reached up to fidget with a tie that wasn't there, scratched his stringy throat instead. "Notes? Ya gotta take notes?"

The ghostwriter choked back exasperation. "Vincente, try to understand. This thing we're doing, it might take a year, two years, it might come out eight hundred pages. I can't remember—"

"My business," Vincente said, "we remembered. Sometimes for decades we remembered."

"I'm sorry," Arty said. "I'm not that smart."

The Godfather paused, sipped some wine, glanced at his new associate's wide-spaced hazel eyes, and wondered if the guy was already being a wiseass; decided no, he was just looking for a way to do his job. Fair enough. The older man made the conciliatory gesture of offering the plate of celery and olives. "'Course," he admitted, "fuckin' problem was, sometimes different guys remembered different. Then there was a misunderstanding like, somebody got hurt. Notes—maybe notes coulda saved a coupla guys."

Arty didn't push, he ate an olive.

"On'y thing bothers me," Vincente went on, "ya got these notes, they exist like, like evidence. Evidence a what, don't ask me. But say somebody gets ahold of 'em, say some crazy way they get subpoenaed?"

Arty had a pit in his mouth and didn't know what to do with it. He was trying to grasp the dangers in Vincente's world, looked for words to describe the jungle alertness, the unrelenting wartime suspicion that was called for in it. He fished the pit out of his mouth, put it on the edge of the plate, hoped that was the right thing to do. "They can't be subpoenaed," he said. "First amendment. I don't have to give them up; I wouldn't give them up."

"School, they teach ya that at school?" Vincente asked.

Now it was Arty who had to decide if the other man was getting in a dig. Maybe he *had* sounded a little too Columbia, a little righteous and shrill with untried certitude on that one. He just nodded.

But when the Godfather spoke again, his tone was

empty of sarcasm. "I like that, a school that teaches ya not ta bend over, ya don't gotta spread your cheeks just 'cause the fuckin' government . . . What if someone steals 'em?"

"Hm?"

"The notes. Say somebody steals 'em."

Arty groped toward an answer. "My handwriting is so bad," he said, "I have this sort of personal shorthand, used it for years—" He broke off, realizing that his reassurance was beside the point. "Vincente," he ventured, "can I say something here?"

The Godfather made a steeple of his hands and nodded.

Arty leaned low across the metal table. He was wearing khaki shorts, and his bare shins were against the edge of it. "You wanna write a book," he said. "Sooner or later, that becomes a very public thing. A separate thing. Old cliché: it becomes like a child, you can't control it anymore. You see what I'm saying?"

Vincente nodded. He had sons, he knew what it was to watch his offshoots become unruly and at moments unrecognizable.

"So OK," Arty resumed. "Now everything you've been saying, it's with this habit, this obsession, to keep things private. And I think you have to understand that if we do this thing, at some point it's gonna get away from us, it has to, and I don't care who you are, there's no guarantee you can pick the moment when it happens. You sure you wanna chance it?"

Crickets were rasping. From inside the house came the flat ring of tap water spilling into the pasta pot.

Vincente answered the question by going on as if it had never been asked. "Another thing," he said. "The ground rules heah, we gotta get 'em settled. First off, I ain't rattin' anybody out. I ain't takin' bread outa anybody's mouth. What I want, it ain't gossip, it ain't this guy clipped that guy, this other guy drove the car. No. It's the tradition, the reasons. So mostly what I'll talk about is myself. Maybe some other old guys, dead guys. Maybe some guys inna can for life. Which means a lotta things could change inna middle. Ya know, a guy keels over, I can talk about him. A guy gets mercy parole, he's onna street again, we take 'im out. Outa the story, I mean. It's gotta be, ya know, loose."

Arty Magnus had begun to scrawl some things in his notebook. But now he paused to scratch an ear, then left his pen hand suspended in midair. The Godfather regarded him.

"I'm bein' a pain innee ass?" he said.

The ghostwriter felt a quick jolt of that jumpy freedom and was on the brink of answering.

The Godfather spared him by going on. "Ahty, you could tell me. A book, fuck all I know about writin' a book? Am I makin' it impossible?"

Arty Magnus considered. An ever-changing, wildly disorganized, presumably posthumous oral memoir by a paranoid recluse who spoke in coded fragments and whose entire life had been dedicated to covering his traces. Was this impossible? Any more so than the dozen other books he had thought to write and never written? "No," he said. "Not impossible. Just a little difficult."

Vincente made a hissing grunt, picked up a celery spear, pointed it at the other man. "*You* want out, Ahty? Last time I'm askin'."

Reluctance and thrall stretched the ghostwriter from

either end, thinned him out like taffy. In the midst of faint panic, he reminded himself he could still stroll back to the end of the diving board that had the stairs attached. Who, after all, was watching? Who would ever know?

"No," he said. "I don't want out. I said I'd do it, let's do it."

The Godfather smiled. It wasn't much of a smile but it was more of one than Arty had yet seen. The full lips pulled back a little from the long teeth stained with half a century of coffee and red wine, the thin flesh of the grizzled cheeks bunched up into crescent wrinkles. Something eased in his high and narrow shoulders; inside his open collar his neck appeared to seat itself more comfortably in his chest. "So we've stahted," he said.

"Yeah," said Arty, "we've started."

The Godfather's smile didn't broaden but it softened, became the tired, parched, but grateful smile of a man moving past the worst part of a fever. "Ya wrote stuff down."

"A few lines," Arty said.

Vincente nodded. A few lines, nothing really, but something quietly amazing had taken place: his lifelong flow of secrets had been reversed. It was as surprising in its way as a river running backward. "I feel better, Ahty. Thank you."

He produced from nowhere an envelope stuffed with hundred-dollar bills and placed it softly on the table next to the dish of celery and olives.

CHAPTER THIRTEEN

MARK SUTTON wore his shirts just a little bit too tight, to show the muscles in his chest. He wore wide ties and put big knots in them to point up the thickness of his neck. He stood now, short legs slightly apart, veins protruding here and there, before Ben Hawkins's desk. "What's the supe wanna see us about?" he asked.

Hawkins was serenely trimming his fingernails, pushing down cuticles with the flat end of the file. He looked up languidly and said, "He wants to chew our ass about Carbone."

"Carbone?" said Sutton. His voice got high, he went into the pinched tenor of the wrongly accused. "Our target's Delgatto. What the hell's Carbone got to do—"

The fastidious Hawkins kept working on his nails. "Mark," he said softly, "how old are you?"

Sutton shuffled his feet and admitted with due shame that he was twenty-seven.

That seemed to end the conversation as far as Hawkins was concerned. He stood up in no great hurry, slipped into his suit jacket, and led the way to Harvey Manheim's office.

Frank Padrino was already inside. He looked feverish; the tops of his squashed ears were flaming red. In New York it had been a week of alternating snow and thaw, a week of slush. Everyone was coming down with something.

"Almost three weeks, guys," Manheim said, when everyone was seated. With him, the problem was the throat. His voice was hoarse, and it brayed when he reached for emphasis. "And whadda we got on the Carbone hit? What we got, we got the DA pretending he just can't understand why we haven't solved it yet. We got the tabloids reporting every day that there's nothing to report. I've been eating shit for the whole squad. So what gives?"

Mark Sutton sniffled. Aha, Ben Hawkins thought, even the young and musclebound got colds.

Then Frank Padrino spoke through the blockage in his nose. "We know who ordered it," he said. "Aldo Messina. It's a power play within the Fabretti family."

"That's your theory," said Manheim. "But Messina wasn't a shooter, he was watching boxing in Atlantic City. Everybody saw him."

Padrino coughed into his fist. "We'll trace it back to him."

"Yeah?" barked Manheim. "When?"

"Harvey, look," said Padrino. "The shooters expect to be rewarded. The reward won't be enough. It never is. There'll be a grudge. Sooner or later—"

The supervisor rapped his pipe against his metal desk, it made a sharp thin ugly sound, a sound like the pain of an ulcer. "Sooner or later isn't good enough. Where's Delgatto?"

"We tailed Delgatto for two weeks," said Mark Sutton.

"We lived with him," said Hawkins. "There wasn't the slightest indication—"

Manheim rasped on as though he hadn't heard. "And where's the old man now?"

"He's back in Florida," Hawkins said. "Where he was when the hit—"

The supervisor folded his hands and leaned far forward over them. "Doesn't it strike you as awfully convenient that just when everybody needs an alibi, old man Delgatto makes sure he's seen fifteen hundred miles—"

"Harvey," Hawkins said, "he's got family there—an illegitimate son who's not connected. His legit son, Gino, who *is* connected, he's been down there too. Like we told you, the old man's wife—"

"Fuck's his wife got to do with it?" said Manheim, his voice cracking like a French horn badly played. "I think Delgatto's behind it. I think he made the call. I think we're not talking RICO now, we're talking murder one."

"Big stretch," said Frank Padrino. "Carbone's death, where's the benefit to Delgatto?"

"Carbone was moving in on things," said Manheim. "Restaurants, trucking, a couple of important unions—"

Frank Padrino was shaking his head. "Harvey, it doesn't wash. Carbone, OK, Delgatto had his beefs with him, but he was a known quantity, they could work together. Messina, he's younger, more ambitious, crazier. Net-net, he's a much bigger problem for Delgatto."

Harvey Manheim swiveled in his chair, looked out the dirty windows at the huffing smokestacks, the rusting skeletons of groaning bridges. When he swiveled back again, he had a bleak wry look on his face. "Question, guys: Why are we sitting here talking about Delgatto's problem? I wanna talk about *my* problems. I have two: Delgatto's one, Carbone's the other."

Mark Sutton chewed his lower lip, felt a twinge of pleasure in his groin. Something sparked behind his eyes and suddenly the path was revealed to him; he could picture promotions, commendations, a handshake from the Director. "So if we could find a way to put the two problems together—" he intoned.

"Then I'd only have one," said Manheim. "And wouldn't that be nice."

"But Harvey—" said Frank Padrino.

The supervisor cut him off. "Frank, you wanna keep looking at the Fabretti family, fine, you keep your crew on that." He fixed Mark Sutton with a soupy stare. "But it is the working assumption of the Bureau that Vincente Delgatto is linked to the murder of Emilio Carbone. Ben, Mark, your job is to find that link. Got it?"

Ben Hawkins tugged skeptically on the points of his natty glenplaid vest. Suddenly his own throat felt sore, his eyes were itchy. Oh, well, he thought, a break from winter wouldn't be the toughest thing to take. It would be nice to feel some good hot sunshine on his chest. "So I guess that means you're sending us to Florida."

Manheim hesitated. It killed him that his charges should be warm while he was cold, that they should sniff salt breezes while he sniffed Dristan nasal spray. "Yeah," he said at last, his voice thick with phlegm and with resentment, "I'm sending you to Florida."

CHAPTER FOURTEEN

GINO AND his bim had left Key West the day before Vincente did, the morning of the day, as it happened, that Emilio Carbone was whacked in Brooklyn.

Debbi had left with a freckled sunburn, twelve Key limes in a plastic bag, and a slowly ripening inclination to dump the boyfriend. Gino had departed with unfinished Florida business, a festering frustration about an undone deal, and neither awareness nor concern that yet another large-breasted small-hipped female was working up the confidence to kiss him off.

Now, three days after the Godfather's return, the two of them were back as well. They'd come by way of Miami, where Gino went once again to see a guy. He'd dropped Debbi off at a café in South Beach. She'd sipped a Negroni and watched the models, crossed and uncrossed her skinny legs and tried out different positions for her hands, and pretended she was a model, while the real ones slunk past with their beribboned shih tzus, their sheepdogs buzz-cut for the tropics.

Arrived in Key West, they checked into the Flagler House just before sunset, had a shower, a room-service cocktail on the ocean-front balcony, and went unannounced to Joey Goldman's house.

Joey was watching the evening news. The news was

that the economy was a little up and a little down. As if he didn't know it: Real estate sputtered, his listings ran week after week in the paper, everybody looked and nobody bought. It was really Sandra's end of the business, the housecleaning and rentals side, that kept the steady money coming in. Short hair, simple clothes, a soft voice, down-to-earth ideas that worked; thank God his wife was practical.

Joey was surprised to hear the bell ring. He swung his bare feet off the wicker hassock and went to answer it. In the dim light his half-brother was glutting the doorframe like a feed-lot steer, Debbi squeezed off to the side like a cat that had wandered into the stall.

"Gino," Joey said. "I didn't know you were in town."

"Yeah," said Gino, by way of explanation. "I'm heah. Pop around?" He leaned close. Joey smelled aftershave, bourbon, and cheese spread.

"He's onna patio, talkin' with a guy."

"Yeah? What guy?"

"Guy you met," said Joey, standing aside as Gino barged into the living room, Debbi following. "Arty. The editor guy."

But Gino was not much interested in the editor guy. "Ah," he said. "I gotta talk to Pop."

"Pop wants ta talk ta' us," said Joey.

"What about?" said Gino.

"I think I know, but I'm gonna let him tell it, he wants ta tell us both together. Hello, Debbi."

"Hi, Joey," said the bim. The traveling had knocked her hair down, it lay flat this time, was parted in the middle, and framed her face the way girls' hair used to frame their faces, following the lines of their jaw, in high school. The tan from her last visit was already gone, the only remnants some pink spots where she had peeled. Hoping for some company, some talk, she asked, "Is Sandra here?"

"Nah," said Joey, "she's at a benefit. Guy who works for us. Got burned, needs skin, more operations."

Gino wasn't much interested in the guy who got burned. He pointed his stomach toward the patio and charged off after it, Joey and Debbi trailed behind because they didn't know what else to do.

Outside, seated at the metal table softly lit by flood-lights tucked tastefully into shrubbery, the Godfather was talking to his ghostwriter.

"So Ahty," he was saying, "I'm depending on you ta say this nice, make it elegant like, polished, ya know, so it moves people, but the first thing we gotta get across is tha' Sicily, the people, the whole island—what we gotta tell 'em is tha' Sicily, from the beginning a time, has been fucked right updee ass."

Arty was dutifully scrawling in his notebook *Sicily fucked in ass* when Gino burst through the vacant doorway like a fat sprinter straining toward the finish line. "Hi, Pop," he said. "I gotta talk ta ya."

Vincente paused, blinked, reached toward the low metal table as if to ground himself, and raked his hand slowly across its cool top. He had been, if not serene, at least crawling toward serenity, beginning to skim griev-ances from his stuffed heart, starting to excise rancid memories from his cluttered brain. And now here was Gino, blustery, urgent, loud, insistent on reversing the flow, cramming more crap through his father's eyes and ears. The old man could not keep a sudden weariness out of his voice.

"Gino," he said. "When ja get back?"

"Just a while ago. Can I see ya, Pop?"

"Say hello t'Ahty," Vincente said. It shamed him that he still had to coach his thirty-six-year-old son in manners.

Gino said a grudging hello, then stood there leaning forward, damp under the arms, shifting weight from foot to foot. Joey and Debbi were standing in the doorway, leaning against the frame, as if to steady themselves in the turbulence left by Gino's passage.

"I'll talk ta you and your brother," the Godfather announced.

"But Pop," said Gino, "what I gotta talk about, it's important, maybe just the two of us—"

Vincente had begun the slow and stately process of rising from his chair. Halfway up, he said, "Gino, he's your brother. We're guests in his house. Ya don't leave 'im out. Besides, I got somethin' to tell yuhs." He straightened gradually, and only standing could he see around his bulky firstborn. "Oh, hullo, Debbi," he said.

She was opening her mouth to answer when Gino wheeled and said to her, "You stay out heah wit' Ahty."

He slammed back toward the doorway. Joey and Debbi flew off in different directions, like bowling pins. Joey backed inside; Vincente excused himself and walked slowly toward the house.

In the sudden and disarming absence of the father and his sons, the world grew oddly peaceful. Debbi dropped into the Godfather's chair, she and Arty sat a moment in a silence that was both awkward and delicious, a respite from the noise and tumult that pulsed off Gino like hot blood around a boil. A breeze riffled through the hedges, carried smells of coconut husks and seaweed, moved the shrubs in which the floodlights were embedded so that shadows danced around the pool.

Finally Debbi put on a slightly bent half smile and said, "So I guess that just leaves us unimportant people."

"Looks that way," said Arty Magnus. He would have said more if he could think of more to say, but he couldn't just then, and Debbi took his terseness to mean that maybe she had offended him.

"I guess I shouldn't put you in that category," she said.

"It's an OK category to me."

"But you're a friend of Mr. Delgatto's."

"This makes me important?"

Debbie gave her head a tilt, pursed her lips, and lifted a plucked red eyebrow.

Arty went on. "You're a friend of two Mr. Delgattos."

That wasn't something the girlfriend especially wanted to be reminded of. She pulled her green eyes away a moment, then changed the subject. "You still working for the paper?"

Arty saw her looking at the stained blue notebook on the metal table. No one could handpick the moment when a book became a public thing, and it made him nervous that she noticed it. "Not tonight," he said. Then *he* changed the subject. "But what about you, Debbi. Up in New York, whadda you do?"

Surprised to be asked, she raised a hand to her chest. Her long pink fingernails looked both elegant and goofy against her freckled throat. "Me? You're gonna laugh."

"Try me," Arty said.

She paused. Palm fronds rattled, ripples ran across the pool, caught the light like fish scales. "I groom dogs," she said.

Arty didn't laugh and Debbi was nonplussed.

She studied him a moment, then felt a perverse urge to goad him into laughing, poke his ribs, tickle his feet, anything to call forth the expected mockery. "I shampoo their fur. Trim their bangs. Poodles, sometimes I put nail polish on their paws."

Still Arty didn't laugh, so Debbi Martini laughed for him. "Such a dumb job," she said.

Arty considered. "You like dogs?"

"I love dogs."

"Well, you're ahead of me. I don't love newspapers."

Debbi didn't buy the comparison. "Yeah," she said, "but to work for a newspaper, ya gotta be really smart."

"Wanna bet?" said Arty, and now he laughed.

She watched him laugh, it relaxed her like a bath. His eyes crinkled up, his lean shoulders jostled, it made him less forbidding, less severe, less *something* than she had imagined him to be. In her relief she leaned a little closer to him and amazed herself by saying, "I wanted to be a vet."

He said nothing, just came to the end of his chuckling and looked at her.

"I wasn't bright enough," she said.

"Who told you that?" he asked.

She made a small harrumphing noise and a dismissive gesture with her painted hands. "Everybody. My father, the nuns. My report cards mostly."

"Ah," said Arty. Report cards were hard to argue with. But now Debbi got feisty, decided to argue with herself. "'Course, I coulda done better if I went to school more often."

"So why didn't you?"

She shifted in her chair; the metal frame rang slightly with her squirming. "Trouble at home," she said. "Boring stuff."

She waved it away, then felt herself retreating, shrinking back. She stared off toward the pool and the low stars that dangled just above the aralia hedge. "I wonder what they're talking about in there," she said.

Arty Magnus shrugged. "Must be something very important."

He said it deadpan, it wasn't meant to be a test and yet it sort of was; she would either get it or she wouldn't, would choose to be a party to his secret wry subversion or would play it safe and let it pass.

She hesitated just an instant, then she crossed her arms against her midriff, gave her chin a gutsy and rambunctious tilt, and met his eyes. Something like a smile happened. Palm fronds scratched and rattled like maracas, light and shadow poured in waves from the illumined shrubs, and from the house came sharp contentious voices that were drowned in the outdoor mildness like scorpions in the swimming pool.

CHAPTER FIFTEEN

"GINO," VINCENTE had begun, "it's like extremely obvious you got a hard-on and it hurts, so g'ahead, you talk first. I'm listening."

The three of them had settled into Joey Goldman's study. It was a Florida study, airy and sparse. There was a glass block wall where up north there might have been a fireplace, recessed lights on dimmers filled in for old silk-shaded lamps, the chairs were upholstered in white cotton where you might have expected cordovan leather. Still, it was a serious and manly room; it had a globe and it had liquor. Gino had asked for a bourbon, and Joey poured him three fingers' worth. Then the younger brother backed away, propped himself on the arm of a settee, and let the urgent Gino have his say.

But Gino didn't find it easy. He dropped his head so that his chin went double, pawed the floor like a bull. "Awright, Pop," he began, "it's like this. While I been heah, heah in Florida, up in Miami, Key West, ya know, I been goin' back and fort'—"

With his glass he gestured up and down Route 1; then he took a swallow. His father propped his elbows on Joey's limestone desk, rested his chin on his folded hands, and waited.

"Ya know," Gino went on, shuffling his feet, "I been

seein' you, visitin', I figured, Hey, lemme do some business, get somethin' taken care of, make a few dollahs. So what I'm saying—"

He broke off, scratched his neck, felt a brute frustration that in his rough mouth language shredded up, scraps of it peeled worthlessly away like when you start a roll of off-brand tape.

"So this Miami business," he labored on. "Pop, I think you'll be proud a me, I was doin' a right thing, standin' up for the family—"

Vincente did not look proud. "Gino," he said, "fuck kinda business ya doin' in Miami?"

The son stared at his father, saw the bristly brows roll down to shade the sunken eyes, and a hint of panic now chopped his speech into even more shapeless pieces. "Miami. Ya know. Cholly Ponte."

The Godfather's voice grew no louder but it rumbled, seemed to soak into the walls and work its way under the tile floor. "Cholly Ponte's a boss. Ya talk ta Cholly Ponte wit'out ya ask me?"

Gino's face caved in a little more, lost its luster and went cock-eyed like a dented hubcap. "Pop, I knew ya got a lot on your mind, I didn't wanna bother ya."

"Well, y'are botherin' me. You're botherin' me a lot."

Gino swigged his bourbon, paced a step in one direction, a half-step in another, measuring the box he was building for himself. Suddenly he was mad.

"Pop," he said, "it ain't fair I should get grief from you on top a the shit I been takin' for the family. Miami, I been insulted, jerked around, I'm gettin' like zero satisfaction—"

"Gino," said Vincente, "stop bitching, slow down, put

85

the drink away, and tell me what the fuck is going on. Joey, bring a chair over for your brother."

The recessed lamps threw disks of light, broke the room into sectors a little bit like circus rings with arcs of shadow in between. Joey slid a chair into the bright circle opposite his father, then made a point of slipping back into the darker place himself.

"OK," said Gino as he sat. "OK." He took a deep breath, glanced over at his whiskey glass. It glowed a tasty amber. He told himself if he got through this conversation he could have it. "Cholly Ponte, he's got this racket, he runs stolen cars, rent-a-cars mostly, ta South America."

"I know that," said Vincente.

"Well, ta get the cars onto the ships, he needs the Miami longshoremen."

"I know that too," the Godfather said.

"So I figure," said Gino, "hey, if he's usin' those guys, we oughta get—"

"Gino, that's a Miami local, that's not our union anymore."

The bulky man tugged at the collar of his shirt; the cloth bit into the rolled flesh of his neck. He looked longingly at his bourbon. "Since when?"

"You know goddam well since when," his father told him. "Since a year or so ago, when I cut that deal wit' Emilio Carbone. We keep the International, the Fabrettis get the locals."

Gino chewed his lower lip, looked down at his lap. He knew there was something he shouldn't say, and he knew he was about to say it. "That wasn't a deal, Pop, that was a giveaway."

The son braced himself to get smacked. A crack like that, in the old days it would have earned him a brisk backhand across the cheek, not hard enough to leave a mark, not hard enough to really hurt, but placed artfully so that the eye would tear, and in that involuntary squirt would be a ritual and necessary surrender. But now Vincente didn't hit him, didn't even visibly rile, just frowned and said, extremely slowly, "Gino. Big man. Putz. Now ya tell your father what's a deal and what ain't a deal?"

In some peculiar way Gino was infuriated, humiliated not to get belted. *My dad can lick your dad.* The childhood taunt had for him become the first article of a lifelong creed; it shook him to his roots, made him quail inside, when his father declined to kick ass. He pushed his thick chin forward and egged the old man on. "A deal, Pop, is ya give somethin', ya get somethin'. Fuck we get for givin' up the locals?"

Vincente's mouth was slack, the wrinkles at the corners of his eyes looked waxy. His voice was soft, it sounded like someone dancing on sand. "A little peace a mind," he said.

There was a pause. For Gino, the answer might as well have been Chinese; for Joey, silent in the background, hardly breathing, it seemed no more than obvious; and it was strange but natural that the two brothers' understandings were so different. A father didn't really teach his sons; his life threw lessons in the air like scraps to gulls, and different mouths latched onto different morsels.

After a moment Gino went on the attack again. "So Cholly Ponte, he tells me he's already payin' tribute ta

New Yawk, ta the Fabrettis, he doesn't have to pay double."

"He's right," Vincente said.

"Maybe," said Gino. "But what I'm thinkin', this deal you made wit' Carbone, it died wit' Carbone."

Vincente shook his head, and the sinews in his stringy neck rose and fell on either side. "The deal's between the families."

Gino waved away that notion. "Messina, that geek, I don't see what it's got ta do with him."

Vincente had nothing to add. He sat there very still.

"Listen, Pop," said Gino. "Here's what I wanna do, and I want ya ta back me on it. I wanna go ta Ponte, tell 'im things are back the way they were, he pays us again."

The Godfather put his hands flat in front of him and leaned a little closer to his son. He cocked his head; the angle put his eyes in shadow. "Gino, you fucking deaf? The deal stands. Leave it alone."

Gino sucked his gums. He looked down at his lap, watched his meaty fist flex and unflex against his thigh, felt his palm grow slick with oily sweat, but he was taken by surprise when his hand flew up in the air and came down hard, made a bruising, stinging sound against the cool stone of the desk. When he spoke, outrage and helplessness were wrestling to a strangled stalemate in his throat, his voice was pinched and shrill. "Pop, you're lettin' people walk all over us, they're losin' respect, you're lettin' 'em take what's ours—"

Vincente raised a single finger and spoke in a voice that seemed to rumble up from underground. "Ours?" he said. "Gino, listen a me. Ya live long enough, an' if there's anything left ta run, maybe someday you'll be running things. But that day ain't heah yet. So do like I tell ya. Stay outa Miami. Keep outa Cholly Ponte's way. And fuhget about that fuckin' union. Ya got that, Gino?"

Gino didn't answer. He sat there hangdog, brooding, taking weird solace from the pins and needles in his smarting hand; the sting was some evidence of action, proof of contact, some rub against his father's strength. He wrapped that aching hand around his glass and sucked the bourbon down; too bad if his old man didn't like it.

The silence went on too long, too long even for family, and finally, from the shadows, Joey Goldman said, "Pop, ya said there was somethin' ya wanted ta talk t'us about."

Vincente raised a heavy salt-and-pepper eyebrow, managed the beginnings of a small smile devoid of pleasure. He'd almost forgotten. It was supposed to be an evening of talking to Arty, his writer, an evening of cleaning out, of shedding garbage, not taking garbage in. Air whistled in the old man's nose, came out as a hissing grunt. "Another time," he said. "I'll tell yuhs another time. I had enough aggravation for one night."

CHAPTER SIXTEEN

THE NEXT morning a cold front came through, one of those unwelcome reminders that not even Key West was totally removed from the embarrassing and frozen continent above it, that appalling people and rotten news and lousy weather could still plop down from the mainland like droppings from some gargantuan internal beast. The wind veered till it was due north and carried foreign smells of pine and granite. Smeared and moody clouds raced through the sky; fronds and leaves tore loose from trees and landed in roiled swimming pools.

The Godfather, drained from the conversations of the night before, stayed in bed till Joey and Sandra had gone to work. Then he rose, washed, dressed. Drinking coffee, he looked out the window. The chill and the gloom reminded him he had some calls to make.

He went to Joey's study, sat down at the limestone desk. Usually circumspect about the telephone, here Vincente felt secure. This was Florida, not New York. His son Joey had a spotless record; he was a respected businessman. No judge would sign off on a warrant to tap the phone. Besides, what did Vincente have to talk about that was so awful? Petty things, administrative things. Things where a few soothing words and a couple dollars could keep the peace. Of a mobbed-up shop in the garment district: *Our guy gets six-fifty and car?* the Godfather would say; *So give* their *guy six-fifty and a car.* On a rigged construction bid in the Bronx: *Bring the steel down three percent, you'll make it back on the cement.*

Referee of greed—that's what his job really came down to. Keeping the larceny within sustainable limits. Now he picked up the phone to cajole a certain supermarket boss to give more space to a certain brand of chickens.

"I thought the chicken man was on our shit list," said the supermarket man.

"He's playing ball," Vincente said. "He's using our trucks. You'll ease up on 'im."

"The butchers don't like he don't use union butchers."

Vincente didn't answer right away; he was distracted by a just-noticed dripping in the bathroom down the hall. "One thing at a time," he said at last.

"The meat cutters," stressed the supermarket man, "they have big cleavers. I don't like to see 'em unhappy."

Vincente heard another drip. It seemed suddenly more pressing than chickens. "The union thing," he said. "I'll look into it."

He hung up the phone, went down the hall. Sure enough, the faucet in the bathroom sink was leaking, a bulbous drop just then growing at the end of it as at the tip of an old man's nose. For a moment the Godfather watched the drop, confirmed that it would fall. When it did, a secret joy suffused him, the quiet joy of simple purpose. He was alone in his son's house. He felt he'd been a burden, a bother, a taker. Suddenly there was some small thing he could offer in return, an honest useful project a man could do with his hands.

In a gesture almost worshipful, he fell to his knees in

front of the sink. He opened the cabinet, took out towels, toilet paper, scouring powder. He arrayed things neatly around him on the cool tiles of the floor, then looked in past the drainpipe, which swooped down and up again like a saxophone, to the oval handles of the intake valves. He'd close them; then he'd get tools to take apart the faucet. He'd remove the bum washer, keep it to show to Joey. They'd go to the hardware store together to get a new one. That would be nice: a father and a son together in the hardware store.

Vincente leaned in under the sink. His neck ached as he craned it; the floor tiles were hard and cold against his knees. It was an awkward reach toward the handle of the valve, his shoulder complained at the angle of it. But finally the thing was in his hand. He tried to turn it but it would not turn.

He shifted his knees, dropped into a lower crouch, and tried again. That was when the throbbing in his head began. It started as a warm and not unpleasant pulsing at the top of his neck, then crawled upward to the bony place behind his ears, the place that still remembered the childhood pain of German measles. He wrestled harder with the unmoving valve handle, small grunts escaping past his teeth. The throbbing crept up both sides of his head, moved up almost soothingly, like hot fingers on his scalp. The light was bad under the sink, Vincente couldn't see the red rust and green corrosion that glutted the valve's old threads. He only knew that it was meant to turn, that a man was meant to be able to turn it.

He was sweating now, his legs were cramping. He began to be dizzy. He pulled back for a moment to summon strength, blinked around the tiled bathroom, but saw only a shrinking tube of brightness. He hunkered down again, stretched his neck, seized the handle like the windpipe of a deadly enemy. The throbbing crested at the top of his head and now was pushing outward from behind his eyes. He gave a final twist and a whimper of frustration, then, he didn't quite know how, his hands had lost their grip and he had gone from kneeling to lying backward on the tile floor. The floor sucked warmth away from his flank. He saw a white glare smeared with acid yellow; it was ugly, and he was grateful when his eyes fell closed.

Confusion lingered for a moment, but it passed, and then the Godfather felt weirdly, deadly happy. He was floating, empty, on a brief vacation so splendid as to undo his life. Behind his eyelids, different colors scudded past; he tried them on like ties. He saw a color he especially loved and locked it into place. It was a reddish purple streaked with black; he recognized it instantly as the color of the pressed grapes when his father made wine in the basement sixty years before. He smelled the mash—musky, woody, more like wine than the finished wine itself—and then he smiled, or thought he did, when he remembered what was done with the squeezed-out fruit. They had a fig tree in the backyard, a fig tree that bore figs in Queens. It was a thousand miles out of place, this tree, but it would live the winter if you took care of it, if you decked it out. So the pressed grapes would be spread around the tree, would ripen again into a gorgeous reddish-purple mat of stems and skins and mold. Tarpaper, ashes, old linoleum held down with tires—everything was blanketed around the tree, built up in a cone that sometimes gave off steam. And in the summer there'd be figs, their skins sticky with oozing juice, their insides warm as thighs. And basil, huge bouquets of it, and tomatoes, red as fire engines even at the core . . .

The Godfather stirred. Flat light filtered through his eyelids. His ears hummed though the throbbing in his head had eased, flattened into a steady ache. He remembered where he was, remembered that some six decades, a little more, had passed. He'd have to tell Arty about the fig tree, the mat of grapes. He told himself, Remember ta tell Ahty.

He opened his eyes. He saw the porcelain of the commode, the open cabinet of the leaky sink he'd failed to fix. A drop fell from the faucet, mocking him.

He rested awhile, telling himself there was no reason he shouldn't stay there on the chilly floor next to the toilet. Finally he got to his knees, put things back into the cabinet, closed it up. He didn't want to leave a mess, didn't want anyone to know he'd fainted or that he'd tried to do a simple job and couldn't do it. He paused a moment more, then slowly stood and went on thin unsteady legs to his bed.

CHAPTER SEVENTEEN

"'Lo, Bert," said a voice from over his left shoulder.

The resurrected mobster, his clogged chihuahua dozing on his lap, made only a slow and grudging effort to turn around. He was on the beach, sitting in his folding mesh-weave chair; it was nearly sunset and he wasn't feeling sociable. The cold front had passed through, leaving in its wake a crystalline blue sky and a brisk wind that chased the ocean ripples back to sea. He wanted just to watch.

But, grudgingly, he turned. He saw two men, one of them an old acquaintance from New York. His name was Hawkins, and a decade or so before he'd been a most aggressive and resourceful cop, the agent who, almost single-handedly, had built the so-called I-Beam case and had subpoenaed Bert the Shirt to testify at the trial of his bosses. Bert had been walking up the courthouse steps, rehearsing the words of the Fifth Amendment, when the pressure got him and he died.

"Well, whaddya know," he said, and with no further comment he turned back toward the green ocean and the sinking orange sun.

His two visitors strolled around his chair and stood in front of him in the crumbled coral that passed for sand. Bert took a moment to size up the other guy: short, white, thick-built in a sleeveless shirt and running shorts. He said to Hawkins, black, tall, almost gangly, "Congratulations, Ben. I didn't know you had a son."

Mark Sutton's sprayed hair moved no more than a building in the wind, but his neat bland face crawled with affronted dignity. He moved his mouth, but before he could speak he doubled over and gave a wrenching sneeze.

"*Salud*," said Bert. "Y'ain't dressed warm enough."

The sneeze woke up his dog. It whimpered and he petted it back into its habitual half-sleep.

"This is Agent Mark Sutton," Hawkins said.

Bert ignored the introduction. "Those winter colds," he said. "I remember 'em. The mucus, postnasal drip, the way your nostrils get all crusty inside, after a few days they bleed." He put his hands behind his head, sucked in a deep breath of salty air. "Mus' be mizzable up theah."

Ben Hawkins crinkled up his stuffed nose and sniffled. "Don't gloat, Bert," he said. "Man your age, it's unbecoming."

The old mafioso motioned like he was composing a photograph, then waved the younger agent a little to the right. "Yo, Muscles, you're blockin' my view."

Sutton slid over an inch or two.

Hawkins said, "Nice shirt."

Lovingly, Bert caressed his billowing sleeve. The blouse was of a heavy, nubby linen, a forest-green background with tiny pastel boomerangs. "Good clot', good tailoring, seams ya could swing on . . . Ya come alla way down heah to compliment me on my habbadashery?"

"Checking out the hit on Emilio Carbone," said Mark

Sutton. He set his mouth in a purposeful frown and gave a slight flex to his abs.

Bert jerked in his chair, threw his hands up like in the Wild West. "How'd ya know it was me, kid? OK, ya got me fair and square."

Hawkins shook his head. "Same old Bert. Always taking credit."

Bert didn't answer, he just stared at Ben Hawkins's feet, stared at them so long that eventually Mark Sutton and Hawkins himself glanced down at them as well, looking for an answer to some mute mystery. "I was just tryin'a think," the old man said at last, "if ever in my life, even once before, I seen a black guy wearin' boat shoes."

"Vincente Delgatto's in town," said Hawkins.

"And speakin' a habbadashery," said Bert, "you, Hawkins, you think you're dressed for Key West? Creased chinos? Gingham shirt? You're dressed for fuckin' Palm Beach. Muscles heah, he's dressed for Key West. Tank top. Tight shorts. The fellas on Duval Street are gonna love 'im."

"Must be nice having an old friend around," said Ben Hawkins. "Been seeing him?"

"Nah," said Bert. "Busy schedule. Ya know, hot dates, gin rummy. Lotta women after me." He scratched Don Giovanni behind the ears and looked out across the ocean. Windblown ripples skidded southward, toward the sun. For some reason Bert found it sad to see the water move that way, receding.

"Some people think Delgatto called the hit on Carbone," said Mark Sutton.

"That's fuckin' stupid," said the Shirt.

"Gino's in town too," said Hawkins. "We thought maybe there's a confab going on."

The sun went a shade redder and seemed to spin as it made its arcing dive for the horizon. "You try havin' a confab wit' Gino," Bert suggested. "See if ya can follow two words he says."

A moment passed. Then Hawkins said, "Bert, there's no hard feelings between us, right?"

He petted his dog. "Ya mean just because ya killed me? 'Course not. Best thing that ever happened. Wit'out ya killed me, I could be standin' theah like you. Red eyes, runny nose—"

"So maybe you'll help us out this time," Ben Hawkins said.

"Don't make me laugh, I got chapped lips."

"You're an easy guy to talk to, Bert," said Hawkins. "Maybe Vincente said something, maybe the Fabrettis have been in touch."

"I'm retired," said the Shirt. "Thanks to you."

Mark Sutton put his hands on his hips and bent forward with a show of menace. "You're not retired as far as we're concerned."

The Shirt looked deeply unimpressed. "Where'd ya find this guy," he said to Hawkins, "the high school gym?"

"Be nice, Bert," urged Ben Hawkins. "Who knows, maybe sometime there'd be something we could do for you."

Bert peered off at the ocean. The sun was a finger's breadth above it now, pouring an endless stream of molten stuff that put a red trough in the water. The line of flame spilled straight toward Bert the Shirt but then was intercepted by the bulk of Mark Sutton's quadriceps. "There is," the old man said to Hawkins. "Ya could ask Muscles heah ta please stop standin' in my light."

CHAPTER EIGHTEEN

THAT EVENING, sitting outside on the patio, Joey Goldman said, "Pop, I think that's great. Terrific. I'm happy for ya."

The bastard son half rose from his chair, leaned across the low metal table, and touched his father's shoulder. The touch was part squeeze, part pat on the back, it seemed more like something a father would do to a son than vice versa, and the upside-downness of the moment made both men feel a little shy. Vincente looked down and almost smiled. Writing a book—OK, *telling* a book— the newness of it, the unlikeliness, did in fact make him feel somehow boyish, pleasantly green. For a couple of breaths he basked in the quiet pleasure of realizing that even now, at the age of seventy-three, he could still surprise himself, still strike off toward the unexpected. He savored that realization until he could no longer ignore the fact that Gino, his firstborn, his heir, had made no response whatever to his news.

Finally he could not help asking, "And you, Gino, you got anything ta say?"

The heavy man shifted in his chair, he turned onto a hip so that his ample backside was lifted slightly toward his father and his jowly sulking face was held away. He sucked his teeth, pushed out his lips, and said at last, "I think it's wrong. Ya want the truth, I think it fucking stinks."

Overhead, crisp winter stars were shining; the cloudless sky seemed empty of all movement. A blue gleam hovered above the lightly rippled surface of Joey Goldman's swimming pool. Gino's vehemence came as a rude insertion in the stillness.

"You of all people, Pop," he went on. "Blabbin'. Spillin' your guts. Tellin' everyone about us. It ain't right."

Joey watched his father, waited for the old man to defend himself, to put Gino in his place. But Vincente just sat, his hands folded in his lap, his long hairy ears apparently unstung by his son's complaints. It was the younger brother who could not keep silent.

"Gino, it's a different world out there," he said. "What're we talking heah, Sicilian passwords? Secret handshakes? Ya think Pop's gonna give away any deep dark secrets, ya think he's gonna say things that could hurt—"

"That ain't the point," said Gino.

"No?" said Joey. "Then what is the point?"

Asked for logic, Gino swiveled farther in his chair, presented a wider swath of his ass. He chewed a fingernail, grunted, then finally said, "The point is that who we are, what we do, it's like . . . separate."

Joey crossed his legs, hugged an ankle. "Separate from what?"

Gino gestured broadly, tried to pluck an answer out of the cool and empty air. "From everything. From how the other jerks live, how they do their business, how they settle things—"

"All the more reason," Joey said, "that someone should tell the story from the inside—"

The Godfather interrupted. He broke in with a rumble; there was a low rasp that readied the air before the words came out. "Gino, you got any money?"

The question seemed to come from nowhere, it made the big man squirm. He gave a short nervous laugh that was meant to sound offhand. "Plenny, Pop. But I don't see where money has to do—"

"I just thought," Vincente said, "maybe it bothered you, what I'm payin' Ahty, that after I'm dead it's his ta sell."

Gino tried to wave that notion away with a gesture that was a little too emphatic. "Nah, Pop, nah. It ain't the money. It's just that—"

He broke off, twisted in his seat, shook his head, and wriggled in his choked quest for words.

"I'm listenin'," said the Godfather.

"He's an outsider," Gino spluttered. "He ain't even Italian. Fuck is he, Jewish? So now you're gonna be spendin' all this time wit' 'im, gettin' close wit' 'im—"

"Gino, you jealous?" asked his brother.

"Fuck you, Joey. It ain't about that."

"It ain't about money," Joey said right back. "It ain't about bein' jealous. Gino, the more you shoot your mouth off, the more things it comes out it ain't about."

Gino's flat black eyes picked up blue light from the pool and zinged it at Joey. The big man's hairline crawled, the cloth of his trousers chafed him, his glower flicked back and forth between his father and his brother, and he couldn't figure out who he was madder at. When he spoke again his voice was dangerously calm. "Look," he said. "I don't wanna be embarrassed. 'Zat so fuckin' hard t'understand?"

"Gino," Joey said, "Pop ain't gonna—"

Gino cut him off. "You ain't a Delgatto. Fuck's it to you? For all I know, your Jew friend's givin' you a cut—"

"That's enough, Gino," Vincente said. He said it very softly. His hands were folded against his shrunken stomach. He looked at his two sons and wondered how much power and how much wisdom it would take to do right by more than one person at a time. A breeze stirred, just cool enough to tickle the backs of necks. Finally Vincente spoke again.

"Gino," he said, "look at me. I'm doin' this thing, my mind's made up. But my word as your father: I won't do or say anything that would embarrass you."

The two of them locked eyes. Gino's pudgy face was a mix of umbrage and defiance; Vincente's expression held determination and a dim unlikely hope. He wanted Gino to believe him, and he wished that Gino would return his promise, his pledge not to dishonor their common name, though he understood that was probably too much to wish for.

Gino went away mad.

He climbed into his rented T-Bird, floored it in reverse, and drove the few short blocks to Flagler House. But when he got there, saw the valet coming to take charge of the car, he decided he wasn't ready to go in yet; he wanted to ride around and think. He peeled out of the driveway and started over.

He drove up A1A, along the beach toward the airport.

A lopsided moon was just coming up over the Florida Straits. A powdery orange pocked with gray, it threw a reddish beam that ran along the flat water and tracked the car as it barreled up the road.

The white lines slipped past, the coastline curved, and meanwhile Gino was thinking about obedience and respect. Or at least that's what he thought he was thinking about. In truth, he was thinking more about what he could dare to get away with. Not that he was against obedience. No, obedience was a handy thing, it made it nothing personal if, say, you were called upon to hurt someone; it justified holding back, say, from something that deep down you were scared to do. You obeyed out of respect, which was fear dressed up in fancy clothes, and the respect gave the whole business its dignity.

Still, there were times when obedience was a burden, a cramp, a real pain in the ass, and in those situations it was only natural that a guy would find a reason, many reasons, to disobey. Who wouldn't? If other guys played by the rules no matter what, that would be one thing, but hey. . . . Gino squeezed the steering wheel and thought about his old man's book. It broke the rules in every way. Telling secrets. Trusting outsiders. Did you still have to follow orders from a man who did things like that? Especially if the orders held you back from something where there was a nice buck to be made?

Gino didn't quite notice where he'd made a U-turn, but at some point he'd spun the car around; the moon was on the other side. He was heading back toward Flagler House and something had been decided.

When he bulled into his top-floor oceanfront room, he did not at first see Debbi. He found her out on the balcony, sipping a martini and looking at the stars. She was holding her fingers at peculiar, pained, arthritic angles, and it took Gino a moment to understand her nails were drying.

"Tomorrow we're drivin'a Miami," he announced.

"Jesus, Gino. Not again."

By way of answer, Gino said, "Juh order *me* a drink?"

Debbi looked through the railing at the palm trees on the beach. "Other people," she said, "they come ta Florida ta relax. You, ya come ta Florida, ya run around like a cockaroach."

Gino went inside to call room service.

Debbi kept talking to his back. "Can't we sit still five minutes? Can't we settle in a little bit?"

Gino ordered a bottle of bourbon, switched the TV on, and poked his head just for a second through the open sliding door to the balcony. Obedience could sometimes be a cramp, a pain, and so could the company of a complaining broad. "I'm drivin' up for a day or so. You wanna stay, stay. I don't give a fuck."

CHAPTER NINETEEN

"Look," said Sandra Dugan, as she rummaged through the refrigerator for romaine, endive, hearts of palm, "it's always a gamble. When I started in with Joey, that was a gamble too."

Debbi Martini leaned against the counter and sipped a glass of water. She was happy to be standing in this kitchen, pleased with herself for having had the nerve to call Sandra that morning. When Sandra invited her to come by and have lunch, gratitude had closed her throat. Now she gave a little laugh and said, "Joey, a gamble? Joey's so nice, so regular."

Sandra's head was in the fridge, her voice was muffled by lettuces, muted by the pith of grapefruits. "When I met him," she said, "he didn't know it yet."

"Didn't know it?" Debbi said.

Sandra wheeled, handed the other woman some greens, kicked the fridge door shut. "We were living in Queens. He was still very close with his family, that whole group. You know what I'm saying. Joey was the kid brother. He thought he had a lot to prove."

Debbi considered, and realized all at once that she felt like a kid sister, standing there with Sandra. They were pretty much the same age, give or take a year or two, but Sandra had a husband, ran a business, was mistress of a real house with matching plates. Sandra hired and fired people, picked out furniture. She had a sense of the future—her stocked refrigerator told you that. Sandra, in short, was a grown-up, had lucked or bluffed or willed her way to some mysterious graduation, while she, Debbi, seemed to keep repeating the same dreary classes in remedial life. From bad in school to frustrated at work. From Mr. Wrong to Mr. Trouble to Mr. Cokehead to Mr. Slob.

"You like sprouts?" Sandra asked.

"Hm?" said Debbi. "Yeah, love 'em. . . . So with Joey—what made him change?"

Sandra took a sun-warmed tomato off the windowsill behind the sink. She cut into it and seeds spilled out. "Hard to say."

"Coming to Florida?" suggested Debbi.

"Nah, the change had to come before the move. Otherwise he never would've made it south of Staten Island." She pointed toward a high shelf with her nose. "Grab that salad bowl, would ya?"

Reaching up, Debbi said, "I guess people have to get pretty fed up before they change, pretty sick and tired of not being happier."

"And they have to believe they *could* be happier," said Sandra.

She finished cutting the tomato, then tested an avocado with her thumbs. Debbi shredded romaine and looked out the window. She saw trees, light, air; the clean spaciousness sucked the deflating truth right out of her. Absently, she said, "Gino—Gino's never gonna change."

The avocado wasn't ripe enough, Sandra put it back on the sill. She bit her lip, weighed how far to get involved.

She was chewing back the words *So dump him, girl*, when the doorbell rang. Glad to escape, she wiped her hands on a dish towel and went to answer it.

It was Bert the Shirt. His lean form was framed by glaring sunshine and he seemed to be fresh out of the shower; his white hair with its bronze and pinkish glints was brushed back in neat damp bundles. He was wearing a canary yellow pullover of polished Egyptian cotton and carrying his drowsy dog. "Hullo, Sandra," he said. "Your father-in-law around?"

"He's in the garden," Sandra said. "Puttering as usual. Come in."

She led the visitor through the living room, into the kitchen. He saw the food on the counter. "Hey, if you're having lunch, I'll come back—"

"Vincente's not eating," Sandra said. "Doesn't want to break off pruning. But Bert, say hello to Debbi. She's down here with Gino."

"Charmed," said the old mafioso, and he extended his hand. Debbi took it and smiled at him, but almost instantly her attention shifted to the dog.

"And who's this little fur face?" she asked.

"This?" said Bert. He put on a dismissive scowl and held the chihuahua away, as if it were a smelly little parcel he was taking to the trash. "This is Don Giovanni, world's oldest, laziest, most worthless dog. This is a rug-wetting curse from my late wife. This is a brainless four-legged bundle a aggra—"

"He has some problems, doesn't he?" said Debbi.

There was something in her tone that Bert had not expected, something knowing, serious. It instantly pulled him out of his old routine. "Yeah," he said. "He has some problems."

"Cataracts," said Debbi. "Probably arthritis."

Bert looked at her more closely. Red hair, probably perked up from a bottle. Long fingernails perfect as wax apples. Nose-cone boobs scoring a dramatic but temporary victory over gravity. So far, standard equipment for a woman traveling with the Ginos of this world. Still, there was something in the blue-green eyes that didn't fit the mold. Bimbos' eyes—you could look at them but never into them, they were blank and opaque, like the paint on a car. But Debbi's eyes invited you in; behind the colored part was a room as comfy as a paneled den. "He's got other problems too," confided Bert.

"Like what?" asked Debbi.

Bert glanced at the salad bowl, the glistening tomatoes. "You ladies are about to eat," he said. "It ain't the pleasantest subject."

"Tell me," Debbi said. "Maybe I can help."

Bert looked at his sneakers, pulled an earlobe. "Well," he said, "ya want the truth, he's constipated somethin' awful. I can't think the last time he had what you could call a successful walk."

"Poor puppy," Debbi said. She said it to the dog, and the dog lifted up its white and ancient head. It weakly shook its whiskers, a ray of hope seemed to flash in its milky eyes like dim lightning buried in the clouds. The pet groomer reached out and felt the creature's abdomen; it was hard and nubbly as a potato. "There a health food store around?" she asked.

The old mobster found the question droll. "Debbi, I

live on meatballs, sausage. I smoked t'ree packs till I was sixty-five and had a haht attack—"

"There's one on Southard Street," said Sandra.

"Get some flaxseed," Debbi told Bert.

"Flaxseed?"

"Just ask for it. Take a tablespoon of it, slow-simmer it in a quarter cup of mineral oil—"

"How 'bout olive oil?" asked the Shirt.

"Whatever," Debbi said. "Simmer it like half an hour, let it cool, mix it with his dog food."

Bert was leaning forward now, avid at the prospect of a cure. "Yeah? Then what?"

"Wait an hour, take him for a nice relaxing stroll, and sing to him."

"Sing to 'im?" said Bert.

Debbi petted the dog. "That part I made up. But the rest, really—"

Bert looked hard at her, took the measure of her wisdom. Then he said, "How you know all this?"

Debbi felt suddenly bashful and only shrugged.

"You're a clever kid," Bert told her.

She looked down at the tiled floor. "No," she said, "I'm really not."

Certain things you could only do when your hair was white, when your teeth were loose, when the sleeves of your shirts flapped like hung laundry around your shrunken arms. Bert reached out a hand and lifted Debbi's chin. "Don't contradict an old man," he said. "I tol' ya you're a clever kid."

Out in the garden, the Godfather was trimming bougainvillea. Streamers of the stuff hung over him as he worked, he half disappeared behind a curtain of fuchsia flowers and wicked ocher thorns. Fallen petals lodged in his straw hat that was unraveling at the edges, a line of sweat traced out his backbone beneath the old blue shirt. He was barefoot, he had a red bandanna tied around his stringy neck, and he was too immersed in his task to see or hear Bert the Shirt approaching. He kept right on clipping until his old friend gave a low chuckle and said, "Vincente, Jesus, no offense, but ya look like a real *paisan*."

The Godfather brushed aside a strand of vine and turned around. "Bert, what could I tell ya—I *am* a real *paisan*."

He stepped out from the canopy of flowers, put his shears point down in the soft imported dirt, and raked a forearm across his sweating brow. As he did so he felt Bert's eyes on his naked feet, his soiled insteps.

He shook his head and said, "Poor fuckin' immigrants, huh? They get shoes that pinch, they try ta grow basil onna fuckin' fire escape; they get a job wit'out a window, their wives start wearin' girdles. They tell themselves they're doin' good, but down deep . . . Ah, screw it. What's up, Bert?"

"Siddown a minute?"

Vincente didn't answer, just started walking toward the low table on the patio. It bothered him to take a break, but since his fainting spell it bothered him less. This surprised him, and he thought, Thank God that people— some people—got less pigheaded when the alternative was dropping dead, that they could give some ground without totally losing pleasure in the things they loved to do.

"The FBI's in town," Bert said when they were seated.

The Godfather said nothing.

"Hawkins and some new boy wonder," Bert informed him.

Vincente nodded. He'd never met Ben Hawkins but he knew who he was. His roving circle of cops and robbers—at the more select levels it was a very small club.

Bert petted his chihuahua, plucked a ghostly dog hair from his yellow shirt. "They know you're here. They were askin' me 'bout the Carbone thing."

Still the Godfather said nothing. He put a hand under his nose, smelled soil and sap; the smell pulled him back to ancient summers and memories of greater strength.

Bert paused, then cleared his throat. "Vincente, I know better than t'ask—"

"Then don't," said the Godfather, not unkindly. "It's simpler that way."

Bert looked down at his lap. Vincente glanced over at the bougainvillea. The papery flowers were fluttering in the breeze, the leaves were a lush green but the sound they made was brown and dry.

"The Feds," the Godfather went on, "they can set me up, arrest me any time. I knew that when I took the job, Bert. The power they have, it's unbelievable."

"Big power," his friend agreed. "Like the whole fuckin' world's their neighborhood."

"But I don't want 'em in my face down here," Vincente said. "I don't want 'em botherin' my family. 'Zat too fuckin' much t'ask?"

Bert stroked his dog reflectively, like the dog was his own chin. "Nah," he said, "it ain't too much. They should at least be whaddyacallit, discreet."

"'Course," the Godfather mused, "wit' the Feds, it's tough ta know how much decency t'expect."

"Hawkins is OK," said Bert the Shirt. "He won't bust your balls wit'out he's got a reason."

The Godfather toyed with some loose strands of his unraveling straw hat. "And the new guy?"

Bert smoothed the placket of his shirt. "The trut'? Him I didn't like. He's two things that worry me: young and short. Tries too hard, double. I'm just not sure he'd give a guy an even break."

"An even break from the Feds?" Vincente said. "Bert, you always were a dreamer."

CHAPTER TWENTY

ARTY MAGNUS raised his right arm high and let the thin and tortured spray of lukewarm water chase the soap out of his armpit and down his flank.

His showerhead had annoyed him every day for just over six years now. It was a small, cheap, fake-chrome job to begin with, and over time many of its holes had silted up with minerals. Water squeezed through it painfully, it was like a man with kidney stones. Instead of forceful parallel streams, it hissed out dribs and jets at random angles, a lot of the water missed his body altogether and clattered uselessly against the aluminum stall, which was painted a lumpy, ugly shade of tan, a sort of nuthouse beige. Some years before, something had gone wrong with the floor of the shower; the drain was no longer at its lowest point. Water pooled in a corner, and tropical algae, mold, and fungi often grew there. Sometimes the growths were green, sometimes black—it just depended what spores were in the air. Once the stagnant puddle had turned golden and begun to foam like beer.

Rinsed now, drying off, Arty looked around and wondered for the thousandth time why he'd stayed so long in the rented four-room transient-looking cottage on Nassau Lane. When he'd first come to Key West, he'd been reluctant to take a more expensive place—the job at the *Sentinel* was brand-new; what if it didn't pan out? As he became more entrenched in the town, he'd wrestled with the question of buying something. But at first the prices seemed too high, and so he'd hesitated. He'd been tempted when values began to decline, but stalled, waiting for the bottom of the market. Two years into the slump, he was no longer convinced that a house was necessarily such a great investment. Besides, did he really think he'd stay in Key West that much longer? He was reluctant to commit to it.

And anyway, in the main he was comfortable where he was. OK, the shower sucked. The frying pans were dented, the coffee cups were chipped, the tines of the forks were snaggled. The maroon Formica dinette had been in appalling taste thirty years ago and time had not redeemed it. But so what? The bedroom got a nice breeze, the garden was open to the southern light, and besides, Arty didn't need luxury. He didn't even *like* luxury, or, more precisely, luxury had been soured for him because it somehow put him in mind of a goad he had heard too often and never really been able to refute: that he lacked direction, was short on drive, deficient in ambition. He would never find success because he didn't want it bad enough.

That had been a heavy charge, a terrible accusation, when he'd lived up north. The attitude behind it was almost as good a reason as the weather not to live there anymore.

The weather, yes. He walked on damp feet to the bedroom and sat down bareass on the bed. It was a February dusk, the windows were wide open, and he was about to pull on a winter evening outfit of khaki shorts and a polo shirt, a cotton sweater just in case. He could not resist a quick thought of all those heads-up, savvy folks freezing their ambitious butts off in New York; in the rosy glow of picturing their hunched shoulders and chapped lips, of remembering how much a tweed jacket and woolen topcoat weighed, he could recall with serenity the goads he used to hear. He wasn't very suave at cocktail parties. Well, that was true; while smoother colleagues schmoozed their way to positions at the *Times*, the *Voice*, the glossy magazines, he hung back, wasted evenings on people he already knew. He was a washout at the high art of the query letter, not even a contender in the race for fellowships. Maybe most blameworthy of all, he'd had a no-respect job as editor of a neighborhood weekly, a dreary little rag kept afloat by ads for yoga classes and tap-dance lessons, and he'd stuck with it. Why change? The truth was, he didn't believe one job was much different from another.

This was heresy, of course, and could not go unpunished. His punishment? Condemned to live in a funky four-room cottage in paradise.

And to live there alone, but that was another story.

Arty tied his sneakers and went to the living room, one corner of which did service as his study. On a rickety table with rusted metal legs stood a small computer, some ill-assorted pads and papers, and a stack of timeworn spiral notebooks, maybe twenty in all, their covers stained with coffee and liquor, their pages fattened up with dampness. In these notebooks were almost two decades' worth of floundering, false starts, dumb ideas, proof positive of just how much Arty Magnus didn't want success. Sketches, epigrams, first paragraphs of essays, vague outlines of eccentric novels. . . . Then there was one notebook off to the side, separate from the others. This one, by God, would be a book: the story of the Godfather, the story of the end of something.

Arty reached for it, made sure his ninety-nine-cent pen was clipped into the spiral binding. Then he walked past the sagging rattan sofa, through the front door with its porous screen, and out into the day's last light. As he climbed onto his old fat-tire bike, the gruff jazz of Vincente's speech was already tapping in his ears, though, as ever, he had no idea what rages and remembrances the old man would talk about tonight.

As Arty was bicycling through Key West's quiet streets to his appointment with the Godfather, Gino Delgatto was driving his rented T-Bird up the gross ribbon of Dixie Highway to meet with Charlie Ponte. He barreled past South Miami, snaked his way across Coral Cables, and wound at last through the narrow avenues of Coconut Grove to the boss's headquarters on the waterfront.

The headquarters were at the back of a restaurant called Martinelli's, insulated from intruders by a pair of giant bubbling lobster tanks, a dim and gloomy bar, a barnlike dining room full of people wearing bibs, and an enormous kitchen stocked with short Cubans in tall hats.

As on previous visits, Gino announced himself to the maître d', who then signaled to a broken-nosed bouncer on a stool by the cigarette machine. The bouncer led him past the lobsters, past the people eating lobsters, and through the kitchen where the lobsters were prepared. Beyond the brushed-chrome freezers was a locked door that gave onto an anteroom manned by two thugs. The thugs took charge of the guest, patted him down for weapons, then took him through to the boss's inner sanctum.

This was a big room, but low-ceilinged and almost empty of furniture. Its bare walls threw back a shrill and tinny sound like cheap speakers; dim fluorescent light mixed unpleasantly with a smeared glow that came through very narrow windows of bulletproof glass. Beyond those grudging portals could be seen, distorted, the red and green channel markers of the Intracoastal. Along the docks, blurry yachts bobbed gently in their slips. A metal door with several locks gave directly onto the catwalk of the wharf, and Ponte's cigarette boat looked like a restless horse tied up right outside.

"So you're back," said the Miami boss as Gino was led in. The fact seemed to cause him no great happiness. He was a small neat man sitting slouched behind a vast and weighty desk. He had dull gray hair combed mostly forward, Caesar-style; his skin was taut and waxy except for pebbled sacs the color of liver beneath his eyes. He wore no shirt, just a silver jacket with a zipper, it was like something race-car drivers wear.

"I said I would be," Gino told him.

Ponte pressed his hands together, brought them to his mouth, and blew some air between them. He lifted an eyebrow toward one of the thugs, and the thug brought Gino a chair.

Sitting, the guest said, "I talked to my father, and it's like I tol' ya: The deal he made, it wasn't wit' the Fabrettis, it was wit' Carbone. It ain't a deal no more."

Charlie Ponte reached up a hand and rubbed his

cheeks. The tugging stretched the sacs beneath his eyes, put a morbid shine on the brown-purple flesh. "No offense, Gino, but I'd be happier hearin' this from your old man direct."

"Mr. Ponte, he's in mourning for my mother. He's not doin'—"

Gino's words were lost in the sudden bustle of Ponte rising from his chair. Standing, he was not much taller than sitting down, but there was a dangerous impatience, a violent nervousness in his posture. He paced the width of his desk and back again, then put his knuckles on a corner of it and leaned across them. "Gino, try ta see it my way, huh? I use that union, I pay tribute ta New York. I got no problem wit' that. The system's in place, the money's comin' in, everybody's happy—"

"I ain't happy," Gino said.

Ponte talked right over him. "And now you're leanin' on me to change everything aroun', risk a beef wit' the Fabrettis—"

"You don't worry about a beef wit' the Fabrettis," Gino said. "A beef wit' the Fabrettis, that's a New Yawk problem."

Ponte leaned farther across his desk, and his tone was tinny and mordant. "Yeah? And who settles a New York problem these days?"

Gino pushed down on the arms of his chair, slid forward on the seat. He was very near the end of his nerve, but he hadn't reached it yet. "You forget, Mr. Ponte? The Puglieses are still the leading family. My father is still *capo di tutti capi. We* settle New Yawk problems."

Ponte straightened, turned his back. He went to one of the narrow windows and looked out at the Intracoastal.

For what seemed a long time he watched the boats, the dirty pelicans, the channel markers flashing red and green. When he wheeled again toward his visitor, he had the look of a man who'd swallowed nasty medicine. "OK, Gino," he said, "you win. You say it's back the way it was, fine."

Gino squeezed the arms of his chair and struggled not to smile. His old man had taught him that it didn't do, was undignified, to smile.

Ponte raised a finger and went on. "But the Fabrettis—your problem, not mine."

The visitor gave the slightest nod, the way he'd seen his father do it.

Charlie Ponte moved back toward his desk; he seemed to think the meeting was over. Gino didn't budge. Ponte dropped into his chair, then finally met the other man's eye.

"The money, Mr. Ponte?"

The Miami boss made a harried nervous gesture, like his time was being wasted on niggling details. "Gino, I need a couple days. I gotta, like, reroute things, retool the machine. You understand."

Gino had the rare thought that it was now his place to be magnanimous. He gave his head a gentle tilt.

"Day after tomorra," Ponte said. "Can ya come back then? We'll do the first month's tribute. Thirty thousand."

Walking out through the kitchen and the restaurant, Gino tried with all his might to hold his face together. He wanted to grin, to cackle, to slap his chest and howl. He'd done well, extremely well; his father would be proud of him if he'd seen how smart and bold he'd been, would admit that he, Gino, had been right about this union bullshit from the start.

Or maybe he wouldn't. What then?

Gino, in his glory, strode between the tables and entertained a queasy but intoxicating thought. If the old man didn't come around, it only proved his time had passed, made it obvious that he was no longer fit to lead, that Gino, by dint of balls and independence, had himself become the Man. The notion put an itch in his scalp and a tingle in his pants, and the barnlike dining room swam before his eyes as he bulled past the people who sat there, oblivious in their lobster bibs, sucking legs and claws.

CHAPTER TWENTY-ONE

"Aut'ority," the Godfather was saying. "That's what this whole thing is about—aut'ority."

"What about it?" Arty asked. They were sitting on the patio. There was a bottle of Chianti and a plate of strong cheese and roasted peppers on the low metal table between them.

"How ya deal wit' it," Vincente said. "Ya see what I'm gettin' at?"

"Not yet," the ghostwriter confessed. His notebook was open on his lap; he'd scribbled the word *Authority* on the top of a fresh page and was looking at it hopefully. He'd been thwarted before in his efforts to put Vincente's raves into something resembling outline form. The Godfather would start off on a promising tack; Arty would give it a heading. Then the old man would carom off onto something totally different, and the heading would sit there unembellished, lonely and inexplicable as a single tree in the middle of a vast and weedy plain.

Vincente took a sip of wine. "The way I see it," he said, "aut'ority, there's like three ways ya can think about it. First way, there shouldn't *be* any aut'ority. It should be like . . . whaddya call it when there's nobody in charge?"

"Anarchy?" said Arty.

"Right, yeah. Anarchy. A very appealing idea, let's face

it. But more when you're young than when you're old. You're young, ya figure, Hey, great, nobody's tellin' me what ta do, I can play the mandolin, pull my pants down, get laid, travel—terrific. But then ya get ta realize it wouldn't work. People, ya leave 'em alone ta do what they want, they go ta these crazy extremes. Some guys, they'd get too greedy, they'd want money, power, more alla time. Other guys, they'd be just as happy sittin' home jerkin' off. Pretty soon the greedy bastards would be runnin' everything, tellin'a happy jerkoffs what ta do, an' it wouldn't be that different from like it is now. Am I right?"

Arty looked up from his notes and only nodded.

"Have a piece a cheese," the Godfather told him. "Put a pepper on top, 's good that way. . . . So the next way wit' aut'ority, ya just accept it like it is. This is what most people do, right? Cop pulls y'over for speeding—ya don't look out the winda and say, Wait a second, who the fuck are you? IRS says Pay us—ya don't tell 'em they should kiss your ass. Y'accept it."

"Not because you want to," Arty could not help putting in. "Because they have the power."

Vincente sipped wine, moved his skinny haunches to the edge of his chair, and raised a finger. "Right, they have the power. Exactly. And at some point, ya have to make a choice. Ya have ta decide which of two pains innee ass is less of a pain innee ass—t'accept that they have the power, or ta look for ways ta get around it. And what that decision rides on is whether, down deep, ya believe that whosever in charge has any fuckin' right ta be . . . Y'ever been ta Sicily?"

Arty nibbled cheese, shook his head. Wind moved the

shrubs that the floodlights were embedded in; shadows danced across the patio and over the surface of the pool.

"Sicily is like . . . how can I describe it? Sicily is a little like New Jersey. Ya know how New Yawk and Pennsylvania are always fightin' over who gets ta dump their gahbidge in New Jersey? It's like nobody gives a fuck what Jersey wants, right? Well, that's how it was wit' Sicily, on'y people weren't dumpin' gahbidge, they were dumpin' churches, fortresses, castles. Lemme tell ya somethin': Sicily is fuckin' beautiful. On'y problem is it ain't Sicilian.

"Say you're goin' down a road by the ocean. Over here, there's a beautiful temple, a ruin. But it ain't Sicilian, it's Greek. Over there, onna water, there's a big-ass fort. But it ain't Sicilian, it's Moorish. Up onna hill there's a mansion, a fuckin' palace. But it wasn't built for a Sicilian, it was built for some French fuck who once gave the King a Spain a blow job. Ya get the picture? We're talkin' thousands a years a this bullshit. So the Sicilian, he's got this very old habit a thinkin', Hey, wait a second—who put these sons a bitches in charge?"

The Godfather paused, Arty made bold to pour him more wine. Palm fronds rustled, a parched exotic sound.

"OK," Vincente resumed, "so ya don't believe in anarchy, ya don't respect the aut'ority that's there—wha' does that leave? Ya *become* the aut'ority. Unofficially, of course. *Cosa nostra*. Ya know what that means, Ahty? *Our thing*. That's all it means. It don't mean, This guy, ya break his knees. It don't mean, That guy, he goes inna river. It means *our thing*, the thing we keep no matter what, the thing these fuckin' Greeks and Moors and Spaniards can't fuck with."

Arty scrawled, flipped a page, and scrawled some more, his private shorthand getting ever more minimal with velocity and finger fatigue. He waited for the Godfather to continue, but the old man just reached forward rather daintily, put a slice of roasted pepper on top of a slab of cheese, and started nibbling. Arty was deciding whether he would challenge him—point out, say, that New York was not Palermo or that the nation where Vincente had made his career had never been invaded—when Bert the Shirt came steaming through the doorway from the living room, his dog nestled in his arms, Joey and Sandra following behind.

"Ya shoulda seen it," the retired mobster was saying. "Ya shoulda seen it!" His white hair with its pink-bronze glints was less than perfectly in place, the big sleeves of his salmon-colored linen shirt were quivering. "Jesus, ya hadda see it. It was beautiful."

"Wha', Bert?" Joey said. "What was beautiful?"

"Don Giovanni," said the Shirt. He lifted the chihuahua in his upturned palms, and it did seem that the tiny creature was proud of itself. Its whiskers turned upward at a jaunty, almost rakish angle, and its black nose sniffed the air with a quickened curiosity about the wonders of the outside world.

"Wha'd he do?" asked the Godfather.

Bert paused, looked momentarily confused. "*Marrone*, Vincente, I gotta paint ya a picture?"

No one reacted. The awkward silence only seemed to drive the doting dog owner onward.

"We were onna beach," he said. "I gave 'im the flaxseeds, just like Debbi said. She's a peach, that kid, I'm gonna send 'er flowers—Sandra, don't lemme forget.

S'anyway, we're onna beach, walkin' along, almost sunset, and the Don goes inta his squat. I'm thinkin', Oh Christ, here we go again, another failed attempt. He hunkers down inna coral, gets comfortable, looks up at me with those pathetic white eyes. I see the muscles start strainin' in 'is sides, I'm like heartbroken. Then whaddya know? The breakthrough! I don't know who was more surprised, me or the dog. . . . He shifts around a little, finishes his business, I swear ta God he smiles. Yeah, smiles! Then he starts kickin' like crazy. Sand, rocks—I mean, he's *excavatin'*. He prances off like a fuckin' whaddyacallit, a Clydesdale, like he could lick the world, the little stud."

Bert paused. The silence around him was perfect except for the soft rustling of the foliage.

"I guess ya hadda be there," he concluded, suddenly embarrassed.

The Godfather cleared his throat. "Bert, say hello to a friend of mine. Ahty Magnus, Bert d'Ambrosia."

Arty rose, smiled, extended his right hand. From his left dangled the spiral notebook, and Bert the Shirt, confused, abashed, but never altogether out of it, didn't fail to notice.

"Glass a wine?" Vincente said. "Piece a cheese?"

"Nah, Vincente, nah," said Bert. "I'm interruptin'. I shouldn'ta come bargin' in like this, but I was all worked up. I hadda tell someone."

"We're honored it was us," said Sandra. "Come inside, have a cup of coffee."

Bert shook his head. "Thanks, nah. The truth? I'm like emotionally drained, I gotta go lay down." He started turning, then hefted the chihuahua the way a butcher hefts a steak before slapping it on the scale. "But ya know,

I don't think it's my imagination. The dog is definitely lighter. Ahty, nice ta meet ya."

He went into the house. Sandra and Joey followed him.

Arty settled back into his chair, put his notebook on the low metal table. The atmosphere had gotten churned up, like water when a big boat passes; he waited for the air to flatten out. He refilled Vincente's wineglass and his own; the two men batted a shy droll smile back and forth.

After a time, the ghostwriter said, "So Vincente, we were talking about authority."

A cloud crossed the moon. It seemed to carry with it a parcel of wind that rattled the aralia hedge and put choppy little ripples in the pool. "Ah," said the Godfather. "Were we?"

CHAPTER TWENTY-TWO

Gino was feeling so pleased with himself that he spent the night at the Eden Roc in Miami Beach and availed himself of the services of a five-hundred-dollar popsy. In the morning his eyes itched, his mouth felt woolly, and the hot glary ride to Key West was four hours of irritation. When, around one, he opened the door to his top-floor oceanfront room at Flagler House, all he wanted was to crawl into bed and complete his short night's sleep.

Debbi wasn't there, and the first thing he noticed was the vase stuffed full of extravagant roses, so red they were purple. He narrowed his eyes, lumbered suspiciously to the dresser, and read the little folded card that lay next to a fallen petal. A jolt of blind jealousy flashed through him, lighting up his gut and his muscles; the adrenaline left a glow like the tail of a comet. Had Debbi been there, he would have berated her on the spot, maybe grabbed her hair while demanding an explanation. But she wasn't there, and he was sleepy. With no one watching, no one to defend his honor to, his spasm of rage soon petered out. He drew the curtains, stripped, and went to sleep.

Around three, Debbi came up from the beach. She unlocked the door; the click and the squeak brought Gino past the last stages of his nap. His righteous jealousy woke up with him. Debbi slipped into the room, dark save for the wand of sunlight that squeezed between the panels of the drapes, and the first thing she heard was, "Who the fuck is Don?"

She was wearing flip-flops; there was sand between her toes. She stepped out of the rubber thongs and said, "Gino, what're you talking about?"

"One night I'm away," he rasped, "and you're fuckin' around. I oughta slap ya silly."

"I'm turning a light on, Gino. Cover your eyes."

She switched on a night table lamp. The yellow gleam showed Gino propped on pillows, a wrinkled sheet around him like bunting. His skin was blotched with sleep, his face was wrinkled. He looked like a gigantic hairy newborn.

"So who is 'e?" he insisted. Then he put on a fey and sour voice and quoted the little card. "*You set me free. Don Giovanni.* What kinda faggot poetry bullshit is 'at?"

Debbi slipped out of the smock she wore over her bathing suit. Sunburn had freckled her shoulders; wisps of red hair escaped from the clip at the nape of her neck and tickled the peeling skin. "You're pathetic, Gino." She wanted a shower. She went into the bathroom and locked the door behind her.

Gino sat bolt upright in the bed. His glands were telling him he'd been insulted, wronged; now he couldn't even get an answer to his question. Naked, hairy, furious, he bounded off the mattress, lumbered to the bathroom, and hammered on the door. "Who is 'e, goddammit?"

Debbi turned the shower on, got ready to step in.

"Answer me, you tramp!" screamed Gino.

Serenely, Debbi eased herself into the hot rain of hissing spray. Gino punched the door. Then he slammed it

129

with his shoulder; the wood creaked on the hinges. Debbi thought, Oh hell, let's not have the police. She reached around the shower curtain and undid the lock. Gino bulled against the door again. This time it opened easily. The big man's momentum carried him skating naked across the damp tiles of the bathroom floor. He bounced off the far wall, hit his chin on a towel rack, and ended up sitting on the toilet. He'd used it last; the seat was up.

Above the hiss of the shower, Debbi said, "He's a dog, you asshole."

Now Gino was confused. "Who's a dog?"

"Don Giovanni," she said. "Your father's friend Bert? His dog. I gave 'im a laxative."

Gino said nothing, just sat there on the pot. Debbi poked her wet head from behind the curtain. "Maybe you should take one too, Gino. Improve your disposition. When we gettin' outa here?"

The big man shifted on the lip of the bowl, groped for a way to get on top of things again. "Gettin' out?" he said. "You're the one who's always sayin' why don't we stay awhile, settle in."

It was Debbi's turn not to answer. She put her head under the full force of the shower, reveled in the streaming oblivion of it. She was over wanting to settle in. She'd crossed the line. Probably she'd crossed it days before, but now she knew she'd crossed it. All she wanted now was to be done with Gino.

At around four o'clock that afternoon, Marge Fogarty, the silver-haired copy editor and receptionist at the Key

West *Sentinel*, stepped into Arty Magnus's cubicle and told him there were two men who wanted to see him.

The editor looked up from his computer screen. "Who are they?"

"They wouldn't say," said Marge.

"Dirtbags? Crackpots?" That's who usually clamored for the attention of newspaper editors: people with festering grievances, paranoid obsessions, people who had worn out the ears of everyone they knew.

Marge peeked over the top of her bifocals. "They don't look local and they seem respectable."

Arty gave a resigned shrug, and Marge went to fetch the visitors.

In a moment she was back with a white man and a black man. The black man was tall, with wide-spaced eyes and a grayish dusky skin; his hair was silver on the sides and he was fastidiously dressed in pleated poplin trousers and a mint-green oxford-cloth shirt. The white man was short and knobby; he wore khaki shorts and a polo shirt whose banded sleeves were snug against his bulging triceps.

"What can I do for you?" Arty said to them, polite but not too welcoming.

For a moment they didn't speak. They waited for Marge Fogarty to withdraw, waited to see if she would close the door to Arty Magnus's office. But this was Key West; there was no door. The only modicum of privacy was afforded by the rumbling, groaning air conditioner at the editor's back. The FBI men eased forward to get within the shadow of its noise and presented their credentials.

Arty glanced at the badges, the ID cards. He felt a

flutter of that absurd inchoate guilt that even saints must feel when confronted on any pretext by a cop. He tried to smile but his lips stuck to his teeth. "What brings you to Key West?"

If this was the old we-know-that-you-know game, Mark Sutton had no patience for it. "A friend of yours," he jumped right in. "You visited with him last night. You arrived by bicycle at six-thirty-six P.M., you left at eight-fourteen. We took the liberty of following you home."

Arty folded his hands in front of him. He did not consciously decide to fib; he fibbed, rather, on a protective hunch, an instinct, though he could not have said who he was protecting, or precisely why. "You mean Joey Goldman? Yeah, he's a friend of mine. But what—"

"You met his father?" asked Ben Hawkins.

"Yeah, I've met the old man. Sure."

"You know who he is?" Mark Sutton asked.

It dawned on Arty quite suddenly that his guests were standing and he was sitting. His tiny office had no extra seats. Fetching a couple might be a good way to gain some time to think. Rising, he said, "Lemme grab some chairs—"

"We don't need to sit," Mark Sutton said. He leaned down, not very far, and put his palms on Arty's desk. "Do you know who Joey Goldman's father is?"

Arty sat again, considered. He'd blurted one fib already; that he could forgive himself. But two fibs made a lie, and soon there was a pattern, a universe of lies, and the thought of that put a sick taste in his mouth, a revolting taste as of biting into something rotten. "Yeah," he said. "I know."

The young agent gave a vindicated nod, then blew his

nose into a red bandanna. "He's a lifelong criminal. A dangerous man. Scum."

"He sits in the shade and putters in the garden," Arty could not help answering. "Not very dangerous as far as I can see."

Ben Hawkins crossed his arms; his crisp clothes all but creaked as he changed positions. "No offense, Mr. Magnus, but you can't see very far. A few weeks ago, there was a gangland killing in New York—"

"I've read about it," Arty said.

"All right then," said Ben Hawkins. "Listen, we're here for information. You know these people. You're welcome in their house . . ."

Arty splayed his hands out on his desk. Behind him, the ancient air conditioner dribbled out a drop of condensation that splashed dully on the rotting floor. Tension was crawling up the back of his neck and making his scalp clamp down around his brain, and yet he almost smiled. He was hearing Vincente rasp and rattle on about authority. You can accept it, resist it, become it, or just shut your mouth and try to live an unbowed life as though you were free to decide things for yourself.

"Sorry," said Arty. "I like these people. You guys, I don't know you from Adam. I don't want to get involved."

"It's your duty as a citizen to be involved," said Sutton.

That made Arty scratch an ear. He was at the age when he'd just begun to notice that there were people in the world who were considerably greener, sillier, more confidently stupid than himself.

Ben Hawkins understood that his partner had laid an egg. He took another tack. "You know what the RICO statute is, Mr. Magnus?"

"Sure."

"Not a favorite law of mine. But our boss enjoys noodling around with it. Personally, I think he stretches it a little far, tries to make it reach all the way to friends of friends. Bottom line—you can't always pick where you're involved."

Arty poked his tongue around inside his cheek. To his surprise, he was feeling feisty, getting mad. "Gentlemen," he said, "my dealings with cops have been limited to my work as a reporter. So bear with me if I seem a little slow. Are you threatening me?"

Mark Sutton looked at Ben Hawkins from underneath his mat of too-neat hair. Hawkins's eyes were urging him to go easy, but of course the young agent did not. "Threatening?" he said. "No. Not threatening. Not yet. Just suggesting that it might be in your interests to co-operate with us."

He reached for his wallet, coaxed it from his back pocket, past the knotted muscles of his buttocks. He produced a business card, let it flutter down onto Arty's blotter. "Maybe you'll reconsider."

The agents left. Arty leaned back in his chair, his wet shirt stuck to his shoulders. He picked up the card with the Bureau seal and made a move toward the wastebasket; then, without quite knowing why he did it, he dropped it into the back of his Rolodex instead.

CHAPTER TWENTY-THREE

VINCENTE WAS home alone when Gino and his bim came to say goodbye the following afternoon.

In a shady spot out by the pool, the father and the son embraced, but things were wrong between them, the clasp was awkward; chest to chest they came no closer than before.

"Take care, Pop," Gino said as he backed away. "I'll see ya in New Yawk."

Vincente could think of nothing to say that would not ring false, and so he only nodded.

Debbi reached out her hand, and the old man surprised them both by taking her in his arms. Perhaps he did it mainly to erase the empty feel of Gino. The hug put a catch in Debbi's throat. It had nothing to do with feelings toward Vincente, only with his uneasy gift of drawing out the truth from others.

Debbi asked him please to say goodbye to Sandra and to thank Bert for the flowers.

Gino floored the rented T-Bird in reverse, the tires spit gravel onto his bastard brother's lawn, and he headed for Miami.

On the long hot drive up U.S. 1, they saw pelicans skimming green water with their wing tips, ospreys perched on lampposts with fish still wriggling in their talons. Gino hardly spoke. Debbi figured he was being surly; it was all the same to her. But in fact he wasn't being surly. He was happy, excited, and he was hoarding his excitement, savoring it, trying with the clenched pleasure of a man withholding semen to prolong it. He was on his way to pick up thirty thousand dollars. More than that, he was on his way to claim a prize, clinch a victory that would in turn confirm him as a leader.

They passed Key Largo, made the unmomentous crossing to the mainland. On the MacArthur Causeway to South Miami Beach, Gino said to Debbi, "So I'll leave ya at a café, you'll have a drink. I'll see dis guy I gotta see, I'll come back for ya in an hour, hour and a half, we'll go straight ta de airport."

"Fine, Gino," Debbi said. She was looking out her own side window at the cruise ship docks. The mention of a drink made her realize to her slight bewilderment that she didn't feel like having one.

On Ocean Drive she got out of the car in front of a place called Bar Toscano. Gino's tires squealed and he was gone before she'd rounded the rail that stretched along the sidewalk.

Alone, he allowed himself to vent a little glee. He squeezed the steering wheel, indulged in a brief carnivorous grin, came forth with a short percussive laugh.

But by the time he drove into the parking lot at Martinelli's he was composed again.

It was with a certain gravity that he gave his name to the maître d' at the podium, with a kind of pomp that he followed the broken-nosed bouncer past the lobster tanks and through the dining room to the kitchen. His dignity was undiminished as he let himself be patted down by the thugs in the outer chamber of Charlie Ponte's office, and when the inner door was opened he stood still a moment, reviewing his posture, straightening the placket of his shirt. Charlie Ponte, in his silver jacket, was sitting at his desk. His small hands were folded, and he gave Gino a little smile.

But when Gino moved through the doorway, something went terribly wrong. There was a sudden agony in the small of his back, a splintered fiery pain arced up under his ribs. The pain made him go rigid, and when the blow came at the base of his skull he didn't roll with it, he caught it the way a house absorbs a wrecking ball, and it knocked him full length to the floor. He fell so fast he couldn't get his hands out under him; he landed on his chin and split it open. Maybe he was knocked out briefly or maybe he was just confused. The next thing he noticed was that the sole of a boot was on his neck, and Charlie Ponte, looking a great deal taller than he really was, was standing over him with his arms crossed against his stomach.

A small pool of blood was spreading away from Gino's chin, he couldn't move his head to get away from the iron smell of it. Fish-eyed and nauseous, he looked up at Charlie Ponte. "Ya crossed me, ya little cocksucker. Ya set me up."

Ponte only smiled. "I didn't cross ya, Gino. I'm givin' ya a chance to keep your word."

The boot came off of Gino's neck; he crawled and rolled and managed to sit up on the floor. He saw four muscle guys – Ponte's bodyguards and two others. One of the new guys was holding the lead pipe with which he'd bashed him in the kidney; the other still palmed the sap he'd used to pummel in his brains.

Ponte went on calmly. "Gino, you distinctly said the Fabrettis were your headache, you settle New York problems." He gestured toward the new guys. "So here's your problem, Gino. Settle it."

Close to shore, inside the protective barrier of Key Biscayne, the waters of the Intracoastal were flat and viscous, the surface had an oily gleam like that of cooling soup. Back to the west, the sky was red and acid yellow with the last heat of sunset; ahead, over the deep enveloping Atlantic, it was already night. Charlie Ponte's cigarette boat, piloted by one of the Miami boss's bodyguards and moving at a speed that would not attract attention, plied the clement waters, carrying Gino toward the darkness.

The doomed man sat on a wraparound settee at the stern. He was flanked by the two Fabretti thugs, who were smoking cigars and looking at the scenery: the mangrove islets, the diving birds. Gino's chin still bled slightly: a line of crimson flowed slowly down his neck; now and then a drop broke free and splattered on his chest. His hands were cuffed behind him. From the middle of the cuffs a chain hung down; at the end of the chain was a clip. In front of Gino, a two-hundred-pound mushroom anchor took up much of the cigarette's small cockpit. The anchor was designed to bury itself in the muck of the ocean bottom and stay buried for eternity. It had a metal stem with an eye to which the clip at the end of the handcuffs would be attached.

Terror made Gino feel lonely. He wanted to chat. "Where we goin'?" he asked his executioners.

The thug at his left puffed on his cigar. He was very handsome for a thug, with dark eyes, chiseled nostrils that were almost feminine, and the thick and wavy hair of a fifties crooner. His name was Pretty Boy and he ate amphetamines like candy. "You're goin' ta hell," he said.

"Out to de edge a duh Gulf Stream," put in the other thug. He was ugly but not nasty; he liked geography and had a philosophical turn of mind. A long curved scar paralleled his jawbone. His name was Bo. "Water gets nice and deep out theah," he added. "Mile deep. Maybe more. Dark blue onna map."

There was a pause, the boat's twin engines popped and purred, water lapped against the hull. Gino moved a notch closer to the impossible knowledge that he was about to die. "That fuckin' Ponte," he said. "That midget cocksucker."

Bo tried to produce a smoke ring, but the breeze tore it instantly to shreds. "Now Gino," he said, "don't be bitter. Ya gotta think about the psychology of it. You gave Ponte the chance ta make an enemy and the chance ta make a friend. He figured the Fabrettis are comin' up, the Puglieses are goin' down—"

"The Puglieses are fucked," Pretty Boy put in. "They're history." He spat out a tobacco fleck.

"Ponte made a choice," said Bo. "That's nothin' ta get mad at."

The boat slipped under the Rickenbacker Causeway, past the golf-course end of Key Biscayne. Gino caught a whiff of lawn, of soil, he tasted dry land at the back of his throat, and the flavor carried with it the unspeakable poignance of childhood memories. He again tried on the thought of death and was instantly filled with a great and all-forgiving tenderness toward himself. Things should not have turned out this way for him; it wasn't fair. He'd been gypped somehow, given a bum steer somewhere along the line. The bunglings and the lies that had brought him here—he divorced himself from them, they were not his fault.

Beyond the marker at Northwest Point, the sea grew featureless and infinite. The earth smells vanished, overwhelmed by the tang of iodine and salt and kelp and fish. The first stars were coming out. Ponte's thug goosed the engine and brought the sleek hull up on plane; the mushroom anchor clattered as the boat bounced from crest to crest, and Gino scavenged through his aching brain for a way to save himself.

After a time, he shouted above the motor noise. "What if I tol' ya that Ponte's choice, us or the Fabrettis, it don't make a fuckin' bit a difference, the whole goddam thing is comin' down?"

"I'd tell ya ta shut the fuck up," said Pretty Boy.

Bo thought a bit more deeply about the comment. "Gino," he said, "just 'cause you're havin' a bad day, it don't mean—"

"What if I tol' ya," the captive cut in, "that while we're sittin' heah inna middle a the fuckin' ocean, the biggest ratout in history is gettin' ready ta be sprung?"

"Calm down, fuckface," Pretty Boy told him. "You're bleedin' all over ya'self."

The powerboat slammed on. The water now was indigo, it rose and fell with the heavy evenness of open ocean waves. Perhaps two miles up ahead, the fuller surge of the restless Gulf Stream could be glimpsed beneath the brightening stars.

Gino flexed his cuffed arms and prattled desperately on. "Your boss," he screamed. "If someone was gonna blow his world right open, ya don't think he'd wanna know? Ya don't think he'd be grateful to the guys that brought de information?"

Pretty Boy and Bo still clutched their cigars, but it was too windy to smoke them now; the ash had blown away and the tips glowed a hellish red. The two thugs leaned forward in front of Gino and held a silent conference by the light of the smoldering tobacco. Gino held his breath. Then Pretty Boy said, "Fuck 'im, he's jerkin' us around."

Bo didn't disagree. They leaned back again. Gino took a deep breath of salty air and hoped he wouldn't start bawling.

The cigarette reached the heavier chop; spray hissed up along its sides. Ponte's thug cut the engines and the mighty boat became a raft, a cork, a passive thing being cradled by the ocean. In the sudden silence the stars seemed nearer, the teasing slap of water on the hull was terrifying in its mildness.

"Stan' up, Gino," said Pretty Boy.

Shakily, he did so. His handcuffs chattered with his fear; the chain hung over his buttocks and down his legs like an obscene mechanical tail. Almost gently, Bo took him by the shoulders and turned him around. He grabbed the chain and fitted the clip to the eye of the anchor. It locked shut with a dry and bell-like *ping*.

Ponte's thug looked on, his feet spread wide for balance, his arms crossed on his chest. In the tone of an expert adviser, a connoisseur, he said, "T'row him in first, *den* de anchor. Udder way, ya yank his arms off, the body's still layin' there."

The boat bobbed and slowly spun, the astonishing power of the current could be felt right through the fiberglass. Bo puffed on his cigar. "So Gino, ya wanna jump or ya want we should t'row ya?"

The captive looked down at the water. It was black. He couldn't see into it one inch. He wet his pants; the piss ran down his leg like tears. His ribs compressed around his burning lungs and he might as well have been already drowning. Past the locked sinews of his throat he managed to squeeze a weak whisper. "Someone's writin' a book."

"Lotta jerks write books," said Pretty Boy. "Take a dive or we t'row ya."

"Someone inside," Gino rasped. "Someone who knows enough ta fuck us all."

"Yeah? Who?" said Bo.

Pretty Boy did not wait for an answer. He leaned in on Gino's flank, started bulling him toward the gunwale. "Come on," he said. "We're wastin' time. Let's drown the piece a shit and get some dinner."

The mushroom anchor dragged around the cockpit. Gino strained for balance, his locked knees screamed and his cramped spine arched like a palm tree in a gale. "You're makin' a big mistake," he croaked.

Pretty Boy bore down on him, spun him so that his wet thighs squished against the gunwale. "And you're gonna make a big splash."

"Who's writin' a book?" said Bo.

Gino smelled piss and ocean and flailed within himself

for one more ounce of moxie. "I ain't talkin' heah. I'll talk on land. I'll talk to Messina."

Bo considered.

Pretty Boy yelled out, "Fuckin' shit, let's do the fuckin' job." He slammed the captive in the kidney, hacked him across the back of the neck to bend him double, was reaching now for the manacled hands that would serve as a lever to heave him overboard.

Bo grabbed his colleague by the elbows, wrestled him away. "Nah," he said. "Ya don't drown information."

Pretty Boy, panting and manic, wriggled free and glared at him. Bo paused, then tried to cheer him up. "New Yawk," he said, "same water as Miami. Whatsa difference we drown 'im tomorra or today?"

Gino didn't move, didn't breathe. The boat rocked and slowly twirled, the stars seemed to leave faint tracks as they wheeled. Finally, Ponte's guy shrugged and turned the key in the ignition. The engines thundered into life, the boat spun toward the faint and hazy lights of land, and Gino Delgatto, still chained by his metal tail, stumbled back to the stern settee and began to wonder what he'd say and how he'd say it when he stood before his enemies and ratted out his father.

PART THREE

CHAPTER TWENTY-FOUR

THE WAITER at Bar Toscano had not minded when the single redhead took a first-row sidewalk table and ordered nothing but a Pellegrino water. It was early, five-thirtyish, the fashionable crowd was not yet swarming in, and the place was mostly empty. Besides, the redhead was pretty in a hokey, brassy, touristy kind of way, and it never hurt to have large-breasted females on the rail.

But something over an hour later, with the sun down and with the neon and the streetlights giving the dusk a restless dappled gleam, the South Beach regulars began appearing in their skin-tight leggings, their big shirts with the top buttons cinched shut around elegant necks. People were jostling for places, and now the single red-head had become a liability. The waiter wanted her to be gone.

"Anything more?" he asked her. The tone was as welcoming as a faceful of bleach.

Debbi glanced at her watch. Gino was not yet late but he was pushing it, as he often did. A tentative exasperation set in and she asked for a Campari.

She sipped it slowly, and before it was three-quarters gone, the waiter, moving sideways between the close-together tables of the now-packed café, was back to ask if she would have another. She sighed, said yes, and the waiter flashed a sour little smile, as if politely telling her to choke on it.

The traffic was heating up on Ocean Drive. Four-somes of gorgeous men, their shirts the colors of lolli-pops, cruised slowly past in vintage Chevy convertibles. The occasional Rolls went by, driven usually by some devilish little fellow with a silver ponytail.

The second aperitif made Debbi feel feisty, and when the waiter once again confronted her, she shot him a look that said, Fuck you too, buddy. Over the buzz of chat and giggles, she ordered a martini, straight up, two olives, very dry.

It was getting on toward nine o'clock. Models slunk past, vacant as cats, and with a cat's knack for holding the eye while giving nothing in return. Smells of garlic and mushrooms came forward past the stink of car exhaust and the faint hint of ocean just a few hundred yards away. Debbi felt suddenly maudlin. She was getting smashed and she didn't want to be. Nor did she want to be sitting in this café. Places like this—they made you feel like you were missing something, yet the longer you stayed, the more you felt that what you were missing was no better than what you had, however crummy what you had might be. She called for her tab, put down a somewhat overgen-erous tip, and left.

On the other side of Ocean Drive was a park. This was still the old Miami Beach; there were slatted benches where ancient people could sit and rest their swollen ankles and brag about their grandkids. Debbi decided that's where she would wait for Gino.

She picked her way across the bustling avenue and plopped down on a bench that faced the sidewalk. She stayed there a long time. During rare lulls in the traffic she could hear the ocean. Waves broke, but the sound was less a crash than a slow boiling hiss against the sand.

After a while she noticed that a police car had been cruising past again and again, pausing a moment in front of her each time. Now she met the eye of the cop on the passenger side, and the bleak condescension in his gaze made her realize something galling. My God, she thought, they think I'm a whore.

The mute accusation made her mad and also made her feel ridiculous, pathetic, lonely and exposed as a lighthouse on a single rock. A tourist with no one to talk to and nowhere to go. A woman ditched by her date, an easy object of false pity and true scorn. It was after ten and she was furious.

The alcohol was wearing off, it left in its wake a groggy edginess, a grouchiness as from an interrupted nap. Where the hell *was* he? She opened her purse. She had no credit cards and about a hundred dollars in mad money. If ever there was a time for mad money, this was it—but what would her lousy hundred bucks do for her? It wouldn't get her to New York; in this neighborhood it wouldn't even get her a hotel room. Besides, if Gino came back and couldn't find her, what then? Frustration made her face flush hot, she wished to her soul she had never met Gino Delgatto.

The wish made her feel guilty. There was something murderous in it, some impulse not just to escape the boyfriend but to undo him, erase him, blot him out. She made amends for the evil thought by letting herself realize she was worried.

By eleven she was very worried and by midnight she

was panicked. Gino did dangerous things with dangerous people. She knew that. She didn't let herself think about it very much, but she knew it.

By 1 A.M. the procession on Ocean Drive was just beginning to slacken, the crowd at Bar Toscano just starting to thin. Debbi wandered back across the street, sat down at a table near the rail, and ordered a double cappuccino. She nursed it unharassed till four; then the place closed up and she went back to her bench.

An exhausted numbness had set in against the sinister sparseness of the predawn hours. Homeless people drifted by with shopping carts stacked up with tin cans, beach toys, shoes; furtive men, their blank eyes on the sidewalk, stole glances at her breasts before slipping off to the shrubbery to masturbate. Debbi was afraid to sleep but now and then she briefly dozed—her nodding head would trip a trigger in her neck and she would jerk herself awake. Around six, day began to break. The sky floated free of the black ocean; the palms, heavy with night, showed their slack outlines against the faint horizon. A hazy orange sun came up from out beyond the Gulf Stream.

At exactly seven Debbi went to a pay phone, took from her purse a piece of notepaper from the Flagler House, and dialed the only person she could think to call in Florida.

Sandra reached out blindly toward her night table and picked up on the second ring. "Hello?"

"I hope I didn't wake you."

"Debbi?"

"Yeah. I'm sorry."

Sandra tried to rouse herself, came up on an elbow.

Joey gave a little grunt and seemed to will himself back to sleep. Soft light filtered through the thin bedroom curtains. "Where are you?"

Debbi paused a moment because she could feel her throat clamping shut and the tears simmering behind her itchy eyes. She bit her lip, swallowed hard, but still her voice caught when she said, "Miami Beach."

"Lemme change phones," said Sandra. She slipped out of bed and went to the kitchen.

When she returned ten minutes later, she was carrying coffee mugs. Joey was awake. He'd propped himself on pillows and put on his blue-lensed sunglasses to ease the shock of the early light. "Who was 'at?" he asked.

Sandra sat down near her husband and stroked his hair before she answered. "Debbi. Gino dropped her off in South Beach yesterday and didn't come back to get her."

Joey reached for his coffee but didn't drink, just held the mug in front of him and looked past the rising steam at the window. He knew his brother was a shit with women, but the knot in his gut was telling him that Debbi's stranding meant something else entirely. Guys who lived like Gino—they had to believe that some rogue saint was looking out for them, deflecting bullets, bending enemies' knives. At the same time, somewhere at the bottom of their brains, they had to know that they were diddling death, heading crotch first toward the buzz saw.

"Where'd he go?" asked Joey. "Who'd he see?"

"She doesn't seem to know," said Sandra. "She was rambling. She's very tired and very scared."

Joey pulled a deep breath in, pushed it out, sipped some coffee. "The old man," he said. "Jesus." He shook his head and let it go at that.

"I told her to get a cab and come down here," said Sandra.

Joey just nodded.

"Look," said his wife, "why don't we try to keep it to ourselves for now, give it some time. Maybe he'll turn up, maybe he'll call."

Joey nodded again. Maybe he'd turn up, maybe he'd call. The younger brother didn't think so. He stared through his sunglasses, past the thin bedroom curtains at the brightening day, and wondered how it would be when he could no longer stall and had to tell Vincente.

CHAPTER TWENTY-FIVE

SOMEWHERE IN the Carolinas, sometime after dawn, Pretty Boy pulled his Lincoln off the Interstate and swung into a Shoeless Jimmy truck stop. He parked in a distant corner of the lot. Not that he was seriously worried that Gino would draw attention to himself. The captive was handcuffed, his mouth sealed with duct tape, his legs bound up double so he couldn't kick against the carpeted walls of the trunk. Still, he could bounce a little, he could groan. Better to leave him where the highway hum would drown him out.

The Fabretti thugs got out of the car and stretched. Less than twelve hours from Miami, it was already a different world, an ice age. Against the red sky, frost-loving pine trees, ramrod straight, were wreathed in frigid mist, the vapor wound through the branches like a corkscrew.

Pretty Boy did a little dance, shifted his weight from foot to foot. "I hate the fuckin' Sout'," he groused. His breath showed opaque white as he said it. "You're gonna freeze your ass off, why call it Sout' to begin wit'?"

"It's called Sout'," said the philosophic Bo, "'cause, like, back inna Civil War—"

"And they got such stupid fuckin' names for things down heah," interrupted Pretty Boy. He gestured disgustedly toward the frosty neon sign above the restaurant. "Shoeless Jimmy Truck Stop. Betty Sue Biscuit's White Trash Café. Whistlin' Darkie Trailer Lodge—"

"Go easy onna pills, huh?" Bo suggested. "They're makin' you, like, irritable."

Pretty Boy flapped his arms to warm himself. "What's makin' me irritable is that dog turd inna trunk. I still say we shoulda—"

"How many more states I gotta listen ta dis?" protested Bo. "Florida. Georgia. Sout' Carolina—"

"And fuck geography too," said Pretty Boy.

"Ya fuck geography," said Bo, "how ya gonna know where you're at?"

His partner didn't answer, just fumbled in the pockets of his sharkskin pants for his bennies. A couple more pills, three, four cups of coffee, he'd be driving over the Verrazano Bridge, looking at the skyline, getting ready to deliver his half-dead cargo to Aldo Messina on the seafood docks in Brooklyn.

Over breakfast, Joey said, "Take a ride wit' me, Pop? I gotta look at some property up the Keys, I'd like to know what ya think."

The Godfather looked up from his grapefruit. He knew nothing about real estate, and his son had somehow come to be an expert, as much an expert as a briefcase guy who went to a fancy college. But it wasn't Joey's know-how that Vincente was reflecting on; it was the deeper mystery of his kindness. The kindness to coddle an old man's vanity, to let him believe he wasn't in the way, he was helping. Vincente thought, His mother was very kind. He musta got it from his mother. He said, "Sure, Joey, I'm always happy ta take a ride."

The two men left the house around nine-thirty, comfortably before Debbi would arrive in her taxi from Miami. Sandra would have a chance to talk with her alone. Maybe Gino would call while Vincente was out.

It was a beautiful morning, with just enough breeze to animate the palms, and with scattered puffy clouds whose flat bottoms were tinged green by the reflecting water of the Straits. The old El Dorado hummed along, archaic and imperial beside the rented compacts, its enormous tires gripping the pavement like giant paws. There was something goofily erotic about the knobs and swellings of the dashboard. Vincente stroked the orifice of the AC vent. "I'm glad you kept this car," he said. "Car this nice, ya can't find 'em anymore."

Joey just gave his father an absent glance from behind his blue-lensed sunglasses.

They looked at lots on Summerland Key, three rocky parcels overgrown with grayish scrub and fronting on a silted-up canal that smelled like anchovies. While Vincente listened in with pride, Joey and the seller talked about flood plains, dredging regulations, rights-of-way. The seller wanted eighty-five a lot, and Joey said he'd think about it. He said it with a perfectly unreadable neutrality that the Godfather could only admire.

It was now eleven-thirty, and Joey suggested continuing on to Marathon, twenty-five miles farther up, for lunch. It seemed a long way to go for a bowl of chowder, but Vincente didn't argue.

They went to a place on the Gulf side of the highway and sat outside, under an umbrella made of thatch.

155

Between spoonfuls of soup, Vincente said, "Joey, I never really thanked ya for gettin' me together wit' Ahty, for pushin' me on 'at."

"Pop, hey," said Joey, "it's—"

"It's a good thing, what ya got me ta do," the old man said. He dabbed his full lips on a napkin; his dark eyes twinkled in their deep nests of brows and wrinkles. "Ya know, it's a crazy thing: ya can be an old fart, ancient, and there's still so many things, you're like a kid, a virgin, ya just don't know how they're gonna feel. Like talking. I mean really talking, lettin' things out."

Joey broke a soggy saltine; it didn't snap, it folded. He managed only a distracted nod.

Vincente looked out across the water, at the distant mangrove islands that seemed to float a few inches in the air. "But there's somethin' I don't understand," he said.

"Whassat, Pop?"

"Writers. Ya hear about 'em, they're supposed ta be unhappy. They drink too much, they blow their brains out. . . . I don't get it. I think they oughta be the happiest guys on eart'. Somethin' bothers 'em, they write it down. Someone fucks wit' 'em, they make 'im the bad guy, they make 'im an asshole. Ya know, they spit stuff out, get rid of it. They don't gotta carry shit around for forty—"

The old man broke off abruptly. Some flatness in the air made him realize, not with anger but with a slight embarrassment, that he wasn't being listened to.

"Somethin' on your mind, Joey? Somethin' botherin' ya?"

The younger man looked up from his chowder and met his father's eyes. The old man could not be lied to, lies wilted under that gaze like lettuces in August—but still, in the name of compassion, the truth could some-times be deferred. "Yeah, Pop," Joey said. "Somethin' is. But it isn't somethin' I can go inta right now."

Vincente nodded, swallowed. He was a parent, it wounded him to be shut out from his child's pain. But Joey was a grown-up, a husband, an expert in real estate; he'd earned the right to deal with things his own way. The old man reached out and put a hand on the young man's wrist. "OK," he said. "I unnerstand. But Joey, I'm your father, you can talk to me. You know dat, right?"

Around two o'clock Debbi woke up from her nap.

It took her a moment to remember where she was, and then she was seized by an infinite and nameless gratitude, a gratitude like waking up in the hospital, comfortable and cared for, after thinking one would die. The clean sheets felt delicious against her skin; smells of sand and jasmine filtered through the guest bedroom window. She nestled her head against the pillow and luxuriated awhile in the pure, supreme delight of safety.

After a time she got up and dressed. She found herself wanting to touch things. She ran her fingers across the weave of the wicker bureau, traced out the grooves in the paneled walls. Everything about this airy house seemed a pleasure and a solace; it seemed a house where a person could be happy.

She left her room, went to look for Sandra, and found her sitting on the patio, the low metal table now a make-shift desk littered with ledger books and yellow pads. Sandra wore big square glasses as she did accounts; the lenses smeared her eyes when she looked up at her guest. "Good morning. Coffee?"

Debbi gave a sleepy smile. "I can make it. Bring you some too?"

They took their mugs and sat on lounges near the pool. The afternoon sun had lost most of its bite; its heat was not searing but cozy. The breeze picked up a hint of coolness from the surface of the water and tickled ankles as it skittered by.

"Feeling better?" Sandra asked.

Debbi nodded, her lips against her cup. "I don't know what I would've done if you hadn't—"

The other woman shushed her with a wave of her hand, and for some moments the two of them sat in silence. Then Sandra said, "Debbi, I hate to ask you to go through this again—"

"No, I understand," said Debbi, and she reviewed her awful sojourn in Miami. But there was no more she could explain. Gino never told her anything; he didn't believe she could keep a secret. He said he had to see a guy, that's all. He said he'd be back in an hour, hour and a half.

Sandra looked down along her legs to the shimmer in the pool. She said softly, "He might be dead, you know."

Debbi held her coffee mug in both her hands. It made her look very young. She only nodded.

After a moment Sandra said, "Debbi, can I ask you something?"

"Sure."

"In your own mind, you were finished with him, weren't you?"

The other woman hesitated, glanced at the flickering tops of the aralia hedge. "I think I was. I hope I was."

"Stick to that," said Sandra. "Dead, alive—don't remember him as better than he was, more than he was to you. Don't do that to yourself."

Overhead, a flight of ibis went past. They seemed to be scudding lazily but their tiny shadows on the apron of the patio went by very fast.

"And you?" Sandra resumed. "What'll you do?"

Debbi gave a shrug that brought her freckled shoulders almost to her ears. "Scrape together some money and go back home, I guess."

"Back to Queens," said Sandra. It was not a question, more like a sentencing.

Debbi nodded.

"That what you wanna do?"

"I dunno. There's my job and all."

"You care about the job? The job make you happy?"

"I like dogs," said Debbi.

"That isn't what I asked you," Sandra said.

Debbi kept quiet. She couldn't put her finger on it, but something was making her afraid again. She recalled the nasty stylishness of Bar Toscano, how glum and lonely it had made her feel. She pictured the lost souls and the creeps who stalked the night, and the world beyond her old neighborhood seemed a difficult and thankless place.

"Debbi," Sandra said, "you and I once had a talk about what it takes for a person to change. Remember?"

Debbi swallowed, looked down at the pool. She remembered. But that had been a safer subject when the person who needed changing was someone else.

"Why don't you stay with us awhile?"

Redheads blush easily, and now Debbi felt her skin grow warm, the spaces between the freckles were colored in. "Sandra, I couldn't—"

"Take a break. Give yourself some time to think things through."

Debbi inhaled, and the breath didn't seem to want to come out again. She lifted a slender eyebrow, and the eyebrow hung suspended. She remembered the nice feel of the wicker bureau, the grooves in the paneled walls. "I don't know what to say."

"Say yes," said Sandra, "and let's get you some breakfast."

Joey dragged Vincente on some errands and managed to stay away from home till five o'clock. But as he drove the El Dorado up the gravel driveway and underneath the carport, his stomach clamped down and started to burn, and his fingers began to tingle with the first squirts of unwanted adrenaline.

Father and son walked into the living room.

Vincente saw Debbi, glanced quickly at Sandra, and understood at once that something bad had happened, Joey's distraction instantly made sense to him. The old man held himself very straight. This was a vintage trick, an act of bravado that sometimes worked: you took the bad news full on an unbent chest, and if it didn't knock you down, if it didn't bowl you over, you were ready to straighten your collar and press forward.

Joey looked at Sandra and knew beyond a doubt there'd been no word of Gino.

For a moment no one moved and no one spoke. The ceiling fan turned very slowly; the air pushed in gentle viscous waves. Joey dropped his sunglasses in the pocket of his shirt. "Pop," he said, "we gotta talk."

CHAPTER TWENTY-SIX

"Hour, hour an' a half," murmured the Godfather. "How long's it take to get from Sout' Beach ta Coconut Grove and back?"

"About that long," said Joey.

They were in his study, Vincente sitting at the lime-stone desk, Joey pacing in front of him. Through the glass block wall gleamed the lavender light of dusk. The Godfather reached up to fidget with an absent necktie and tried without success to find an alternative to believing his son Gino had disobeyed him. To be disobeyed—it made him angry, of course, but more than that it disgraced him; it showed that he had failed in his authority and therefore failed in his ability to protect.

"Joey, can ya think of any other—"

His son was already shaking his head, and now a kind of embarrassment was heaped on top of the old man's shame. He was losing his grip, getting soft. He shouldn't need to consult. He shouldn't need help or confirmation. It was his place to know, to act. He reached for the phone and dialed a number from memory.

After a moment the line was picked up and an oily voice said, "Martinelli's. Good evening."

"Do you have gnocchi?" asked the Godfather.

"No," said the maître d'. "No gnocchi."

"Then lemme get a calf's head."

"How you like it, sir?"

"Eyes open, facing forward."

"Hold on," said the oily voice. "I'll put you through."

Bad music played through the phone. Joey paced. The light outside went gray. Then Charlie Ponte picked up the line.

"Yeah?"

"Where's my son?"

The voice was like a rumble underground, it seemed to come from everywhere at once. For a moment Ponte didn't answer; then he sounded knocked off stride, confused.

"Vincente—"

"Where is 'e, Cholly?"

Again there was a pause, a clinch, but this time Ponte came out of it swinging. "How da fuck should I know?"

"Don't bullshit me. I know he was there."

The Miami boss chewed a thumbnail and tried to figure out what else his adversary knew. "Yeah, he was here. And he left."

"Who wit'?"

"Some friends from New York."

"Wha' friends, Cholly?"

Ponte sighed, sucked his teeth, and when he spoke again his voice was harried, whiny. "Vincente, I'm just a guy tryin'a make a living. Don't put me inna fuckin' middle a this."

"Middle a what?"

"This New York bullshit."

"Explain 'at, Cholly. You're talkin' out your ass."

"I'm talkin' unions, jurisdiction," Ponte said.

"You ain't talkin' nothin' so far," Vincente said, but a dread suspicion was clawing at him, it raked over him the way a dull knife frets the surface before it slashes through.

"Look," said Ponte, "ya wanna change the game wit' the Fabrettis, I don't give a fuck, it's alla same ta me. But work it out with the Fabrettis, don't send me Gino ta tell me things are back the way they were."

The Godfather held the phone a few inches from his hairy ear. The nostrils flared in his bridgeless nose, his thin cheeks went sickly yellow. He found he had nothing more to say; there was nothing more he could ask. To ask more would be to let this stranger know that his own son had lied to him, misrepresented him, had borne false witness to his words and wishes. It would be both useless and impossibly humiliating to let Charlie Ponte, or anyone beyond the tight circle of family, find that out.

Slowly, dazedly, Vincente put the phone back in its cradle.

"Pop?" said Joey Goldman. He said it very softly, the way you talk to someone when you're not sure he's awake. A minute had passed since the old man hung up the phone, and his lean form had remained unnaturally rigid, his sallow face impassive.

"Hm?" The Godfather gave a little jerk, then turned his head slowly toward the younger man and spoke in a quiet monotone. "He went against me, Joey."

"'Zee alive?"

His father took a deep breath. It seemed to be the first air he'd had in a while. "I don't know. I don't think Ponte

164

clipped 'im. Doesn't have the balls. I think it's like he says—he just passed 'im along ta the Fabrettis."

Joey paced. The evening light had faded, the study was nearly dark, but he didn't turn a light on. "Should we call New Yawk?"

In the dimness the Godfather allowed himself the beginnings of a bitter smile. He shouldn't need to consult, he shouldn't need advice, but there was something sweet as well as galling in this talking as equals in judgment, equals in bafflement, with his younger son. "Ya know somethin', Joey?" he murmured. "I just don't fuckin' know. I need ta go outside."

He put his palms flat on the desk and used his arms to help him get up from the chair. Less than steadily, he moved to the door, opened it, and went down the hallway to the living room.

The light there seemed very bright after the dimness of the study. It was mostly a white room to begin with, and now everything looked bleached out, as in an overexposed snapshot. It took the old man a moment to realize that Arty Magnus was sitting there, along with Debbi and Sandra.

"Ahty," said the Godfather, "I fuhgot all about—"

"No problem," said the ghostwriter. "If it's a bad time—"

Joey had followed his father down the hall and now stood at the old man's shoulder. "Maybe it is, Arty. 'S'been kind of a hectic day."

"No problem," the writer said again, and he stood up with the blushing quickness of a man who's just walked in on someone naked. "We can talk tomorrow, whenever."

"Hey," said Sandra, "we're not chasing you away. Sit awhile, have a glass of wine."

Arty stood with his calves against the couch and did an awkward little pirouette. Too many people were talking at once and in his shy desire to get along he wanted to please them all.

A long and indecisive moment passed and then a low rumble moved the air, got it ready to carry sound. "Nah, stay," said the Godfather. He'd realized that he wanted, needed, to sit quietly under starlight with a sympathetic or at least a tactful listener and to think aloud, to open the valves and tell his version of how things should be. Too much evil stuff had been forced into him today; he doubted whether his insides were still elastic enough to contain it. He had to bleed some pressure out, stay within a certain range, like an old and rusty boiler. "If Joey and the ladies will excuse us, Ahty, you and me, we'll sit outside and talk awhile."

CHAPTER TWENTY-SEVEN

THE GODFATHER dove into his ramblings the way some other men, faced with grinding insurmountable sorrows, dive into drink.

"So here's the difference," he was saying, when he and his ghost had settled in around the low metal table on the patio. "Most people—prob'ly you too, Ahty—they believe that friends, associates, come and go, but what's right is always right and what's wrong is always wrong. Am I right?"

Arty was scrawling in his private shorthand in his cheap blue spiral notebook. Without lifting his eyes from the page he gave a noncommittal nod.

"Sicilians," Vincente went on, "we believe the opposite. Laws could change tomorra. Ya could have a different cop onna beat, a different judge inna courtroom. The whole fuckin' government could change. But your friends, they ain't goin' nowhere. World ain't that big. Where they gonna go? You'll be dealin' wit' 'em next week, next year; ya couldn't shake 'em if ya wanted to, believe me. So the bottom line? If ya gotta do somethin' wrong to keep things easy wit' your friends, ya do it."

Arty looked up from his notebook. "We saying wrong or illegal?"

"An excellent question!" said Vincente.

He raised a finger, his cavernous dark eyes picked up glints from the stars and the floodlights; for the moment his grim preoccupations seemed to fall away, the relief was like a cramp letting go. He came forward to the edge of his seat, and despite the wrinkles he seemed suddenly young, as spry and bold as a sophomore in a dorm, talking philosophy in his pajamas.

"Wrong or illegal?" he parroted with zest. "Who's ta decide where one stops and th' other starts? Fuckin' government, they want ya ta believe the laws are right, period. Ya think about it, ya know that's bullshit. Prohibition—right one day, wrong the next? Gambling—wrong for four guys inna back of a candy store, right for four thousand ol' ladies in a casino? Obvious bullshit."

He broke off, sipped some wine, wiped his full lips with the back of his hand.

"But there's gotta be some way—" Arty put in.

"Some way a what?" Vincente interrupted. "Some way a keepin' things orderly? Which is another way a sayin' keepin' people in their place? I agree. But my point is this: ya got blond hair, ya been ta college, y'own stock and got a house inna country, then yeah, the laws look pretty reasonable; ya say, Hey, I'm playin' by the rules and I'm winning, so this must be a fair game and I must be a helluva fella. Ya got black hair, ya start off broke, ya talk funny—it all looks a little different, don't it? And this is where your friends come in. Ya see what I'm sayin'?"

Arty wasn't sure he did, but he nodded and kept scrawling. He thought vaguely of the terrifying day when he would have to sit down with this jungle of notes and bushwhack a trail that a reader could follow.

"Mafia," Vincente rolled on. "In Sicily, ya know, it

goes by a lotta different names. I'll tell ya my favorite: *gli amici degli amici*. The friends of friends. That says it all. It's an us-and-them kinda thing, that simple—a system outside the system."

The Godfather paused for a sip of wine. Crickets rasped, blue light shimmered softly above the pool.

"Not that the system runs perfect," the old man acknowledged. "The legit world has its fuckups; so do we. And this is where it comes back to right and wrong."

Arty pricked up his ears; he'd stopped believing it ever would.

"Someone fucks up inna legit world, the legit world decides how ta judge it. Someone fucks up in our world, *we* decide. We judge hard, very hard, but we judge fair. And we judge accordin' to what *we* think is right and wrong. What I'm sayin', we don't dodge th' obligation, we don't go runnin' ta lawyers, we don't hide behind robes and flags and fancy words and mumbo jumbo. We judge. And lemme tell ya somethin', Ahty, I ain't braggin', but that takes balls. Someone needs punishing, we don't leave it to a buncha strangers—we punish. We clean our own house; we don't ask for help. Takes nerve."

The old man stabbed the air with his index finger, cleared his throat, and reached for his wine. He took a hurried shallow sip and then continued.

"And this is how it's gotta be. Ya know why, Ahty? Because *gli amici degli amici*, the whole network, like, it's just a big outgrowt' a the family. Ya got a problem in your family, ya run to a cop? Ya think a cop has any fuckin' business nosin' in when it's a question a fa—"

The old man broke off suddenly, the last fragment tailed away in a slow and labored whistling hiss. Arty kept on scratching out his notes, and when he finally looked up he saw Vincente bent and slouching in his chair, as limp as if he had no bones. His eyes were dull and distant, his neck was frail and stringy inside his shirt. Arty had seen him run out of gas before, but never this abruptly; he had no way of knowing that the old man, in his meanderings, had fallen into a thought as into a muddy ditch with chill and fetid water at the bottom.

"Go ahead, Vincente," the ghostwriter coaxed. "What you were saying, it was—"

"It was bullshit," the old man said bitterly. "I don't know what the fuck I'm talkin' about." He picked up his wineglass, twirled it by the stem, put it aside without drinking. He looked past Arty at the blue gleam of the pool, stared off at the dead heavens and seemed to want to be there.

Arty put his pen down, sipped wine, and discreetly observed Vincente in his funk. It made him wonder about the boundaries of a ghostwriter's job. Where did his duties and his privileges begin and end? Should he only listen, or should he probe? Concern himself only with his subject's words, or with his moods, his quirks, his sadnesses? Be a scribe, an employee, or presume to believe that by dint of the affection that comes from paying close attention he could perhaps become a friend?

"Vincente," he said softly, "is there more we wanna talk about?"

The Godfather stared away a moment longer and then just shook his head. Arty had the feeling that he didn't speak because he was afraid that if he spoke he would begin to cry.

"Call it a night then?"

The old man nodded. Arty closed his notebook, then scooted forward in his seat, put his elbows on his bare knees, and said, "Vincente, maybe it isn't the perfect time, but can I tell you something before I go?"

By way of answer, Vincente only cocked his head. There was something resigned and automatic, priestlike, in the gesture. He might be weary, he might be crammed full of evil stuff, but he would listen, it was his job to listen; he would never have the luxury to stop his ears.

"Two guys from the FBI came to my office," Arty said. "They wanted to talk about you."

Vincente raised a finger to a bushy eyebrow, scratched it lightly, nodded. "Thanks for tellin' me, Ahty. Lotta guys, they wouldn'ta had the balls ta tell me."

"Why not?"

The Godfather seemed to find the question amusing. He braced his wrists against the arms of his chair and squirmed to a less forlorn position. "I like you, Ahty," he said. "It's a dumb question, but I like ya for askin' it. Ya really don't know?"

Arty said nothing.

"Lotta guys," Vincente went on, "they'd think it was dangerous if the Feds were on to them and I knew it. They'd think I'd see them as a whaddyacallit, a liability, that I'd doubt them, ya know, be worried that they'd turn on me. . . . That never even occurred to you, did it, Ahty?"

The ghostwriter just shook his head.

"A clear conscience," said the Godfather. He said it wistfully. "Fuckin' amazing. . . . You think the best about people, don't'cha, Ahty?"

The younger man just shrugged.

The Godfather mulled a moment, then said, "Mus' make ya a lousy journalist."

The ghostwriter stood up. It was time to go; he left Vincente with a small gift of candor. "Little secret?" he said. "I am a lousy journalist."

CHAPTER TWENTY-EIGHT

IT WAS snowing in New York, a thin wet snow that was white against the streetlights but turned gray and glassy by the time it squashed itself on the windshields of the cars. From the Verrazano Bridge, the Manhattan skyline was a ghostly smudge. It was the middle of the night. There should have been no traffic, but cars still crawled behind trucks spreading salt and sand between the stanchions; the delay juiced up Pretty Boy's crankiness to the level of psychosis.

"I feel like I got fuckin' curry in my bladder," he said.

"The pills," said Bo. "They're burnin' y'up inside."

"Ya know what's wrong with this fuckin' country?" said Pretty Boy. "Too fuckin' big. Little country, Puerto Rico like, we'd be home already."

"Puerto Rico ain't a country."

"Fuck you too, Bo. I'm sicka you."

On the Brooklyn side they turned off toward the west, following the Belt Parkway as it wound around the crammed, offended shoreline. They exited at Red Hook and slid down steep cobbled streets toward the warehouses and the docks. Disused railroad tracks were everywhere, they arced and looped among the paving stones, standing out like scars. The wet snow made them slick as polished marble, and the Lincoln fishtailed now and then, its rear end whipping crazily. Gino Delgatto, slightly blue and barely conscious, flopped around the trunk like a caught fish in the bottom of a boat.

At the docks, Pretty Boy maneuvered through the narrow opening of a high metal gate and drove to a hangarlike steel building that backed onto the river. He pulled through an open portal to a loading dock, and there, finally, he stopped the car.

He got out, stretched, and opened the trunk. He saw Gino lying curled around the spare tire.

The captive struggled to turn over, his red-rimmed eyes blinking spastically against the sudden light. His arms were still cuffed behind him, his legs were trussed up like a veal. Pretty Boy produced a switchblade and cut the ropes around his thighs and ankles. "Get up, shit-head," he commanded.

But with the bonds removed, Gino's legs were no more mobile than before.

Bo reached down and turned him by the ankles; the stiff body pivoted on its hipbones but stayed in the shape of a chair. Finally the two Fabretti thugs grabbed Gino by the armpits and settled him like a dummy on the lip of the trunk. Pretty Boy yanked the duct tape off his face; it came away with a sound like ripping cloth. Then, for no reason in particular, he backhanded him hard across the cheek and said, "Welcome ta New Yawk."

The blow did Gino good, seemed to aid his circulation. He turned his head a little, tried to point his toes. "Wouldya take the cuffs off?" he asked.

Pretty Boy shrugged and fished the key out of his pocket. Gino's freed hands fell limp at his sides. He had no feeling from the shoulders down.

"We're gonna walk now, Gino," said Bo. "Ya ready ta walk?"

By way of answer, Gino leaned forward on the edge of the trunk, tried to get his feet out under him, and proceeded to keel over onto the cement floor. The floor was very cold; it stank of diesel drippings and the juice of very stale shrimp. He struggled to his knees. The thugs yanked him upright and now, somehow, he was walking between them.

They walked him up a short flight of steps to the level of the loading platform, then through a broad doorway to the main chamber of the warehouse. It was vast, high-ceilinged, dimly lit by bare bulbs; through its silence there seemed to seep a low and ceaseless ringing as the steel sang against its rivets. Boxes of iced seafood—salmon, flounder, lobster tails—were stacked on pallets fifteen feet up; the place smelled of ocean, dust, and damp cardboard. Far away, down a towering aisle of fish, a yellow light gleamed through Venetian blinds in an office window.

Gino trudged that way, still trying to wake up, struggling to reenter the world and reclaim his own skin. Hands, feet, brain—nothing felt like his anymore, it was as if he'd already died. And as if other things had died with him: old loyalties, bonds, his last remaining shreds of decency or caring. He'd died and now he'd been slapped back into being, but not quite as a person, simply as a blob of life, a dollop of animate goo driven solely by the sublimely pointless instinct to preserve itself.

Bo knocked on the office window. Someone used the muzzle of a gun to part the blinds for a look; then the door was opened from inside.

Pretty Boy shoved Gino through. In the yellow light the captive saw three men. Two of them were bull-necked bodyguards in pearl-gray suits. The other was Aldo Messina, new boss of the Fabretti family.

He was a thin, gray, doleful man, quietly, methodically ruthless, a planner and a worrier. His concave face seemed hollowed out with fretting, his cheeks pinched in around his gums, his black eyes threw shadows on themselves. He wore a gray turtleneck sweater and stood huddled in a corner near a space heater, rubbing his delicate hands together. The heater's coils put a red glow on his face and made him hard to look at. "'Lo Gino," he said softly.

"'Lo, Aldo," said the captive.

Messina raised a delicate finger, a pianist's finger. "First mistake," he said. "It isn't Aldo anymore, Gino. It's Mr. Messina. Got that?"

Gino looked down at the floor and nodded.

Messina approached him and pushed his chin up with a lightly balled fist. "So say it, Gino."

The prisoner hesitated, swallowed. This business of a name—it was a small submission but a bitter one. He tightened his face, pulled back as though the other man's penis were being forced into his mouth. "Mr. Messina."

"Better," said the boss. With a ghoulish slowness, he stepped back, brought his bloodless form nearer to the heat. "So Gino, you've been meddling in our affairs in Florida. That isn't smart, Gino."

The captive looked down at his shoes.

"We had a deal down there," Messina said. "It's not like the Puglieses to welsh on a deal."

Gino sniffled, massaged a bruised wrist.

176

"Your old man, Gino, I have to tell you, I really looked up to him. He was a diplomat, a reasonable person. I can't believe he'd pick such a stupid time and a stupid way to try taking something back from us. I take over. I can't show weakness. That's basic. And he tries to grab a union from me? Almost makes me wonder if it was really his idea."

Gino shuffled his feet. He wasn't thinking, exactly; what was going on in his reclaimed brain was something more primitive than that, something like the coded firing of neurons that tells a hunted animal when to zig and when to zag. "My old man, truth is, he ain't sharp like he was, he's losin' it. He's old."

Messina rubbed his hands together near the heater and considered. "Possible," he said. "But Gino, scumbag, what's *your* excuse?"

Gino sucked some air and realized quite suddenly that the office stank of fish. "I ain't got an excuse," he admitted. "What I got is information."

"That's why you're here instead of at the bottom of the ocean," said Messina.

"Where he fuckin' oughta be," blurted Pretty Boy.

Messina softly told him to shut up. "So Gino, let's have the goods."

The captive reached deep for another spoonful of nerve. "First let's talk about what it's worth."

The boss looked up from the heater; red rays played on his sallow face. He nodded vaguely toward the big thugs in the pearl-gray suits. "Your bargaining position," he said. "It's not worth much."

"I ain't askin' much," said Gino.

Messina kept silent, made the other man bid.

"Absolution, that's all," said Gino. "This whole thing, like it never happened."

A gust of snowy wind made the vast steel warehouse sing around its rivets. "And in return I get some gossip about a book," Messina said.

"It ain't just a book," said Gino. "It's a fuckin' time bomb. It's ten times worse than Valachi, it's worse than any ratout—"

"So who's writing it?"

"We got a deal?"

Quietly, Messina said, "For now."

Gino felt his bowels go liquid. Suddenly he was giddy. He'd schemed, he'd lied, he'd wriggled; the grim concentration of the chase had masked his terror. Now he'd played every card but the last one and he had no idea if it had done him any good at all. "Fuck's that mean?" he whined.

"The water was warmer in Florida, Gino."

The captive swallowed; his saliva tasted of fish and bile. The walls of the office seemed to be tipping in; he had the feeling that the Fabretti thugs were looming over him on every side like brownstones about to topple. He couldn't breathe, and when he tried to get his lips ready to make words, his face contorted into a sickly smirk, the horrid glower of an idiot child doing something cruel and senseless. Yet on the brink of foulest treason, he could not quite summon up the guts to be direct. He smirked, and in a glozing whisper he said, "OK, the book. Ya mean, all this stuff about my old man losin' it, ya still ain't figured it out by now?"

The room went silent save for the insane faint ringing of the metal walls. Then there was the dry sound of Aldo

Messina rubbing his hands together in front of the heater. A long moment passed amid the stink of fish and the grainy yellow office light. Finally the boss who had admired Vincente Delgatto said very calmly, "Somebody hit 'im for that. Hit 'im hard."

The thugs in the pearl-gray suits passed a look, deciding who would administer the beating. One of them moved toward Gino and sized him up. He took his time, measured out the distance between his own fist and Gino's gut, and then he walloped him in the soft place underneath the ribs. The blow carried through almost to the backbone. Air popped out of Gino as from a bottle of warm champagne. He doubled over; the thug's jerked knee caught him in the left eye socket and spun him backward. His adversary grabbed him as he twirled; Gino's head bobbed like a buoy in the ocean, but the next punch landed flush on his nose and crushed it. The prisoner stumbled back, and Pretty Boy could not resist the urge to trip him. Falling, Gino slammed his head against the doorframe, then crumpled half sitting on the floor.

He was stupefied but not quite out. His eyes had closed but he was conscious enough to taste snot and blood at the back of his throat and to realize he was still alive. It no longer bothered him to be hurt; in some unspeakable way he liked it, it confirmed him. As for being despised, humiliated, loathed, he had sunk to a place where those things lost their sting, he was as indifferent to them as a roach.

He lay there, woozy, playing possum. Amid the maddening ring of the building he picked up scraps of talk, a confusion of gruff voices. *Bullshitting us*, somebody said.

His own father—that fuckin' skunk. . . . Vincente Delgatto, the last guy inna world. . . . But Jesus Christ, with what he knows. . . . Gotta think, gotta think. . . .

Footsteps came toward Gino; Gino didn't budge. The office door was opened, people stepped over his twisted legs. Someone spit on him while going by, and he neither knew nor cared which one of them it was.

CHAPTER TWENTY-NINE

EARLY THE next morning, in Key West, Bert d'Ambrosia, wearing a teal-blue suit of weightless Chinese silk, was walking his aged chihuahua on the beach.

Over the Florida Straits, the huge sun was going from orange to yellow as it sliced upward through a wisp of purple cloud; the lightly rippled water was moving from indigo to turquoise on its way to milky green. From moment to moment, the air dried out and warmed, came to feel like day, but underfoot the nubbly coral still held the cool and damp of night: the old man felt the tickling refreshment of it through his sneakers.

He meandered a few yards from the water's edge, and now he watched discreetly as his tiny dog hunkered down to do its business. These last few days, since flaxseed had become a regular part of its diet, the chihuahua's approach to the process was almost blasé, and Bert, his relief on the dog's behalf not entirely free of envy, had considered blending a bit of the elixir into his own rations. So far he'd refrained; flaxseed seemed as foreign to his dignity as to his time-honored recipe for meatballs. But as he noted the satisfaction with which Don Giovanni kicked sand and pebbles onto his leavings, as he observed the long-absent lightness in the little creature's step, he felt himself increasingly tempted. The seeds were simmered in olive oil. How bad could they be?

He strolled up the beach and onto the broad promenade that flanked A1A. As was his custom, he sat down on the seawall and watched the early joggers and the power walkers and the roller bladers. They went by in their lime-green shorts, their headbands that made them look like Indians, their humming skates or fancy shoes with waffle bottoms and reflecting tape. Some of them carried little dumbbells; some had tiny radios strapped around their arms like blood-pressure cuffs. Many of them smiled at Bert or waved. They didn't know his name; he didn't know theirs. But for them he was part of the scenery: the old man with the wild shirts and the ancient stiff-legged dog. In his stillness, his predictability, he'd become a feature along their path, like a mailbox or an odd-shaped tree; he took a quiet pleasure from believing that if he was no longer there, some of them would notice, a few would wonder where he was.

He sat there watching, and then one skater caught his eye from perhaps a hundred yards away. He studied her as she approached. She wore a shocking-pink leotard over shiny black bike shorts; she had big boobs that jiggled a bit as she swooped and jerked for balance. Hockey player's knee pads gave an elephantine aspect to her skinny legs; fingerless gloves let her long red nails poke through. Her ankles turned in like the tires of a car with a broken axle, her eyes were fixed on the hard and lacerating pavement, ferocious concentration made her tongue stick out the corner of her mouth.

She was quite close before he realized it was Debbi.

He yelled out a greeting, but she had headphones

on and didn't hear. What made her stop was that she recognized Don Giovanni, who was doing an aimless little dance in the shadow of the seawall. She grated to a halt, flapping her arms like a landing pelican, swept the headset off, and said hello. Twin suns shone in her big sunglasses, sweat glistened on her freckled chest.

"Gorgeous morning," said Bert. It was a treat to have someone to chat with, but he didn't want her to feel obligated. He tried to understand younger people, keep up with what seemed to them important. He made a gesture like urging a baby bird to fly. "Hey," he said, "don't let me mess up your workout."

Debbi made a snorting noise. "You call this a workout? I call it a public humiliation."

She didn't seem very eager to press on, so Bert said, "How long you skated?"

Debbi shielded her eyes. "What time's it now? Never done it before. These are Sandra's skates."

"Sandra, I didn't know she skated."

Debbi mopped her forehead, did a little two-step to keep her footing. "Never used, these skates. She bought two pairs, for her and Joey. Joey wouldn't try, said he'd look ridiculous."

Bert thought that in this instance Joey was right, but he kept the opinion to himself. Instead, he said, "Well, first time, you're doin' very good."

Debbi surprised herself by not deflecting the compliment. She smiled, then, very gingerly, she spun halfway around so her back was to the ocean. She put a hand on Bert's shoulder and was lowering herself to sit, when her skates started spinning and she had to kick like a roadrunner to stay even with herself. When she was settled, she heaved a sigh and said, "Ain't easy, Bert. Day one of the clean-out-and-shape-up program."

Bert indulged himself in a prerogative of age. "Your shape looks pretty good ta me," he said.

She shook her head. "Awful truth? I got a mushy behind, my arms are so puny I can hardly open a jelly jar, and if I don't get serious about my pecs, by the time I'm forty I'm gonna be carryin' my chest around in a wheel barrel."

Out of delicacy, Bert looked away. The runners tramped by, the walkers pumped their little dumbbells; morning traffic grew gradually thicker on the road. After a moment he said, "Debbi, how come you're alla time so tough on yourself?"

She reached down and scratched Don Giovanni behind his outsized ears; the dog whimpered softly in appreciation. She didn't seem to want to answer, and Bert thought maybe he'd gotten a little personal for seven-thirty in the morning. He looked for a way to change the subject, then remembered something that allowed him to. "Hey, I thought youse were leavin' already."

As an attempt to lighten things up, the comment failed. Debbi scissored her feet, let her skates scratch on the rough pavement. "We did," she said to the sidewalk. "I'm back."

The sun was getting white by now, it toasted Bert's shoulders through the teal-blue silk. "And Gino?"

Debbi fiddled with her knee pad. "Gino . . . I don't really know where Gino is."

This didn't sound quite right, and Bert pondered it a moment. He was interrupted in his pondering by two short toots on a car horn, followed by a shouting of his name.

He looked up to see Ben Hawkins making his daily rounds, driving by very slowly in his Bureau car with tinted glass, sunlight fracturing into starbursts on the lenses of his Ray-Bans. The agent gave a delicate little finger-wiggling wave, an insinuating *Remember me?* sort of gesture. Bert waved back in a way that said *Drop dead*. Mark Sutton, crouching on the backseat near the small vent window, balanced his motor-driven camera on a bean bag and, undetected, fired off half a dozen frames of the old mobster sitting there with Debbi.

"Who was 'at?" the young woman asked when the government car had driven off.

"Just a guy," said Bert.

She knew from the way he said it there was more to it than that, and she knew she shouldn't ask.

It was getting hot. The Shirt plucked moistening silk away from his collarbones. Hawkins's pass had succeeded in annoying him. "Little town like this," he said, "island, like, on'y problem is, it don't take much for the place ta feel crowded."

Debbi thought briefly, guiltily, of the pleasure of Gino's absence, and said, "Funny—for me the town feels a lot less crowded all of a sudden." She petted the chihuahua one last time, then put a hand on Bert's shoulder and began the slow and dicey process of rising from the seawall.

She pushed off on a skate and lurched away. Her knees turned inward, her arms flailed for equilibrium, her narrow butt stuck out behind her, seeming not quite part of either legs or torso, a province on its own. She twitched and wobbled as though the earth were moving underneath her, and Bert could not suppress an ungallant image of the old circus trick in which a poodle dances on a beach ball. He watched her till she was lost in the general blur of runners and walkers, and then he reminded himself to wonder just what the hell had become of Gino, what kind of mess he'd blundered into this time.

CHAPTER THIRTY

THE FORKLIFTS had started in at 6 A.M.

They made a droning, buzzing sound as they wheeled in and out of the tall aisles of boxed seafood; the drone rose to a shrill whine as the forks strained to lift the heavy pallets from the stacks. The engines ran on propane, and the exhaust carried a sweetly nauseating smell, a mix of bakery and farts.

The fumes crept under the door of the office where Gino Delgatto, his ankles tied to the legs of a desk, was trying to get a little sleep on the freezing floor, while the thugs in pearl-gray suits took turns napping in squeaky chairs. The propane exhaust mingled with the baked electric smell of the space heater; there seemed to be no room left for oxygen. The prisoner strained for air; each breath hurt as it whistled through his broken nose. Greenish purple bruises were spreading under both his eyes, the lids were puffy. He dozed off and on as the winter wind slammed in from the river and made the warehouse sing a warped note, like a shaken sheet of tin.

Around eight Aldo Messina returned, along with Pretty Boy and Bo. Bo, freshly shaved, looked uglier than before, the scar along his jawbone buffed to a high luster. Pretty Boy's morning bennies were just kicking in, he was getting antsier by the moment. The three men carried big containers of coffee; they brought coffee for their colleagues in the pearl-gray suits but not for Gino. This was a small thing, but it made the captive want to weep with tender pity for himself. He badly wanted some coffee. And aside from that, being denied what everyone else had, being excluded from the morning ritual—it rubbed his nose in his isolation, made him realize how disconnected he'd become from all things comforting, familiar.

Bo untied the captive's ankles and he got stiffly to his feet. Pretty Boy grabbed his chin and examined the discolored face with the eye of a specialist. Messina moved slowly toward the desk and leaned against it.

Today the boss was wearing a black turtleneck that deepened the funereal gloom of his gaze. He warmed his delicate hands around his coffee cup, huddled over it like a refugee. He took a sip, then got down to business. "Gino," he said calmly, "after careful consideration, after sleeping on it, I've come to the conclusion you're a fuckin' liar. You're going in the river."

After all the bad smells of the last day or so, the aroma of other people's coffee was pushing Gino beyond despair. That and the fear of death made his puffy eyes fill up. "I ain't lyin'," he whined. "How could I make up somethin' like that?"

Messina sipped his coffee. "I thought about that," he said. "I thought you were probably too stupid to make it up. That was a point in your favor."

"So—"

"But I've known your father a lotta years," the somber boss continued. "That was a big point against you. Very big point."

The manic Pretty Boy snapped his fingers. "Bottom line, Gino: Kiss your hairy ass goo'bye."

Messina told him to shut up; then there was a pause. Everyone but Gino drank coffee. The forklifts buzzed and the building rang. In his mind, Gino scratched and groped like a cornered mouse, still looking for some gap in the world, some hole in the baseboard, to escape through. "I ain't sayin' take my word for it," he rasped at last. "Check it out."

Pretty Boy's coffee cup had been halfway to his mouth when Gino spoke. Now, instead of drinking, he gave in to a twitch and flung it in the captive's face. The hot liquid stung Gino's eyes; he managed to lap a few sweet drops as they trickled down. Then Pretty Boy grabbed him by the shirt and shook him hard. "Crumb-fuck," he said. "Disgusting asshole. Wantin' ta get your own father clipped."

The words bored through Gino's ears like cemetery worms. Somehow, until that moment, he had managed to hide from himself the full monstrousness of his betrayal. He'd been maneuvering, stalling, improvising blindly: Did the fleeing rabbit take time to wonder what was being trampled in its flight? With his tormentor's mitts still on him, Gino squeezed out miserably, "Hey, I never said that. All I said, I said y'oughta stop this book."

Aldo Messina sat in his fretful calm and sipped his coffee. "So what do we do? We break your old man's pencil?"

Pretty Boy backed off. Forklifts droned.

"First sign of a stupid person," Aldo Messina went on. "Know what it is, Gino? No sense of the big picture. It would hurt me to clip your old man, it really would. But

OK, say we did it. The upshot? War. The Puglieses—they're not what they were, face it, Gino, but they're gonna sit still while the padrone gets whacked? The Commission—on toppa what happened to my predecessor, they're gonna accept it that now the top guy disappears? War, Gino. And for what? We go to war over a half-ass tip from a little twat like you?"

Gino blinked some coffee from his eyelashes. He took furtive looks at Pretty Boy and Bo and the thugs in the pearl-gray suits. Their hands were clenching and unclenching; they were getting ready for some exercise. The prisoner scratched and groped, and suddenly he thought he saw a crack in the wall, a place that maybe he could wriggle into and be safe. "So OK, yeah," he said. "Just break his pencil."

Pretty Boy wheeled on him again and snarled. "Sahcasm? Now ya got the balls ta give us sahcasm?"

"Da pencil," Gino countered. "Da thing that really writes. Ya see what I'm saying'?"

No one did. The forklifts whined, cold winds pounded the building. Gino went on improvising.

"I never said ya should touch my ol' man." He sounded quite convinced of it by now, a little wounded, indignant even, that he could have been so misunderstood. "'Course ya can't, I saw dat. What I'm sayin', ya send 'im a message."

The captive reached out desperately for Messina's hooded eyes. The somber boss met his gaze, looked almost curious, and Gino felt a surge of reckless confidence.

"My father, listen, he don't write things down. He's got a guy he's workin' with, a whaddyacallit, a ghostwriter.

I seen 'em workin' together wit' my own eyes. Writes everything down in a blue note-book. He's a nobody, this guy. A nothin'. Some skinny Yid, works for the paper down there. I'm tellin' ya, ya wanna kill this book wit'out ya got any headaches, *that's* the guy ya clip."

The space heater switched on with an electric hum. Messina put his slender hands in front of the red coils. Pretty Boy, pacing, said, "I still say he's bullshitting."

But now Gino was feeling cocky. "I'm bullshitting, ya t'row me inna river, ya cut my fuckin' head off, I don't care. I'm givin' ya straight goods, ya lemme go. What's it cost ya ta check it out? Ya find da guy, his name is Ahty. Ahty Magnus. Tall guy, frizzy hair. Ya see what's what, ya do what ya gotta do. No more Ahty, no more book."

Aldo Messina looked down at his coffee. His dry and worried skin pulled a little tighter as he fretted and planned, calculated and decided. Forklifts droned. A blast of north wind hit the warehouse like a mallet on a gong. Finally, without lifting his melancholy face, the doleful boss rasped out his orders. "Pretty Boy, Bo," he said. "Go home, go to sleep again. This afternoon you're going back to Florida."

CHAPTER THIRTY-ONE

AFTER BREAKFAST and a shower, Bert d'Ambrosia changed into a loosely woven coral-colored pullover, gathered up his hoary dog, and took a slow stroll down the beach, then two blocks inland to Joey Goldman's house. Joey and Sandra were both at work by then; Sandra had taken Debbi along to help out in the office, keep her occupied. For form's sake, the family friend knocked on the front door. Then he crunched across the gravel driveway, skirted the carport, slipped between a rainspout and a row of oleanders, and went into the backyard.

He found the Godfather sitting in the garden: not gardening, just sitting. His chair was in the shade; his unraveling straw hat threw yet a darker shadow on his face. Either he was unsurprised to see Bert or he just wasn't reacting very much. "Pull up a chair," was all he said.

Bert put down the chihuahua and with some effort dragged over one of the lounges from the pool. He perched on the edge of it and didn't speak.

Vincente looked off past the tops of the aralia hedge, watched an osprey circle in the distance. Then he said, "Bert, you're amazing. Somethin's wrong, you always know." He said it with fondness and admiration and a kind of intimate mockery aimed at both of them, as if he were saying, *You know; I know; what good does it do to know?*

"Ya wanna talk ta me, Vincente?"

The Godfather pursed his loose lips, let out a hissing grunt. His fingers were linked across his wizened tummy. "Before you came, Bert, ya know what I was thinkin'? I was sittin' heah thinkin' it ain't right, it ain't fair, that somethin' goes sour right at de end. It goes sour inna middle, maybe ya got time, strength, ya can fix it. Or maybe you're lucky, ya can walk away. It goes sour right at de end, fuck can ya do? Can't do shit. Ya die wit' a bitter taste in your mouth."

Bert's dog was lying at his feet. He reached down and petted it, took solace from the feel of its veiny ears. A scrap of breeze moved across the yard, brought with it a smell of limestone dust and seaweed.

After a moment Vincente went on. "Gino fucked up bad. He mighta got himself killed."

"Mighta?"

The Godfather looked away, swallowed hard, fought a little battle with himself, and decided at last to confide in his old friend. He told Bert as much as he himself knew of Gino's subterfuge, Gino's fiasco. Bert listened with his chin on his fist; now and then he nodded. At the end, he said, *"Marrone."*

"So what the fuck do I do?" Vincente resumed. "I gotta figure, if he ain't already dead he's wit' Messina. And, Messina, there's no way I can go ta him."

Bert absently petted his dog; white hairs the length of eyelashes came off between his fingers. "Vincente, due respect, maybe this ain't the time for—"

"Pride?" the Godfather interrupted. He was shaking

his head, as at a hopeless position in chess. "Pride's got nothin' to do wit' it, Bert. I'd go on my fuckin' knees ta save my son. But it's this crazy bind Gino put me in. He tol' Ponte *I'm* the one who's takin' back that union. So Messina thinks he's got a beef wit' me. He's gonna make nice while he thinks I'm fuckin' 'im? Or say I try ta set 'im straight, tell 'im it was Gino on his own—wha' does that accomplish? He thinks Gino's that ambitious, that much of a cowboy, he'll take 'im out for sure."

The Shirt looked at the ground and silently thanked God he had no children, thanked Him as well for the massive coronary that had cut the thread of his former life, freed him from its vicious logic and infernal circles of ambush and revenge. Without much conviction, he said, "There's gotta be some way."

"Bert." Vincente sighed. "I been thinkin' nonstop since yesterday. I ain't slept. I'm thinkin' *So we make concessions, we give 'em back that union.* Then I realize *Shit, that does nothin', it's their union ta begin with.* So then I figure, *OK, we give up somethin' more.* But wha' more do I have ta give away? On'y turf I can give away is Gino's— and the Fabrettis'd get alla that by clippin' 'im. The other capos—I can't give away what's theirs; sad truth, I don't have that kinda power. So then I tell myself *Fuck it, get tough, fight.* But Messina just stared down everybody by takin' out Carbone—he's gonna back down now?"

"Ya need a go-between," Bert blurted. "A peacemaker."

Vincente pulled up short at the suggestion. He'd expected a sympathetic ear but not advice. It took him a moment to disengage from his own tangled net of thought; then he said, "Yeah, Bert, that ain't a bad idea, but who the fuck is there? Looka my lieutenants. Sal Barzini: solid guy, but married to a niece of Emilio Carbone. Tony Matera: a hothead. Benny Spadino: I don't trust his loyalty—"

"Nah," said Bert, "'s'gotta be someone y'absolutely trust."

"Someone who knows how ta smooth things out, not make people nervous," Vincente added.

"A diplomat, like."

"A guy that everyone respects."

A small cloud crossed the sun; its shadow slipped over the yard and evened out the shade. The smell of chlorine seemed to grow sharper in the brief coolness. The old men looked away from each other. The same thought was pushing them both toward the same undodgeable conclusion, and neither wanted to presume to give it voice.

The cloud dragged its wispy tail behind it; full sunshine returned. Bert swiveled in his chair, cocked his head, and presented to Vincente a face that for all its ravages—the sagging chin, the wrinkled jowls, the droopy eyes—was full of readiness.

Vincente met his gaze, swallowed, and said, "Bert, nah, I couldn't ask ya."

"Ya didn't," said the Shirt, holding his prepared and willing posture.

"He might not even be alive," Vincente said.

"You're his father. Ya got a right ta know, at least."

Vincente looked away, chewed his lower lip. "I ain't used ta askin' anyone—"

Bert shushed him with a raised hand. The Godfather pushed some air out past his gums, then he reached up, removed his unraveling straw hat, and dropped it gently to the ground. Slowly he rose from his chair and held his arms out to his friend. Bert rose just as slowly; they brought their slack and skinny chests together and kissed each other on the cheek. "Bert," Vincente said, "I don't know how ta thank ya."

"Don't try," the old friend said.

He bent down gingerly, gathered up his brittle dog, and turned to go. There were certain imperatives that went with the decorum of the moment, and Bert and Vincente both knew what they were: There could be no further talk, no hesitation, no looking back.

The retired mobster walked resolutely around the swimming pool and across the yard, maintaining his dignity as best he could while slipping between the rainspout and the oleanders. It was not until he was crunching across the driveway that he realized he was terrified.

His fear did not have primarily to do with confronting Aldo Messina, though he knew that could be dangerous. People had tempers; you never knew when they might take offense. The rules, even back when the rules were obeyed, had been hazy when it came to messengers, ambassadors.

But Bert was frightened mainly because of something else. He was frightened with an old man's quiet panic at the thought of leaving home, venturing out of his routine, sallying through bustling and unfriendly places. Terminals with baffling signs and corridors long as the stroll between the ocean and the Gulf. Devious escalators with oily treads, trampling crowds moving murderously as tidal waves, felonious cabbies and traffic lights that didn't give you time enough to cross the icy street.

He was seventy-six years old, and he hadn't been to New York in a decade. Now that he thought of it, he hadn't been anywhere. He hadn't packed a suitcase, hadn't even looked at his ancient winter clothes hanging in their dusty and forgotten garment bags. Somewhere at the bottom of his closet, buried amid his late wife's undiscarded shoes, was a carpeted carrier for Don Giovanni; the thought of the befuddled dog cooped up inside it, whimpering and cold, caused the old man anguish.

But he'd as much as promised he was going, and he would go. He nestled his chihuahua more closely against his nervous stomach and walked slowly home to begin the daunting chore of making his arrangements.

CHAPTER THIRTY-TWO

IN THE windowless bathroom of number 308 at Key West's Gulfside Inn, Mark Sutton's ankle weights dangled from the shower-curtain rod like salamis in a deli window, his hand squeezers lay on a shelf beneath the medicine chest, and two of his extra-support jockstraps were draped over the faucet in the tub. A mildewed towel had been crumpled up to seal the crack below the door, and by a dim red light the avid young agent was printing the film he'd shot that morning. Exacting with his wooden tongs, he placed an eight-by-ten of Debbi Martini—on roller blades in the company of a known mafioso—in the basin of developer; the image congealed like cooling Jell-O. He washed it in fixer, then clipped it onto a wire to dry with the others.

When he emerged from his portable darkroom, he saw Ben Hawkins standing at the window in his jockey shorts, smoking a cigar and sourly contemplating the vista: a parking lot; a dreary procession of rented cars on U.S. l; then, behind a sparse row of yellowing and scraggly palms, the shallow rocky water of the Gulf. "So wha'dya get?" he asked without much interest.

"Some good shots of the girl talking with d'Ambrosia," Sutton said. "Nice and sharp, even with the sun behind them."

Hawkins said nothing for a moment, just puffed on his cigar. He was bored. He had no stomach for grabbing Delgatto on RICO. Murder one, sure—but he would have bet his pension that the break in the Carbone case would come from somewhere else, that his time in Key West was being totally wasted because of politics and bureaucratic waffling. And meanwhile he was partnered with this hyperactive righteous tyro.

"Mark," he said at last, "let me ask you something about those pictures. Is there such a thing as a card you wouldn't play—in the name, say, of mercy, or gallantry, or just wanting to see someone have a second chance?"

The agent with muscles didn't seem to understand the question. He came up on the balls of his feet and said, "Look, if she's violating her probation—"

"You an agent or a parole officer?" Hawkins asked.

"The information's there to be used," said Sutton. "It's in the computer. I don't see any reason not to—"

"Come on, Mark. She made a mistake. What's it got to do with Delgatto? With the Mob? What's it have to do with anything?"

"It's about leverage."

"Straight from the textbook, Agent Sutton. Very good."

Stung, the younger man flexed his fists and thought ungenerous thoughts about his partner's attitude. Was it the age thing or the black thing that made him so unambitious? "Look, we have a job to—"

"You think that girl's a menace to society?"

"Ben, she has a drug charge on her record. She's Gino Delgatto's girlfriend. She's a guest in the same house as the Godfather, for chrissake. She's supposed to have no contact with criminals, and she's with criminals all the time. If there's a way for us to use that—"

"Use it to what purpose?"

Mark Sutton, girded with the armor of blithe and youthful certainty, was sure he had an answer for that, but when he opened his mouth no words came out. He blamed it on Ben Hawkins's cigar smoke, which, he suddenly realized, was choking him. He longed for fresh air and for the unquestioning simplicities of his jockstraps and his ankle weights. "Ben," he said, "I don't see what you're on the rag about. I'm going for a run."

On the Verrazano Bridge, yesterday's snow was mixed with sand and coated with car exhaust. It had been plowed off toward the edges of the roadway, and it stood there in its gray crags and yellow valleys like a tiny range of sulfur hills.

At two-thirty the traffic on the outbound side was thickening up but still moving briskly, and Bo, taking his turn at the wheel of the dark blue Lincoln, was very pleased with himself.

"We're gonna be there nice and early," he said.

Pretty Boy yawned, put his feet up on the glove box. "Who gives a shit? I coulda slept another half an hour."

"Half an hour," said Bo, "the trucks woulda started, d'early part a rush hour; we woulda stood here gettin' aggravated."

"An' I don't see why we're flyin' outa fuckin' Newark."

"Ya look at a map," said Bo, as they drove under the

second stanchion, "you'd be amazed: different state and all, 'sno farther thanna New York airports."

Pretty Boy didn't care to look at maps; he yawned again. He'd popped a few Halcion to defeat the benzedrine so he could fall asleep. The small blue pills hadn't quite worn off, and he didn't want them to.

The geography-minded Bo went back to a previous line of reasoning. "An' dis half-hour thing? Makes a huge difference. Say we're drivin' straight tru. Dis half hour gets us tru Jersey before it's really da worst a rush hour. Rush hour, we're in Delaware, and Delaware, I don't think they got rush hour in Delaware. By da time we hit D.C., rush hour's—"

"Bo," pleaded Pretty Boy. "We ain't drivin' straight tru. So will ya shut up and drive?"

The scar-faced thug frowned at his partner, shrugged, and looked off at the coastline of Staten Island.

But now the handsome thug gave a bent, carnivorous smile. Something had occurred to him that cheered him up. "Dis time we're flyin', Bo. Ya know what that means, Bo? It means we ain't cartin' anybody back wit' us this time."

"What about I buy the dog a separate seat?" said Bert the Shirt. He was sitting in his cluttered living room at the Paradiso condo, reclining in his oxblood Barcalounger with the phone perched precariously on the arm.

"He'd still have to stay in the carrier," said the travel agent. "FAA regulations."

"The whole trip?"

"Mr. Ambrosia, Key West–Miami is forty-five minutes. Miami–New York is only two and a half hours."

"That's a long time to a dog," said Bert.

"A sleeping pill might be a good idea," the travel agent suggested.

Bert watched Don Giovanni lying white and rigid on his discolored dog bed in the middle of the discolored carpet. Abandoned squeak toys—a plastic hamburger, a hotdog with rubber mustard—were strewn under the glass-topped coffee table and against the skirt of the old brocaded couch. "This dog," he said, "ya give this dog a sleeping pill, he ain't ever wakin' up."

There was a grudging pause. It was a busy time of year for travel agents. "So shall I book the one ticket, the dog to go as cabin baggage?"

Bert just nodded. In his preoccupation he'd forgotten for the moment that he was on the phone, he had to talk. He squeezed out a yes, and the travel agent fired off a salvo of flight numbers, seat numbers, the terminal to transfer to, which airport bus to take. Bert took in none of it beyond the stark fact that he had to be at Key West airport at seven-thirty next morning.

He hung up the phone. His hand was unsteady and he wasn't really watching; the receiver bumped the base and the whole thing clattered to the carpet. Don Giovanni gave a convulsive quiver at the noise, glanced up at his master, and instantly absorbed Bert's debilitating dread. Standing up on its cushion, the dog did a couple of slow yet frantic pirouettes. It managed to lift a leg just slightly; the effort was like an old man's memory of when he had a jump shot. A single drop of urine dribbled out of the distracted creature.

The chihuahua stepped away and sniffed at the damp place as though the drop had fallen from the sky. Bert got up very slowly and walked stiffly to the bedroom to ferret out some winter clothes.

CHAPTER THIRTY-THREE

"Killing," said the Godfather. "Y'ask me what I wanna talk about tonight, I wanna talk about killing."

Arty Magnus spread his cheap blue notebook on his lap and hoped his Adam's apple hadn't jumped too much when he swallowed. He was trying his best to look unshockable. He used his front teeth to pull the cap off his ninety-nine-cent pen, pressed his bare shins against the side of the low metal patio table, and was ready to take notes on rubbing people out.

"Murder. 'Zat OK wit' you, Ahty?"

There was something goading, needling, in the way Vincente said it, and for the first time in a long time Arty felt like he was being tested. He had no idea why— though Joey Goldman had taken him aside when he'd arrived and warned him that it might be a difficult evening. Something was going on within the family, he'd said; the less the ghostwriter knew about the messy business, the better off he was. But Vincente was under a lot of strain. He needed care and he needed diversion. Would Arty stay for dinner? It might not be the cheeriest gathering, but Debbi was cooking sausage and peppers . . .

"Murder," the Godfather repeated. His tone now was not cruel, exactly, but flat with an awful neutrality like that of a desert. "Ya get right down to it, ya cut tru alla bullshit, that's really what da thing hinges on. Murder. Not necessarily ya do it, but ya *could* do it, you're, like, capable. Ya wouldn't back away from it, an' everybody knows 'at."

He paused, reached slowly forward toward his glass of garnet wine. The mild air was very still; it had the sweetly tired smell of flowers closing for the night.

Arty said, "So it's the fear—"

Vincente licked his lips, then cut him off. The writer didn't understand the unaccustomed hardness in his voice.

"'Course it's fear," the old man said. "World runs on fear, ain't ya noticed? But there's fear an'en there's fear. Say I'm gonna beat y'up. You're afraid, it ain't gonna be pleasant, but you'll heal; maybe sometime you'll get even. Say I'm gonna rob ya. You're scared, you're pissed off, but prob'ly you'll make back what I take.

"I kill ya—that's it, the end, it's over. The clock stops. No more chances, ever. Think about it, Ahty. *That's* fear. Ya kill someone, it'see on'y final act. Ya wanna talk about crime, it'see on'y crime that means a damn. Anything else is just a racket, a caper, pissin' around. A rough game, but a game—at most, a warning. Ya kill someone, that's really the on'y serious move, the on'y punishment."

The Godfather sipped wine, then Arty said, "And sometimes you have to punish." He didn't mean to say it; there was something in the mood that pulled it out of him. He heard the words as though someone else had spoken them; they sounded rude, insinuating, and he couldn't decide if they were more like conspiracy or accusation.

But if the ghostwriter was nervous that he'd overstepped, the Godfather didn't seem to notice. He simply nodded with the weary patience of a teacher who's taught the same lesson too many times. "Sometimes ya have ta judge," he said. "Sometimes ya have ta punish." He looked off to the west. Night was stretching toward the edge of the sky, darkness coming down like a sheet being pulled toward the last corner of a bed. After a moment the old man spoke again; the voice was gravelly and barely audible. "And sometimes, maybe a long time later, and maybe indirectly like, the punisher gets punished."

"Hm?" said Arty.

Vincente didn't answer. He reached for his wine, drank some, then pressed his knuckles against his mouth like he was holding something down. "Fuhget about it," he said at last. "I'm bein' a morbid pain innee ass tonight. Fuhget about it, Ahty. What say we try and find a little lighter subject?"

Crouched on the far side of the aralia hedge, armed with a long lens whose casing poked unseen between two knobby stems of the tropical weed, Mark Sutton had captured the meeting on infrared film.

When he walked back to the dark sedan where Ben Hawkins was waiting, he was almost shivering with righteousness and exitement. "That fucking liar," he said.

"Who?" asked Hawkins mildly.

"Magnus," said Sutton, settling into the passenger seat. "Friends with the son, my ass. Ben, he's sitting in there with Delgatto, just the two of them, heads together, sipping wine, talking like best friends. He's taking notes, for chrissake."

"He's a newspaperman," said Hawkins. "It's his job."

"That notebook," Sutton said. "Can you imagine what's in that goddam notebook?"

"Forget about it, Mark," the senior agent told him. "Notebook's off-limits. First Amendment."

"But Ben, he lied to us!"

Hawkins could not work up much indignation. "He wasn't under oath. It wasn't even a formal interview."

"He's hiding something."

"Most people are."

Sutton clutched his camera tight against his chest; for a moment it almost seemed that he would kiss it. "Well, now we've caught 'im in the lie."

"Congratulations."

"Ben, you wait. There's gonna be a way to squeeze that guy. And there's gonna be a way to find out what's in that notebook."

"No more for me," said Debbi, as she placed her hand over her wineglass, her long red nails cantilevered out across the rim. "New leaf. Workout every morning. No liquor while the sun shines. A little wine at night, three, four glasses tops, and that is it."

Arty was holding the bottle of Dolcetto near her wrist, and now he didn't quite know what to do with it. He glanced around the table. No one's glass but his was empty, so he somewhat sheepishly refilled it. Talking about murder had rattled him; Vincente's smoldering bitterness, suddenly flaring, had left him parched. He knew he was drinking a lot, though the awareness was getting vaguer all the time. He ate sausage; it had fennel seeds that warmed his tongue. The peppers had a tiny bit of crunch left in them, the potatoes were dotted with thyme and were perfect for mopping up the cayenne-tinted oil from the meat. "Debbi, you're a terrific cook," he said.

"I'm not," she said, "but thanks." She raised her glass and clinked with Arty. In his elevated state he wanted to believe there was something intimate in the gesture, some private and therefore sexy contact. "It's more a survival of the bachelorette kinda thing," she said. "Ya get hungry enough waiting for Prince Charming to sweep y'off to veal marsala, ya learn to throw some things together."

"Too modest as usual," said Joey, trying to create an ease he did not feel. But it was his and Sandra's dining room; in his mind he was responsible for everyone's good time.

"Modesty is a lovely thing in a woman," said Vincente with a courtly nod toward Debbi. He too was engaged in the silent heroics of the dinner table, struggling not to show his troubles and sour the digestion of the others.

"And a very rare one in a man," said Sandra.

Joey gave her a sideways look but no one picked up on the repartee. Like other avenues of talk, this one seemed to dead-end at the most shadowy hint of anything that might perhaps have had to do with Gino. The man had a gift for squelching conversation even when he wasn't there.

Forks clicked on plates, sausages were pierced with juicy little popping sounds. Then Arty said, "So Debbi, how long are you staying?"

She shot a quick shy look at Sandra, then said, "Don't really know. Playing it day by day."

Arty dabbed his lips on his napkin. "Anything special ya wanna do, see, while you're here?"

Debbi shrugged. It was a wonderful shrug, all-involving, a little goofy and full of curiosity. Her plucked brows lifted along with her shoulders, her blue-green eyes opened so wide that white showed all around, and the lashes spread so they were pointing almost up and down. "I dunno. The beach, the Sunset Celebration. . . . What else is there to do?"

Arty noticed that his glass had somehow gotten empty again. He filled it, then looked over at Joey and Sandra. "Ya tell her about the Key deer?" he asked.

The host and hostess shook their heads. Somehow they hadn't got around to talking flora and fauna.

"Ah, Debbi," he said. "You'll love this. The way you love animals . . ."

He paused to sip his wine, and in that moment each of them felt, hid, and tucked away a twinge of sweet surprise. Debbi was always surprised when any man bothered to remember anything she'd revealed about herself. As for Arty, it just that instant dawned on him that he was flirting. He hadn't flirted in a long time and he didn't realize he remembered how.

"This deer," he went on, "it's only in the Keys and nowhere else. Smallest deer in the world. 'Bout the size of an Irish setter."

Debbi pictured that and laughed. "You're making this up, right?"

He liked hearing her laugh; he wanted to make it happen more. "Antlers? Little toy antlers. Up north,

209

y'ever see a baby azalea bush in winter, those little twigs? That's what the antlers are like. Fawns look like retriever puppies but with spots."

The redhead pulled her eyebrows in, scanned his face for signs of a hoax. Her skin was getting flushed with the pleasure of uncertainty. She turned to Sandra. "Is he making this up?"

Sandra raised her hands, the gesture said *Leave me out of this*.

"Nah," said Arty. "Thirty miles up is where they live. Place called No-Name Key."

"Now I know you're making it up," said Debbi.

They cocked their heads at birdlike angles and held each other's eyes. A long moment passed as they each tried not to be the first to giggle. Then the air moved, rumbled, got ready to carry sound. The Godfather said very softly, "Ahty, it's true?"

The ghostwriter swiveled toward Vincente. "Isn't this what I've been saying? Yeah, it is."

A small sly smile crept almost imperceptibly across the old man's face. He reached slowly forward for his glass. "Then you should bring Debbi up there sometime," he said. He swirled his wine, looked in turn at the young woman and the young man, tilted the glass ever so slightly in what might have been a benediction. "You're the one should show 'er, Ahty."

CHAPTER THIRTY-FOUR

IT FELT late when the ghostwriter climbed somewhat unsteadily onto his old fat-tire bike and pedaled home.

A pocked half-moon was just topping the black and softly rustling trees; away from the tourist haunts downtown, hardly anyone was out, hardly any traffic stirred. The air smelled of iodine and limestone; it was just barely cooler than skin, and Arty savored the feel of it as he weaved among the skulking cats, the stray dogs sleeping against the tires of parked cars.

He skirted the cemetery, its whitewashed crypts stacked up like ghastly file drawers. He bounced down side streets whose old cobblestones were patched here and there with dollops of tar; his spiral notebook and ninety-nine-cent pen clattered in his wire basket. He dodged fallen trash cans knocked over by raccoons and bums. At length he pulled into the cul-de-sac of Nassau Lane, locked his bike to a skinny Christmas palm, then yawned and walked a little drunkenly to his cottage.

The screen on the outer door was torn; a corner of it hung down next to the knob. Arty made nothing of this. It had been slightly ripped before; probably a cat climbed on it. Cats sometimes did.

Nor was the writer particularly concerned to find the inside door unlocked. He thought he'd locked it, but he couldn't quite be sure; he was careless about such things. Hell, when he'd first come to Key West, no one locked their doors.

He stepped into the dark living room and didn't bother turning on a light. After six years his feet knew where to go. His steps creaked slightly on the warped boards of the wooden floor. He dropped his notebook on the ratty table that served him as a desk and continued on to the bedroom.

His hand waved blindly in the still air, found the hanging cord that pulled the switch. He blinked against the rudely sudden glare of yellow light. It was a moment before he saw that the top of his dresser had been swept clean: change, lamp, newspapers, books, scattered on the floor. The drawers were all thrown open; shirtsleeves and pants legs dangled down like the limp limbs of unstrung puppets. His mattress had been lifted, felt under, dropped back crooked.

The awareness that he'd been burglarized bypassed his woozy brain and went first to his readier spine. His body juiced itself and was instantly sober. Muscles twitched, short hairs stood like quills at the nape of his neck, on the backs of his hands. The rage of violation merged with the terror that the intruder perhaps still lurked.

Absurdly, standing there in bright light in the middle of the room, Arty now tried to be stealthy. He slunk to the bathroom doorway, reached a hand around to the switchplate, waited breathlessly while the blue fluorescents hummed and pinged to life. But the bathroom was empty—there was no quailing burglar to confront or perhaps be murdered by. The medicine cabinet had been flung open, its mirrored door bent back on rusty hinges, its meager contents tossed into the sink.

He breathed deeply, tasted salt and iron at the roots of his teeth, felt his heart hammering against his ribs. He swallowed through a clamped-down throat, then moved again toward the living room, propelled by an ancient necessity that went chest-to-chest with fear and could not back down: the necessity to reclaim his place.

He stepped over the scuffed threshold, turned on a light, scanned the corners of the room. Attuned now, he thought he smelled contamination, yet the chamber, for the most part, was weirdly undisturbed. He looked around at the obvious things to be stolen, and because they were all there he didn't notice anything was gone. The small television still stood in the corner, its screen dusty, its top covered in unread magazines. The vintage stereo was unharassed on the bookshelf. The small computer on the table did not seem to have been moved.

He went to check his tiny kitchen. Dirty dishes were still piled in the sink. The cabinets had been thrown open, some canisters knocked over, but damage was slight; not even his small stash of liquor had been taken. He poured himself a glass of bourbon.

Standing in the living room again, he felt a need to touch things. He ran a hand along the back of the old rattan sofa, let his nails click over the woody strands that held it together. Affectionately he slapped the lumpy pillows. He fought against the depression that comes in on the rancid wake of helpless indignation. Like every survivor of every misfortune short of death, he told himself it could have been worse.

He took his drink into the bedroom, sat down on his bed, and thought about the botched and pointless break-in. Clearly, it had been the clumsy work of some pathetic drooling kid strung out on crack. Needlessly, the thief had torn the screen; with quaking hands he'd picked the easy lock. He'd gone straight for the medicine chest, found nothing more potent than Tylenol and Rolaids. He'd scoured the bedroom for cash and jewelry; Arty owned no jewelry and kept no cash at home. Maybe the thief was too lazy to carry out the electronic stuff; maybe by then he'd forgotten why he'd come.

Arty sipped bourbon, weighed the question of calling the police. He knew what to expect from the police, and he decided not to call. The garish roof lights of their cars would only make the ugly business seem yet more sordid. They wouldn't find the intruder, and their failure would only add another drop of bile to the world's supply of futile rage.

He stood up and started to undress. He felt soiled, he wanted a shower. He stood under the random spray of his cheap clogged showerhead until the hot water was all gone, begging his galvanized sinews to relax.

But he was still edgy when he switched off the light and climbed into bed. He tossed and turned, heard sounds that scared him, was assailed by bloody thoughts of some nameless and impossible revenge. He flipped his pillow, took deep breaths. He searched for some serene and decent thought that would sweep away the filth, would soothe him toward sleep, and to his surprise the thought that came was an image of Debbi shrugging, the slightly goofy, all-involving way her eyebrows paralleled her lifted shoulders, the way her bright eyes opened wide as hungry, trusting mouths to taste her life.

In the morning, a mug of coffee in his hand, Arty was crossing his living room when he realized what had been stolen.

It seemed crazy, it made no sense to him at all. It was so ludicrous that his very first reaction was to laugh out loud, though a bleak sound at the tail end of the laugh reminded him it wasn't funny in the least. Why would anybody want his cheap old spiral notebooks? Their covers were stained with outlines of forgotten coffee cups and bourbon glasses. Their pages were fat and wavy with years of spills and dampness. And what was written inside them was both largely illegible and patently worthless— of that Arty had no doubt. His random jottings, sophomoric raves and rambles, his juvenilia. A hundred false starts and not one goddam conclusion.

He stood over the ratty table where the notebooks had been stacked, looked straight down at the bare place they used to occupy, and the longer he looked the less he believed they were really gone.

He squatted down, looked under and behind the table. Nothing. He stood again. As if to confirm the testimony of his eyes, he moved his fingers to where the notebooks used to be. He touched the empty spot, and an unexpected flash of the purest grief, the most perfect, senseless, and irreparable loss, sliced through him and closed his throat. His young ramblings, his solitary jottings, his no doubt embarrassing attempts at learning how to think and feel in written words—in some ridiculous way he would have ached less if he believed his notebooks might be of any earthly use to anyone.

He wasn't crying but his eyes itched. He rubbed them, carried his coffee to the kitchen, left the half-filled mug sitting on the counter. It was time to go to work, and today, uncharacteristically, he was glad to have a job to go to. He wanted to leave the cottage, close the ravaged door, turn his back on the hurt place and not think about it for a while.

CHAPTER THIRTY-FIVE

DUVAL STREET was a grouchy place at 9 A.M.

It seemed tired, sullen, blinky, weighed down by a collective hangover. Yawning retailers grudgingly unlocked their stores, mustering their sarcasm for another day of dealing with the tourists. Drunks and cross-dressers who hadn't made it home the night before wandered aimlessly, stupidly, still looking for the party. The occasional wholesome couple from Michigan, Ohio, Canada strolled in plaid shorts, in futile hope of a genuine local place to get some breakfast.

Arty rode his old fat-tire bike down the middle of the street, tracing out the border of early yellow sunshine that lit up one sidewalk but not yet the other. He was quite close to the office of the Key West *Sentinel* before he noticed the two police cars parked in front. It very vaguely registered that maybe he was less surprised to see them than he might have been.

He quickly locked the bicycle, went through the door between the T-shirt shops, and climbed the narrow smelly flight of stairs. Just inside the *Sentinel*'s frosted door, Clint Topping, the unflappable editor in chief, was leaning against the high reception counter, talking to a semicircle of cops, two in uniform, one in a suit.

"'Course people get mad at the paper," he was saying.

"Politicians. Developers. Guys written up in the blotter for soliciting hand jobs. *Everybody's* mad at the paper, but they don't come trash the office."

"And you say there's nothing to steal?" asked one of the cops in uniform.

Topping waved hello to Arty before he answered. "Your office is destroyed," he said blandly. Then he turned back to the police. "What's to steal? Old papers? Blue pencils? Only thing worth stealing is the computers. And they weren't."

Arty stood on the fringe of the group. From his vantage only a small part of the devastation could be seen. Red and green wires stuck out of the archaic three-button switchboard. The old AP teletype had been toppled from its pedestal like a Communist statue, its unfurled roll of yellow paper wound through the office like a strip of cheap rug. Beyond an open doorway, Marge Fogarty could be seen stooped down, picking up shards of a shattered vase.

"Some offices got it worse than others," said the other uniformed cop. "Personal vendetta maybe?"

Topping shrugged, then gestured toward Arty. "Here's the guy whose office got it worst of all. Anybody mad at you?"

The cops' eyes all turned toward him like they were wired to a single hinge, and Arty found he could not speak. Until that moment he had fought against believing that the trashing of his home and the trashing of his workplace might be linked, might be aspects of the same event. He wanted to imagine the series of invasions was just a grim coincidence, a run of stinking luck; now the extreme improbability of that was flooding in on him like cold and slimy water. Something else was flooding in on him as well: the awareness that he could not talk to the police. If he talked to them, he would have to tell them of his dealings with Vincente, and this was utterly impossible. No one could know about their book. That was rule one. Arty had given his word on it. Not that personal honor was the sole crux of the business; as he understood now with shattering clarity, he'd entered into a contract with the Mafia, a contract that, as the Godfather had made a point of telling him, lived as long as the parties to it lived, and infringements would be handled in the Mafia way.

A long time went by without Arty answering the question his boss had asked. At length he tried to force himself to speak; all that came out was a moist blubbering sound.

"City editor," Clint Topping said to the cops. "Very articulate. I think he's trying to say he doesn't know."

This was not good enough for the cop in the suit. He narrowed his eyes at Arty. "I think maybe he's trying to say he does."

Arty swallowed, looked down, shook his head.

The cop in the suit pursed his lips, dissatisfied. "Dust for prints?" he asked Clint Topping.

"How long's it take?"

"Do it right, couple hours."

"Dust the doorknobs," said the editor in chief. "We still got a paper to get out."

The cluster of men dispersed, and Arty trudged to his office. He was tired of messes, and this mess was a bad one. His file drawers had been yanked out and emptied on the floor; brittle clippings were everywhere, leaning against the baseboards, poking out from folders overturned and spread like tiny tents. His crowded desk had been elbowed clear, the blotter flung aside; the Rolodex was upside down and dripping cards, the telephone hung dead at the end of a tangled cord.

Arty sighed, squatted ankle-deep in paper. He spent the morning trying to restore the minimum order that makes life possible and trying to think through just what the hell was going on.

The foreskin of the jetway was not quite snug against the 767's fuselage, and Bert the Shirt d'Ambrosia was hit by his first slap of northern winter before he'd even entered Kennedy Airport.

He labored up the ramp in a dark gray mohair suit that had been gorgeous before the moths found it and before the slow stretch of a decade on a hanger had given it a flattened and distended look, a shape like that of Gumby. His tie was maroon, his shirt white-on-white, with an elegant pattern of interlocked diamonds, a high collar, and French cuffs pegged with gold and onyx links. On his feet were hard black shoes he hadn't worn in years; they made his toes ride up on one another and didn't keep the cold out.

In his right hand he held the carrier with the perplexed and whimpering Don Giovanni inside; from the left dangled a small suitcase packed with toiletries, human and canine heart pills, dog food, simmered flaxseed, and a single change of clothes. A folded overcoat, double-breasted herringbone, lay over his right shoulder, and with each rocking step it slipped down a little, Bert couldn't help noticing that his shoulder was no longer broad or straight enough to hold it.

The airport corridor was packed and endless, its walls curved like a giant keyhole. Bert plodded along; it seemed to him that everybody was moving a great deal faster than himself. Businessmen jogged past, holding down their ties. Flight attendants raced by, pulling their carts like trotters pulling sulkies. Someone ran into the old man's back and caromed off without apology. Bert's arms were getting tired, his knees ached, but he was afraid to stop against the surge of people behind him.

At length he came to an escalator. Its treacherous and infernal metal steps tumbled endlessly away in front of him; he had no free hand to hold on to the dirty rubber banister. He froze an instant, hoping no one would notice his absurd humiliating terror. He bit his lip and stepped tremulously forward; the tread grabbed his sole and carried him away; he swayed as though standing on a boat in heavy seas. By the time he stepped off he was sweating inside his mohair suit.

He went through an electric door and out into the cold. His breath steamed, his nostrils stung. Little puffs of vapor came through the grating of the dog carrier.

The taxi line was a hundred yards away, and a lot of people were hurrying toward it. Bert knew he should stop to put his coat on, but he was caught up in the hurry now, he didn't want to let everybody get ahead of him. He pressed on through the freezing air that stank of jet fuel and bus exhaust. He looked vaguely off toward the skyline under its dome of soot. By the time he got a taxi his damp chest was clammy and chilled.

The cabbie was a Haitian with red-rimmed eyes and a

green wool porkpie hat. He drove badly, chattering a noisy patois with other Haitians on the radio, but he made no objection when Bert opened the carrier, took out the chihuahua, and held it on his lap. The little dog was shivering with cold or with bewilderment; it looked up at its master with lost and glazed eyes, then licked his hands imploringly with a hot and pasty tongue. Stark white hairs shook onto the old man's dark gray suit.

Bert had asked to be taken to the corner of Astoria Boulevard and Crescent Street, in Queens. There was an old Pugliese hangout there called Perretti's luncheonette. It wasn't a headquarters, exactly—you didn't go to a headquarters unannounced—but it was a good place to find people, or to find out how to find them.

The cab picked its way down the Van Wyck to the Grand Central Parkway. Bert looked out the window at the naked trees, the lingering patches of filthy snow, and tried to tell himself he was at least partway happy to be in New York again. An espresso with anisette would taste good, would warm his gripped and chilly insides. It might be nice to see some guys—Sal Giordano, Tony Matera. And besides, it wasn't a pleasure trip, it was a trip of duty, a kindness to an old friend who would do the same for him.

The Haitian cabbie jerked across three lanes of traffic to exit at Astoria Boulevard. He crawled from traffic light to traffic light, and something almost like excitement began to build in Bert. New York—OK, he was over it, but the city had been good to him. He'd had respect, friends, made money. Now he had the warming thought that he would be remembered, embraced, that a couple of guys, at least, would make a fuss, would treat his visit as a real occasion. He petted his dog, dropped it back into the carrier.

The taxi neared Crescent Street, and Bert tested his memory of Perretti's. A long counter, green, with faded pink and yellow boomerangs. Torn stools with horsehair coming out. Old-fashioned phone booth, with pebbled metal walls, a curved seat, and a fan . . .

The cab pulled off into a bus stop, the driver threw it into park. Bert looked out the window, and now he was confused. "This ain't the place," he said.

The driver didn't answer, just pointed at the street sign.

Bert looked again. Astoria and Crescent. But the place that used to be Perretti's was not Perretti's anymore. It was a place for fruits and vegetables. Pyramids of oranges and grapefruits and half a dozen kinds of apples were neatly piled on staggered crates that cascaded toward the sidewalk. A Korean in a down vest and earmuffs sat on a box and stoically, tirelessly, shelled peas.

"Oh Christ," Bert said aloud.

The cabbie said nothing, just turned his back and drummed lightly on the steering wheel. The meter clocked off waiting time, Don Giovanni whimpered in his cage, and Bert the Shirt tried to figure where'd he go and what he'd do in this freezing town that suddenly seemed foreign as Calcutta.

CHAPTER THIRTY-SIX

AT LUNCHTIME, halfway through the chore of putting his office back together, Arty Magnus ordered in a sandwich and found he couldn't eat it. His stomach was telling him what his brain still denied; along the continuum of fear that runs from vague misgivings to utter panic, he was moving to ever queasier regions. Finally, around three o'clock, he could no longer keep his worries to himself. He called Joey Goldman at work.

"Joey," he said, "remember yesterday, you told me something was going on, there was a problem in your family?"

"I remember," Joey said, a little guardedly. Friend or no friend, it wasn't any of Arty's business.

"Well, whatever it is, it seems to be contagious."

"Say wha'?"

"All of a sudden, I got a problem, Joey. *Coupla* problems. And I'm wondering—"

"Arty, you sound lousy. You OK?"

"I'm not OK. This is what I'm getting to. Outa the blue I got these problems, and I'm wondering if my problem has to do with your problem."

"That's prob'ly impossible," Joey said offhandedly. But after the words were out he thought about them harder. Gino had a long inglorious history of sucking others into his calamities. Still, the only way he could possibly have dragged Arty in. . . . No, it was inconceivable. He cleared his throat. "So inna meantime, what's your problem?"

Arty told him about the break-ins.

Joey said, "Lotta crack-related bullshit goin'—"

"They stole my notebooks," Arty said. "They rifled my files. That sound like crack to you?"

There was a silence. Arty's air conditioner dribbled condensation; his feet were braced against his desk and he leaned far back in his squeaky chair.

"Ya know what ya should do?" Joey continued at last. "Right after work, come by the house. Take the El D, bring Debbi up ta No-Name, show 'er the deer."

The editor let his chair crash forward at the preposterous suggestion. "Joey, are you listening? I'm scared, Joey. I don't wanna go look at—"

The other man broke in, and Arty had a rare glimpse of Joey-his-father's-son, a young fellow who trusted in his own oblique shrewdness, who could take charge, take responsibility. "Arty, listen a me. What's goin' on with you, I don't think it's connected ta what's goin' on with us. But if it is, it's very bad—I tell you as a friend. So lemme take some time, siddown with my father, talk it over. You—stay out of it for now. Take Debbi. Look at deer. OK, Arty?"

At 5 P.M. Duval Street was bustling. Fat people waddled back to their cruise ships like ducks making the inevitable return to water. Pink tourists, their skins sheeny with emollients, twirled postcard racks along the sidewalk.

Early drunks were tuning up for an evening of rude noises.

Arty unlocked his bike and pedaled off toward Joey's. He didn't notice the big dark car that pulled away from curbside a moment after he did and weaved along with him toward the quiet residential streets, keeping a careful block behind.

The ghostwriter cruised under the palms and poincianas, then slowly crunched up Joey's gravel driveway and leaned the bicycle against the house. Joey met him at the door, said a terse hello, handed him the keys to the Cadillac. It seemed clear he didn't want him coming in, upsetting Vincente. The son was handling things his own way for now.

Debbi appeared from the living room. She was wearing skin-tight leggings, cloth shoes, a big shirt over a leotard of electric blue. Her red hair and her freckled throat were swathed in a long navy scarf for the ride in the convertible. She held her big sunglasses in one hand, and she smiled so athletically that the ridges and valleys of her lips stretched away from their coating of lipstick.

The two of them went to the car. Arty settled in behind the wheel, got comfortable, adjusted mirrors. He could not see the dark sedan that had stopped around the corner, hidden by the house next door.

Slowly he backed down the gravel driveway. Debbi touched his arm a second. Her fingers were cool on his skin, he just barely felt the hardness of her nails. "I'm so glad we're doing this," she said. Her eyes were wide, the long lashes spread out almost vertical. "I really thought you were kidding me."

Arty managed a small smile and pointed the El Dorado

toward the beach and up the Keys. It was half, three-quarters of an hour till sunset. The low sun gave the flat water of the Florida Straits a gleam like green aluminum; on the Gulf side, distant mangrove islands seemed to float on top of nests of silver cotton. Here and there ospreys circled, pelicans coasted, their dipping flight paralleling the droop and lift of the power lines strung along the road.

Debbi had as hard a time sitting still as a kid on a school outing. "You say they're like dogs?" she said. "About the size of dogs?"

Arty glanced across at her. He noted, to his great surprise, that her face made him feel better, less worried. "Big dogs," he said.

"Antlers like twigs?" she said.

He looked at her again, at the smile so big it was almost goofy, the avid eyes that seemed to pluck at sights rather than wait passively for things to come into view. His nerves were frayed; sensations good and bad tweaked him as though he had no skin. He heard himself say, "Debbi, I think you're terrific."

She blushed; they rode without talking for a while. Salty air whistled past the chrome edge of the Cadillac's windshield. The dark sedan buried itself in traffic and stayed half a dozen car lengths back.

Around mile marker seventeen, Debbi swept off her sunglasses and said, "Arty, can I ask ya something?"

He just lifted his chin.

"You gay?"

He crinkled up his brows and looked at her. "No. Why?"

"Ya know," she said. "Key West and all."

227

Arty said nothing. Bait shops and seashell stores slipped past.

"You seem like such a nice guy," Debbi went on. "Funny. Nice manners. Ya pay attention. I was wondering why you're not, ya know, involved with someone, married."

"How about: because I was?" he said.

Having got her answer, Debbi now felt qualms at having asked the question. "Listen, I don't wanna pry—"

"No problem," Arty said. The reluctant fellow felt suddenly eager to talk. "Nothing terrible to hide. I was married six years. Most of that time was OK. Toward the end I couldn't help thinking my wife thought I was a failure. I didn't like that part."

"She said that?"

"Never in as many words. She didn't have to."

Debbi pursed her lips. "Wha'd she do?"

"Lawyer."

"Smart, I'll bet."

"Oh yeah," Arty said. "But there's city-smart and then there's life-smart. Ya know what I mean?"

Debbi's slender eyebrows zigged up at the middle of her forehead. "I'm not sure I do."

"I'm not sure I do either," Arty admitted. "But I think it has to do with being able to be happy."

The Caddy barreled up U.S. 1. In the rearview mirror, the pulsing orange sun seemed to be picking its way among the mangrove islands, looking for a clear path to the sea.

After a while, Debbi said, "That's shitty, how she made you feel."

Arty looked at her, not sad, not smiling, just with the

straight gaze you turn on someone when they've got it right. "Yeah," he said. "It was."

At Big Pine Key he turned off the highway onto Key Deer Boulevard, and beyond the prison and the Little League field he took the right that led to No-Name. The road sliced through low gray scrubby woods; the big dark car still stalked, a hundred yards behind.

Debbi looked out at the stunted and distorted pines, the spiky bleached palmettos, the stony earth scarred with veins of scabby limestone. "Not as pretty as Key West, is it?"

"It's the real Florida," Arty said. "No color. Either bone-dry or a swamp, itchy either way. Spiders the size of your fist, leaves that give a rash, alligators that eat Dobermans."

Debbi crinkled up her nose.

They wound through a clot of suburbs, then over the little rainbow bridge to No-Name Key. From the top of the short span they saw the last full daylight; behind the scrub and mangroves on the other side, it was already dusk. A straight road maybe half a mile long dead-ended at a rank of limestone boulders.

"This is where they are," said Arty. He was driving very slowly now, and his tone was that of whispering conspiracy. "Sometimes they come right onto the pavement. Other times you have to find them in the woods."

Debbi nodded. She leaned far forward, her red nails splayed out along the dashboard. Her sunglasses had been put aside; her ardent eyes reached out for deer.

The Cadillac crept on. No deer appeared. Arty looked in the rearview mirror and finally noticed the dark car following behind them. He made nothing of it. They were on a dead-end road where people came to look for deer at dusk.

From moment to moment the light was getting dimmer. A sudden rustling in the undergrowth made Arty and Debbi suck in breath; a raccoon stared back at them and ran away. They peered beneath shrubs, through tall gray grasses, but they heard or saw no other movement, and as they neared the limestone boulders Arty said a little sheepishly, "Ya can't always find them."

Debbi wanted to be a good sport, didn't want to show her disappointment. Besides, she wasn't giving up. "I think we will," she whispered.

At the big rocks, Arty put the car in park, crossed his arms against his belly, and gave his companion an apologetic shrug.

"Can we get out and look?" she asked.

"Be buggy," he said, but he turned the car off and the two of them got out.

They closed their doors very quietly behind them, skirted the limestone barricade, and stood at the indistinct shoreline of No-Name Key. All around them grew tangled mangroves whose roots arced up like tepees and trapped small rank puddles that smelled of sulfur and rotting seaweed. In what had once been a waterfront clearing, an abandoned cistern stood crumbling; tormented casuarinas grew up in it. Lizards scampered; mosquitoes buzzed; frogs croaked. Amid the animal noises came the faint, unnoticed sound of two more car doors opening and closing. Unseen, two more visitors moved furtively beyond the limestone boulders.

Debbi strolled to the far side of the ruined cistern, and there she saw two deer.

They were does, with enormous eyes and beautifully napped brown coats, and they were browsing on a thorny shrub with dusty mottled berries. They really were the size of dogs. Debbi clapped a hand over her mouth to contain a yelp of wonder. With the other hand she pointed. Arty followed the gesture, came along beside her.

The animals looked up without much fear; then they moved off at a leisurely pace, down a path that made a low tunnel through the mangroves. Debbi tucked away the loose end of her scarf, took Arty's hand, and went to follow. Arty, reluctant, resisted the tug for a fraction of a second, then gave in.

They crouched low, held mangrove branches away from their faces, stepped gingerly around the raised and grabbing roots. Mosquitoes hummed around them; spiders swung on half-completed webs. The path wound away from the water; after a dozen steps, scrub pines began to mix in with the mangroves, and under the denser canopy it was dark enough so that colors disappeared and only shapes existed. Fallen pine needles mingled on the ground with limestone pebbles. Up ahead, the deer made the softest rustlings as they ambled.

Debbi paused a second, looked back at Arty, grinned. In that moment of stillness he thought he heard sounds coming from behind them. A jolt of adrenaline put a milky feeling in his legs. Debbi, trusting and excited, pulled him onward.

They came to a small break in the woods. Two miniature bucks were there, their antlers like winter-bare azaleas. Three more does were nibbling at the spiky bushes. Debbi and Arty stood very close together; he felt a warmth like that of fresh-baked bread pulse off her. But he couldn't savor the feeling and he didn't watch the deer; he was listening. There were sounds that were foreign to the woods and he knew now they were footsteps. He tried without success to keep the panic out of his voice. "Someone's following us," he said.

Debbi looked at him in the dimness. Her smile seemed to float free of her face, then shattered like a breaking window; in a heartbeat she had caught the infection of his fear. Mosquitoes swarmed; the metallic groans of toads grew maddening. The two of them stood paralyzed a moment, then bolted across the clearing, scattering the deer, groping with the instincts of the desperate for a path on the far side.

Arty dove through a gap in the twisted pines, Debbi scrambling behind. Low branches lashed their faces; cobwebs wrapped them in appalling gossamer. Their breath came harder in their flight, the sound of it slammed back against their ears. They moved randomly, wherever the woods would let them go. At some point they understood that they were looping back toward water: the pines thinned, the mangroves thickened, a sick salt smell like spoiled oysters weighted the air. Now and again they stepped in slick shallow puddles simmering with rot. Arty wrestled vines, bushwhacked with torn and bleeding elbows.

Then he fell. A mangrove root had grabbed his foot, twisted it as he tried to step. He toppled onto his side; warm muck slapped against his flank, his cheek. He groaned, then tugged his leg like a bear caught in a trap. It came free but his ankle didn't feel right.

Debbi was crouching over him. Her face was close,

mosquitoes swarmed between them. "Go," he said. "Don't wait."

She didn't answer. She didn't go. She put her arms in Arty's armpits and helped him up. For a second he stood on one foot, and in that instant they heard the rustlings behind them, the sharp recoilings of swatted foliage. She threw Arty's arm across her shoulder and they trundled on together.

The ground was getting softer underfoot; there were fewer dry places between the slimy puddles. The mangroves got lower, snakier; flashes of sky broke through here and there, and by the most gradual of increments the woods became a swamp. The puddles merged into an unbroken shallow ooze. The ground beneath melted to an infernal batter, a dense sucking slop like loose cement. Arty's hurt ankle screamed with every step; Debbi's knees ached as she pumped them to lift her sinking feet.

Their progress now was inches at a time. Against the muted splashes of their dire steps, they heard the ever-closer sounds of their pursuers. They heard mumbled curses, gruff breathing fearsome as the wheeze of dragons.

The foul water got deeper, the muck became all-possessing. Debbi sank down past her calves; she struggled to lift herself and tumbled with an awful slowness to a half-sitting posture against a crotch of branches. Arty didn't so much fall with her as reach a certain point of leaning from which he could not deviate. He held a mangrove with both hands, strained every muscle and felt nothing but a stalemate, registered a helplessness more galling than any failure he could ever have imagined.

"Debbi," he whispered, "I'm sorry."

She said nothing. Her eyes were wide, the lashes almost vertical. Tiny lines of blood traced out the scratches on her face.

A flash of blinding light knifed across the swamp. Behind it, two forward-leaning silhouettes could just barely be distinguished. Shoes sucked through the warm morass. One pursuer slowed; the other trudged on with the grim momentum of a dray horse. The beacon panned crazily across the mangroves as the man holding it inexorably approached. Arty's pulse pounded in his neck, he heard blood rushing in his ears. He thought of screaming but went as mute as some toothless thing going down before a lion.

The steps splashed closer, were maybe thirty feet away. The relentless silhouette took on a dreadful bulk and weight. The flashlight pinned Debbi against her branch; lines of black were running down beneath her eyes. Then the beam was turned on Arty. He wriggled like the flash was death itself, there was nowhere he could go.

He didn't know how bullets felt. He waited for them. He swallowed, tasted blood as though his insides were already punctured, gurgling. Then a voice came through the muck.

"What'sa matter, Mr. Magnus, guilty conscience?"

The bright light released his eyes, underlit the face of the pursuer who was holding it. Arty saw a square jaw, a thickly muscled neck, a halo of sprayed hair.

"Jesus Christ," he hissed.

Ben Hawkins neared; his labored breathing wheezed and whistled amid the sounds of bugs and frogs.

"Bad things are happening," said Mark Sutton. "Maybe worse things are on the way. For you too, Miss Martini. I think maybe you could use some friends. Maybe now you'd like to talk with us."

PART FOUR

CHAPTER THIRTY-SEVEN

DEBBI STARTED up the Cadillac. Its headlights found swarms of milling termites and spiraling moths as she turned the car in front of the limestone boulders at the end of No-Name Key.

Her ruined leggings were rolled up above her knees; her shins were lightly coated with dried limestone muck. She drove barefoot, her cloth shoes thrown in the trunk of the convertible, heavy as if cast in concrete. She'd rubbed away the tear streaks beneath her eyes; left behind was a swirled gray smear. When they reached the little rainbow bridge, she broke the frayed silence with a sudden slap-happy chuckle. "The way you told them off, Arty—that was great."

"Left at the stop sign," Arty said. On Big Pine, crickets and tree frogs sang in the scrubby woods, the anemic gleam of television came through people's windows. "Did I tell them off?"

Debbi flicked the end of the thorn-shredded scarf she still wore around her hair and neck. "*Did* you? Arty, you were on a rave. *What kinda lunatic tactics? . . . What kinda crazy SWAT team mentality?* I mean, screaming at them even while they were dragging us outa the mud . . ."

Arty shook his head, scratched a mosquito bite behind his ear, fingered a shallow cut on his neck.

"How's your ankle?" Debbi asked him.

"Throbs a little. No big deal."

"Ice," she said. She'd reached the intersection where Key Deer Boulevard meets U.S. 1, and she pointed the El Dorado toward Key West. The highway was tawdry with bunkerlike bars crouched in chalky parking lots and dim convenience stores that scraped along on sales of condoms, lotto tickets, and potato chips. After a while, she asked, "Arty, the FBI—why'd they wanna talk to you?"

He swiveled toward her, pressed down in his seat by the weight of secrets, of his promise to Vincente. "I don't think I can tell you that," he said.

She nodded, bit her lip.

A moment passed. Then Arty said, "That Sutton guy, he said maybe trouble was on the way for you too. You have any idea what he meant?"

Debbi kept her eyes on the road and said no. Then her hands fretted over the steering wheel and she glanced at Arty. "Maybe I do. It's not something I wanna talk about."

Arty didn't push; he rested his hurt foot and watched the long loops of the power lines strung next to the highway.

Debbi flicked her scarf. "This is crazy."

"Hm?"

"Here we are, the two of us, we almost die, we're alone on this weird road in the middle of nowhere, and there's all these things we're not supposed to tell each other. Like the secrets matter more than we do."

"Secrets matter," Arty said, though before his dealings with Vincente, he'd never realized quite how much.

"Can I ask one question?"

"Sure."

"Your thing with these guys—does it have to do with Gino?"

The question confused Arty. His connection was with the Godfather. It was the Godfather the Feds were asking about. He couldn't imagine what it had to do with Gino, and he mumbled out a no.

But in his own mind the question raised an altogether different matter—the matter of the odd and itchy twinge he'd felt at the mention of Gino's name. He looked at Debbi. The Caddy's top was still down; each passing streetlight unfurled a sheet of brightness over her, then snapped her into shadow until the next beam found her face. Wispy bangs escaped from the scarf and blew across her forehead; her eyes were soft and tired. Arty was amazed to realize that the archaic and almost forgotten thing he was feeling was jealousy.

He tried to keep his voice casual. "Gino—you worried about him?"

Debbi tapped the steering wheel. "Sure I am." Then she added, "But only like I'd worry about anyone in trouble."

"That's all?"

She crinkled up her eyebrows, began to let herself imagine that maybe Arty was angling for an assurance he didn't think he had the right to come out and ask for. She gave it like a Christmas present. "Gino and me," she said, "we're history. That's over, finished, good riddance. . . . You didn't know that either, Arty?"

Sheepishly, he shook his head.

"Sicilians," said Debbi. She gave a half-indulgent, half-exasperated frown. "Always playing us-and-them, whispering games, divide and conquer. . . . Think about it, Arty. With what you know and what I know, we almost know something. If we could tell each other."

He settled back in the seat, looked ahead at the snaking road that hopped from rock to rock to Key West at the end of the line. Gino was history. Debbi was here. Arty hugged his hurt foot and said, "Yeah, if we could tell each other."

Nassau Lane was not much wider than Joey Goldman's car, and when Debbi pulled up in front of Arty's cottage, tree limbs dangled over the convertible and there was barely room left over for cats to slink along the curb. Stars twinkled, were briefly erased by smears of moonlit clouds. Debbi cut the engine, and the sound of rustling fronds flooded in to fill the quiet.

For a moment they just sat there. Then Debbi gave a cockeyed smile and gestured toward her devastated clothing and slightly torn-up face. "Do I say thank you for a lovely evening?"

"We saw deer," said Arty.

"True," she said. "The size of dogs."

Arty made no move to go, and after a pause she added, "Your legs—you'll be OK?"

He nodded, glanced down at his door handle, didn't reach for it. "Ice," he said.

They sat. Moonlight filtered down, hands fidgeted in laps, the faraway perfume of closed flowers came to them. When a man and a woman desired each other and were not lovers, there was no quite graceful way to end an evening, it never quite stopped being high school.

Wistfully, regretfully, Arty said, "Well . . ." and fumbled to open the door.

He looked up from his fumbling to see Debbi's face very close to his, moving toward him, silent, fluid, and mysterious. She kissed him very quickly at the corner of his mouth, at the puzzling cusp between friendly cheeks and amorous lips; then, just as quickly, she withdrew again. Arty, reclutant Arty, saw her retreating, saw her eyes slipping away, her wrapped hair being framed by night and distance, and without an instant's hesitation he reached out both hands to hold her face, to keep it near his own. He kissed her on the mouth, tasted lipstick and salt air.

Then he climbed out of the car, half turned away, and said good night. He felt light and happy but still he limped as he headed for his ravaged front door.

CHAPTER THIRTY-EIGHT

"FUCK IS this supposed ta mean?" said Pretty Boy. "*Juicy pa . . . para . . .*"

"*Paradox*," said Aldo Messina, sitting between his minions at a six-sided table covered in green felt.

"Right," said the handsome thug. "*Paradox. Surest way to fail: aim higher than anybody realizes.* Fuck's 'at supposed ta mean?"

Bo, the philosophic thug, murmured thoughtfully, "I think maybe it means—"

"Or dis?" His partner cut him off. "*Common sense—not very common; does that make sense?*"

"Dat one's like," said Bo, "ya know, a play on—"

"A play on bullshit," said Pretty Boy.

Aldo Messina, looking glum and bloodless, pressed the notebook shut, pushed it aside like a plate of food with bugs in it, and grabbed another from the stack.

This was at the Fabretti family headquarters—the San Pietro Social Club on Broome Street in Manhattan. The club had once been a hardware store; it had display windows covered by steel roll-down shutters that had not been opened since the Eisenhower years; its glass front door had been replaced by a metal one with a peephole. There was a small bar with an espresso machine and some bottles of anisette and Scotch. On the walls hung tilted pictures of Italian-American lounge acts: men with pompadours and bedroom eyes, women in sequined evening gowns with cleavage.

Pretty Boy leaned in toward the new notebook and started in again. "*Remember the as . . . ast—*"

"*Asterisk,*" Messina hissed.

"*Asterisk,*" parroted Pretty Boy. "Fuck's an asterisk?"

"It's, like, inna sky," said Bo. "A little planet, like."

His partner wasn't listening. "*Asterisk. When in doubt, break the scene.* Look, I don't see where any a dis has ta do wit' Vincente Delgatto, and I don't see where dis guy comes off thinkin' he's a writer. Y'ask me, he comes off like a fuckin' nut. Mosta what he writes, ya can't even make out what he's writin'."

"That's what worries me," said Messina. He put his hand on the stained and moisture-fattened notebook, ran a delicate finger across the page as though it were written in Braille. "Could be some kind of code. Look the way he prints one line, a heading like, then scrawls all this other bullshit underneath it."

"Code, no code, who gives a shit," said Pretty Boy, "long's we got the books?"

"We got the books, yeah," Aldo Messina said. "But so what? The problem with writers is it's hard to stop 'em writing. And we still don't have the writer."

"No fault a mine," said Pretty Boy, a note of whining resentment in his voice. He got up from the table and started pacing, it was like the amphetamines pinched him on the scrotum if he sat still more than a few moments at a time. He went to a pool table where no one ever shot pool and rolled the cue ball off three cushions. "I still say we shoulda clipped 'im. Shit. I'm gettin' frustrated, like. I keep gettin' sent ta do a job, then I don't get ta do the fuckin' job."

"Bo did right," Aldo Messina said with finality.

The philosophic thug modestly lowered his eyes. The table they were sitting at had a gutter for poker chips and change; Bo quietly swept lint into it.

Now Messina started pacing, circled wide of Pretty Boy; they were like planes around an airport. The dour boss made a circuit or two, then moved to the table and sat down again. Next to the stacked-up notebooks that had been stolen from Arty Magnus was a small piece of cardboard. He toyed with it; it was a business card. It said Mark J. Sutton, Special Agent, Federal Bureau of Investigation. It had shaken out of the back of Arty's Rolodex when the thugs had rifled his office.

Pretty Boy watched his boss fondling the card and said, "The fuck's workin' both sides a da street, I say dat's alla more reason—"

"Look," said Bo, "he's workin' wit' the Feds, the Feds are gonna be protecting 'im. He coulda been wired. He coulda had a whaddyacallit, one of those things, they know exactly where he is. We take 'im out, *boom*, they got us."

"OK, OK," said Pretty Boy. "But inna meantime, the skinny fuck has gotta go."

"Yeah, he does," agreed Messina. "But in the meantime, Bo did right."

This grated on Pretty Boy's nerves. "Bo did right," he said. "Bo did right. So give Bo a fuckin' medal. But there's still this scumbag writer—"

"The situation's a little more complicated than we thought," Messina said. He pursed his lips, furrowed his bleak tense forehead into a map of perfect pessimism. "But hey—isn't that the way fuckin' life is?"

Arty Magnus had not had time or inclination to straighten up his trashed bedroom. A lamp still lay on the floor and seemed to be groping after its shade, like a man who had lost his hat. Dresser drawers still stood half open; shirt and sweater sleeves hung out at urgent angles, waving mutely, frantically, for help.

The ghostwriter was sprawled across his bed now, his head and his ankle up on pillows, a bag of ice hanging down on both sides of his foot like a cocker spaniel's ears. He lay there and he thought. He thought about Debbi: the shock of finding her face next to his, the salt taste of her mouth. His hands, however briefly, had held her jawbone, his fingers reached behind her ears; such intimacy felt fresh, was astonishing, uncanny. He closed his eyes and imagined he was her lover.

The idyll didn't last long. It was shattered by other preoccupations, by thoughts and worries ruder than slaps and as frightening as a scream in the night. Someone was after Arty. After him. It was an odd phrase, primitive; it suggested a ritual hunt, a ceaseless stalking. Which was precisely how Arty felt: like his steps were being dogged, his range of movement shrinking. He was running out of room, and Key West, this tiny island that had never seemed too small before, suddenly felt confining as a rowboat and as devoid of hiding places.

He lay there on his bed. A mild breeze puffed through the screens, moonlight dusted the tangled foliage outside. He remembered when he'd agreed to become the

Godfather's ghost, the earnest charade he'd gone through, telling himself he was free to say no. He should have said no, he knew that now; probably he'd known it all along. Yet regret was strangely absent from the mix of fear and anger he was feeling. He'd known from the start there'd be some crazy thrall to this business of harboring someone else's story, some lunatic pull into the mad logic and morbid righteousness of gangsters. He'd accepted the danger, in a distant, abstract sort of way, and he'd expected a strict and brittle fairness in return. Vincente's eyes had promised him that, had led him to believe he was entering a realm where justice was severe but simple, ruthless but unerring, a realm where, if you told the truth, and kept up your end of the bargain, you would be safe. What had gone wrong?

He thought. He had no answers, but he had suspicions that started off as vapors then took on human shape, like evil genies, and the more he thought the madder he got. He was surprised at his own grit when, around ten-thirty, he called Joey Goldman and said they had to talk, right now, at his cottage, and to bring along Vincente.

CHAPTER THIRTY-NINE

"GIOVANNI," SAID Bert the Shirt, "what the hell are we doin' here?"

The chihuahua looked up from its ashtrayful of dog food mixed with flaxseed. It blinked its enormous eyes that were milky with cataracts, then went back to its tardy dinner.

Bert got up from the foot of the hotel bed and strolled over to the window. Down the side street, past the darkened theater marquees, he saw the lights and billboards of Times Square. A gigantic ad for color film showed a ski jumper flying off the sign and heading skyward; endless news briefs spelled out in bulbs wrapped themselves around an alabaster building. At sidewalk level, dented wire trash cans lay tumbled in the gutters; homeless people hunkered down on slabs of cardboard tucked into doorways; patches of filthy snow survived in places reached by neither sun nor shovel. The retired mobster put his hand on the cold glass; it left a print in frost.

It had not been a good day for Bert the Shirt. After the disaster of Perretti's, he'd had himself driven to the Airline Diner, near La Guardia, a sometime hangout for old family friends. He was discreetly told that Tony Matera hadn't been around in weeks, and Sal Giordano came in occasionally but seemed to be spending more time in the Village. So Bert directed the Haitian cabbie to Manhattan, where he poked his head into a couple of linguine joints, then made inquiries at a *pasticceria* three steps down from the sidewalk on Carmine Street. There he learned with a sinking heart that he'd missed Sal by maybe twenty minutes; he'd been coming in most days for morning coffee—morning, for Sal, commencing around noon.

Bert's cab fare was nearing a hundred twenty dollars by then, and he knew he had caught a cold. He'd caught it at the airport; he knew the precise instant it happened: as he trudged coatless, with a sweaty back, to the taxi line. The cold was under his right shoulder blade; he felt it knotted there, radiating out to chest, throat, stomach. He'd told the driver to head uptown; he wanted to get a hotel room and lie down.

Manhattan hotels did not take dogs, even dogs in carriers, and after being turned down twice, Bert ditched the chihuahua's cage at curbside and held the little creature under his coat; white hairs the length of eyelashes had come off on his mohair suit. He checked into a semi-dump called the Stafford, was shown to this room, whose waterstained wallpaper was like a foulard tie one wouldn't wear. He'd gotten comfortable, then decided to work the phone.

It was at that point he realized he had no one to call. No wife, no girlfriends. No buddies, no colleagues. No business associates, no people he'd been asked to send regards to. No one. What he felt at realizing this was not loneliness, exactly, but a dislocation so intense that it was itself a kind of death, a numbing transport to a realm of silent shadows, a sphere where there were movements but

250

no events. He felt like he'd outlived all things familiar; he felt like he'd outlived himself, was watching his mortal shell from some great distance.

He was slightly light-headed; he was probably running a fever. He took a nap, slept too long, woke up around 8 P.M. Now it was nearly eleven and he was thoroughly disoriented in time as well as place. He stood at the frosty window, looking with recognition but no connection at the narrow slice of nighttime city.

Then he sneezed. It was a racking sneeze that squeezed his chest and burned his eyes, and it was echoed by a tiny sneeze from floor level, a chihuahua sneeze followed by a snort and a shake of droopy whiskers. Dog and master sniffled, crinkled up their noses, and looked earnestly at each other with glazed and rheumy eyes.

Arty was sitting in the middle of his living room, on an ancient vinyl hassock whose splitting seams leaked oily straw. He'd put his bag of ice away; his ankle was just barely swollen, his bare instep faintly discolored with a purplish tinge like that of spoiled meat. "I'm trying to be logical," he was saying. "I'm trying not to be paranoid. But really, what else could it be?"

Neither Joey nor Vincente answered right away. Joey had been perched on the edge of a wicker chair. Now he sprang up and walked the length of a worn hemp rug; his stride took him almost to the ratty table from which the notebooks had been stolen. Vincente sat far back on the rattan settee. He sat very still and barely seemed to be breathing. His black eyes had settled deep into their bony sockets, his brows hung down like mossy eaves to hide them.

"Debbi had no business saying anything," Joey said at last. He said it not to Arty but to his father; it had the flat and basic sound of a family closing ranks, turning its doors and windows inward toward some somber court-yard where visitors were not allowed.

"She *didn't* say, anything," Arty protested. "All she did was ask me if—"

He cut himself off, annoyed that he felt pressured to explain, compelled to justify himself. "Look," he resumed, "a few hours ago we thought we were gonna get killed. Will ya cut us a little slack on that?"

There was a silence, a long one. Moonlight turned metallic as it filtered through the screens. A cool breeze carried the smell of damp sand. Arty struggled to reclaim the fragile calm that was the hangover of panic.

"Vincente, Joey, we're all on the same side. Let's not arg—"

"But look what you're askin' us to believe," Joey cut in. His face was taut, the slight cleft in his chin grew deeper, darker.

"Gino told people about the book," insisted Arty. "That's why my place was trashed, that's why my office was rifled. You have a better explanation?"

"Be careful, Arty," Joey said. "What you're saying, it's like an insult—"

"Joey, who you talkin' for?" The voice seemed to come from everywhere and nowhere, up from the floor, down from the ceiling. "You talkin' for yourself, Joey? Or d'ya think you're talkin' for me?"

The young man didn't answer, just stared at his father, his teeth clamped tight.

Vincente reached up slowly, stiffly, to straighten a necktie that he wasn't wearing. "G'ahead, Ahty. I'm listening."

The writer leaned forward on his hassock, put his elbows on his knees. "Vincente," he said, "d'you remember, the first time we ever talked, you asked me if I ever spilled a secret? The question, the way you asked it, it scared the shit outa me. But I told you the truth. And it's still the truth."

The Godfather listened in perfect stillness. His skin was drawn and waxy; over his cheekbones the flesh was yellowish and in the hollows it was gray.

"And right at the start," Arty continued, "I told you something too. I told you it was a strange thing about a book, at some point a book becomes a public thing, everybody's property, and no matter who you are, how powerful, you couldn't pick the moment when that happened. You remember that, Vincente?"

The old man nodded almost imperceptibly. He licked his cracked lips but his mouth had no moisture in it; flesh rasped over flesh and no part could comfort any other.

"So what I'm saying now," the ghostwriter went on, "is that our book, the word of it, is out. Why else would someone steal my notebooks? What good are they to anybody?"

The Godfather said nothing. He sat very straight, his hands on his knees; the posture was Egyptian.

"I don't know what's going on with Gino," Arty said. "Debbi didn't tell me anything. *You* told me, Joey—you told me there was a problem in your family, remember? Gino's the problem—for all of us. Am I wrong?"

Arty fell silent. Joey paced. Outside, the wind scratched out island sounds and transported smells of tepid ocean.

Vincente Delgatto was a man who could not be lied to, nor was he capable of closing himself to what was true. He sat there very still, and the truth of Gino's final betrayal seeped through his tissues like swallowed poison. The old man took in a deep breath. It wheezed through his nostrils then came out as a groan. "My son," he said. There was love and bitterness and bafflement and self-mockery in the words. He said them again: "My son."

He got up from the couch, tried not to let it show how much he needed to use his arms to help his legs to lift him. He moved slowly toward Arty, his hands extended. Arty rose, and the Godfather took him in his arms, didn't kiss him, but laid his grizzled cheek against the ghost-writer's, did that on both sides. "Ahty," he said, "the trouble I've caused you, fuhgive me, please."

He stepped away, did half a pirouette between the hassock and the sofa, seemed momentarily to have lost the sense of where he was. Then he added, less to Arty than to himself, "I hope to Christ I have the strength to make it right. Joey, I'm tired. Take your father home."

CHAPTER FORTY

JUST BEFORE eight the next morning, Debbi Martini, dressed in a purple leotard with black tights underneath it, her neck wrapped in a pink scarf against the early chill, approached the bicycle that Arty had leaned against Joey Goldman's house the evening before and climbed aboard. It was an act of considerable courage.

She'd never owned a bicycle. Many Queens kids didn't. Traffic was dangerous, bikes were easy to steal. She tried to remember the last time she'd been on a bike. She thought it was when she was eleven. She remembered that the sidewalk squares had seemed to slip by dizzyingly fast beneath her and that it felt great when the air flew past her ears. She remembered, too, that she'd forgotten to put her feet down when she stopped, had hovered for a moment till gravity noticed her, then had tipped slowly, almost gracefully, into a scraped and bleeding heap at curbside.

Now she climbed onto Arty's high broad seat, bit her lower lip, and launched herself down the driveway. She felt perilously tall, tall and wobbly as on the top step of a ladder. She reached the street, yanked the handlebars to turn, kicked out a skinny leg for balance, and was on her way to Nassau Lane. Arty had a bum ankle and needed to

255

go to work. The least she could do was bring him his bicycle.

The morning was cloudless; stamped tin roofs gleamed like rubbed coins and threw angled shadows that were so precise they seemed painted on the street. Doves sang on telephone wires; dogs lolled, their paws clicking on the quiet pavements; hibiscus flowers yawned themselves awake. Debbi pedaled and grew more confident, she leaned into turns and let one hand dangle jauntily at her side. She smiled as she rode; the air tickled her gums and she almost let herself imagine that maybe she was on her way to make love with Arty, this tall nice guy who asked her things about herself and remembered what she'd said.

Arty at that moment was placing his coffee mug at the edge of the bathroom sink and stepping gingerly over the low sill into the shower. Random spurts and dribbles spilled out of his corroded showerhead. Some of the water hit his flank, some clattered against the lumpy-painted stall. He soaped his armpits and sleepily hummed.

Debbi skirted the cemetery, its blockish crypts shamed by the life-drenched promise of the morning. Palm fronds swayed and lifted, revealing yellow coconuts clustered close as giant grapes. She bounced down cobblestone lanes patched with tar and recalled the feel of Arty's hands around her face. She pedaled and she teased herself by pretending, just pretending, that maybe she was bold enough to appear at Arty's door and seduce him by the light of day.

Arty was shaving in the shower. There was no mirror; the process was one of memory and guesswork. He fingered his sideburns, traced out where they ended. He stretched his upper lip to trim beneath his nostrils. He craned his neck to shave under his chin; he nicked himself above the Adam's apple and didn't even realize it.

Debbi swooped into Nassau Lane, her red hair blown back from biking, her purple leotard just slightly damp with exercise and adventure. She coasted the last twenty yards to Arty's cottage, then attempted a bravura finish to the ride: Rather than hitting the brakes, she tried to stop herself by hooking a Christmas palm with her elbow as she scudded by. It was like trying to do-si-do a partner made of stone. The front wheel jackknifed as the bicycle pivoted around the tree; Debbi hugged the trunk like a koala to keep from falling.

She took a moment to regain her dignity before going to the damaged door.

Arty was brushing his teeth in front of the bathroom mirror when he heard the knock. He'd put a piece of toilet paper on his cut neck. He'd wrapped a towel around his waist; water was still dripping down his legs. Perhaps he should have felt fear at the approach of an unexpected visitor, but fear was a habit he hadn't yet learned, and the knock did not sound sinister. He rinsed his mouth and headed toward the living room.

They saw each other through the screen.

"Hi," said Debbi, as Arty pushed open the door. "I brought your bike."

Arty was a person who woke up blank, had to reclaim his life slowly every morning. "I forgot it wasn't here," he said. "Come in. Have some coffee."

She put one foot over the threshold, hesitated. "You're not dressed."

He looked down at his towel, noticed he was still holding his toothbrush, remembered he still had toilet paper on his neck. He shrugged. She shrugged and came in anyway.

She followed him through the living room into the narrow kitchen. She looked with rueful understanding at his small coffee-maker that had dripped two humble cups, a bachelor's dose of morning brew. She watched him, the long muscles in his back, as he reached into a high cupboard and produced a chipped blue mug. Her legs were tingling, maybe from the ride; her hands felt cold and electric, perhaps the aftermath of clutching handlebars.

She said, "Arty."

She said it just as he was reaching for the coffeepot. He didn't turn toward her right away, just looked over his shoulder. Then her eyes swiveled him around. He put the cup down on the counter. For a long moment she studied him. His arms and face were tan, his body was surprisingly pale. His chest was smooth except for a little tuft of hair along his breastbone; the tuft glistened, still damp from the shower.

Her hand reached out on its own to touch it. Arty's arms went around her and pulled her snug against him.

The Godfather woke up from a fitful sleep with a dull headache so evenly diffused across his skull that it seemed it must have been spreading all his life. His temples surged with tiny tides; thumbs seemed to be pressing on his eyeballs. The soft pillow felt cruel against the back of his head; there was grit, corrosion, in the knob at the top of his spine.

He lay awake a long time and let life proceed without him. He'd heard Debbi leave her room and close the door behind her. He heard Joey and Sandra as they went about their morning routines. He heard the sounds a house makes: the *whoosh* and drips of plumbing, the bells and buzzers of appliances, the inevitable creaks and groans of wood and hinges.

When he was sure that everyone had gone, he arose, put on backless slippers and an old robe of burgundy silk, and shuffled out to the garden. He sat with his back to the sun, let it warm his shoulders.

He thought about his helplessness.

It was a raw line of thought, mean, vulgar, and tactless, and he hated it. Helplessness was what he'd struggled his whole life to avoid, and he used to be able to kid himself he'd done a pretty good job of avoiding it. The helplessness of the poor, the helplessness of the immigrant, the helplessness of the neighborhood schmo without an education—those specters he'd conquered. As a young man, he'd grabbed fiercely, sometimes violently, for the things young men believed could safeguard them from impotence, spare them from humiliation—respect, money, power—and all those things had come to him.

Yet what had he really accomplished except to arrive at a higher, more chastening realm of helplessness? A realm where associates were enemies. A realm where family members schemed, where legal heirs connived like . . . like bastards. A realm where there were no small disappointments, only tragedies. A realm where the final helplessness consisted of being unable to ask for help.

Vincente sat. Sunlight played on the blue water of the pool, breeze shook the mottled leaves of the aralia hedge. He did not believe in sin and retribution, at least he didn't think he did. Still, he could not help feeling that what was happening to him now was some grim comeuppance for unforgiven things done long ago. For the first time in many years the Godfather thought hard and unguardedly about the violence of his youth.

The young Vincente Delgatto had been tough, remorseless—a stringy and quick-handed street guy with a dangling cigarette and a dimpled fedora. He'd intimidated people, grabbed their lapels, thrown them against the hoods of Stutzes and Packards. He'd killed. Twice. Miserable people, loathsome, not worth mourning. Still, they bled, they twitched as they died, their fingers grabbed at empty air, groping blindly for something to hold on to, something to stop their dead slide down to hell.

The Godfather shuddered. Overhead, a flight of ibis went by, a lone osprey circled. Violence. It was appalling, but at least, Vincente reflected, it was not a lie. Believing that violence could be outgrown, put aside—that was the lie, the lie he'd lived by for decades now. He'd told himself that violence had been a tool, a stratagem that set him up, established him, and which he was now in a position to forswear. He could become a diplomat, a peacemaker even, and the violence would seep out of his life, be filtered away by time until the remembered blood ran clear and clean as water.

Only it didn't work that way; he saw that now. Brutality was a virus, once it entered a life it stayed there; it lurked in the organs, it waited with a patient malice, it could take over any time. Vincente sniffed the clement air scented with limestone and chlorine and flowers, and he realized there had never been a moment when his life was not a violent life, that even in the absence of fists and bullets there was the simmering violence of jealousies and grudges, of plots and hatreds, of betrayals and memories that made jagged tearing cuts like rusty knives.

In his top left dresser drawer, back behind his socks and handkerchiefs, the old man kept a gun. It was a thuggish weapon, a snub-nosed .38; he'd had it for many years and never fired it. Suddenly he felt a morbid sniggering compulsion like the sick tug that pulls a former drunk back into the tavern. He wanted to heft the gun, to hold it in his hand. If peace, for him, was sham and pretense, if serenity was something he'd murdered half a century ago, then he might as well embrace the soul and emblem of the violence he realized now he couldn't flee.

He stood up in his robe and slippers, felt the unwholesome excitement of a child left home alone to play with matches or to masturbate. He took a deep breath that did not come easily into his constricted chest; then he padded slowly but with resolve through the sunshine toward the empty house.

CHAPTER FORTY-ONE

GINO DELGATTO, being dull, coarse, and sluggish, dealt with captivity better than most.

After four days in the cramped and smelly office of the seafood warehouse, he'd fallen into a numb docility, almost a bestial contentment. His skin was oily under his stubble beard, ingrown hairs put red splotches on his throat, but he didn't really notice. The swelling under his eyes had subsided; his smashed nose, like a failed soufflé, had become resigned to its flatness and only hurt now when he sneezed. His clothes were wrinkled and dirty, his underwear foul, his armpits stank, and he didn't much care. Time passed and he was still alive. He played poker with the Fabretti thugs who watched over him in shifts. His captors had started taking pity on him; they brought him egg sandwiches, pizza, gave him bourbon now and again. He slept when he could and listened to the insane ringing of the metal building he was caged in.

On the fifth morning of his imprisonment, something happened that was outside the drab routine: Pretty Boy came storming in, bellied up against him, and backhanded him hard across the cheek. Flesh tore inside his mouth as it was crushed against his teeth.

"Some fuckin' tip we get from you, crumbfuck," said the thug on speed. "Fuckin' tip coulda fucked us all."

Gino didn't know what he was talking about. He stood there, one eye tearing, waiting for more information or more punishment.

Messina and Bo filed silently in. Bo took the lid off a container of coffee. Messina, wearing a dark gray coat over a dark gray turtle-neck, moved slowly to the metal desk and leaned against the edge of it. He frowned, took a fleck of something off his tongue, then said to Gino, "The pencil. The guy that's writing for your father. D'you know he's working with the Feds?"

Gino's survival reflexes had come alive. He made a point of looking even more flabbergasted than in fact he was.

"We checked his office," Messina went on. "Know what we found? FBI business card. Agent Mark J. Sutton, of the so-called elite O.C. squad."

A gust rattled the warehouse, made it sing around its rivets. "I had no idea," Gino whined. "I swear on my mother."

Bo slurped coffee; his manic partner went to the Venetian blind and let his fingernails play its slats as if it were a xylophone. After a moment Messina said, "Gino, you've been causing us a lotta worry. First you worry us about that fuckin' union. Then you worry us about your old man's book. Now you worry us about the Feds. That's a lotta worry, Gino."

The prisoner signaled his remorse by putting on his most hang-dog expression and staring at the floor. Messina wrapped the panels of his bulky coat more snugly around himself; worry made him cold.

"So you know what we're gonna do, Gino?" the doleful boss resumed.

Gino didn't know, but he had some ideas. The East River was maybe fifty yards from where he stood; this time of year it was cold enough to stop a person's heart well before he drowned. The captive swallowed, sucked his lower lip, and waited for sentence to be pronounced.

Messina hunched his shoulders and buried his thin chapped hands deeper in the pockets of his coat. He glanced morosely up from under his furrowed brow and said, "We're gonna let you go."

"Bert!" said Sal Giordano, sliding bulkily out of his booth at the *pasticceria* on Carmine Street. "Bert the Shirt! Good Christ Almighty!" The loyal Pugliese soldier, his eyes squeezed almost shut with grinning, lumbered around the table, grabbed the old man by the arms, and beamed at him as though he was a dear and long-lost uncle.

It was exactly the kind of exuberant and showy greeting that Bert had hoped to find on his journey north, but it came a day too late. The foreignness of the city, the archaicness of his being there, had already sunk too deeply into him. He felt self-conscious, felt like he was sleepwalking. He managed only a soft hello.

"What brings ya ta New Yawk?" Sal asked him.

By way of answer, Bert glanced quickly toward the empty place where Sal had been sitting.

The younger man gestured him into it and yelled for another espresso. Once they were seated, Bert leaned confidentially across the table and whispered, "I got a dog under my coat. OK I take him out heah?"

"Bert, hey, you're wit' *me*. Ya do whatever da fuck ya like."

The Shirt nodded, freed the chihuahua. The brittle animal blinked its milky eyes, then patrolled the upholstered bench, sniffed the unspeakable crumb-laden seam where the back joined the seat, and sneezed.

"*Salud*," Sal said. "So Bert, what's the story?"

"It's Gino."

Sal's wry face became a roadmap of disapproval. "He fuckin' up again? He makin' trouble for Joey?"

"Not for Joey dis time," said Bert. "For himself. He got himself in a bad beef wit' the Fabrettis. Don't ask me more."

The young soldier raised his hands in a gesture of surrender. "OK," he said. "More I don't gotta know."

Bert lowered his voice another notch. "But there's somethin' I'm hopin' ya can do for me. I gotta go ta da top, gotta get wit' Messina. Can ya set dat up for me?"

Sal's head snapped back. At least that's what the tiny flinch seemed like to Bert. Bert was studying him hard now, doing what he used to do best, which was reading faces, figuring out what drove guys. Sal was good people, a guy who really wanted to help; at the same time, he didn't want to admit his limits or his fears. If you could get him right at the cusp of his bravado, just at the edge of how far he could go, he'd really push to save face and do you a solid.

While Bert was thinking this, a strange thing happened. His self-consciousness fell away. He forgot about the grippy tightness inside his ribs. He didn't feel young; it just stopped mattering that he was old. It stopped mattering that the world had changed. He was still himself, and if he took on an obligation to a friend, he would find a way to see it through. He reached up and toyed with the silver collar pin of his pale-blue monogrammed shirt.

"Jeez, Bert," Sal Giordano said. "Wit' the way things are, the edginess, like, about what happened ta Carbone—"

Bert remembered another of the things he used to be very good at: pausing. He could put a lot of weight, a lot of nuance, into a pause. Now he poured sugar into his espresso, stirred it slowly with a tiny spoon. His pause was saying, I ain't worried, Sal. I know y'aren't wimping out on me.

After a moment the young man said, "Sit tight, lemme see what I can do." He went to the pay phone at the back of the store.

Bert, suddenly hungry, signaled for the waiter and ordered up a *sfaglatella*. He fed pieces of the hard crust to his dog.

Ten minutes later, Sal came lumbering back. "Here's the deal," he said. "I'll take ya to Brooklyn, leave ya wit' a friend a mine. He'll drive ya ta Staten Island, get ya together wit' a friend a his. That guy'll get ya inta the San Pietro. After dat, you're on your own."

Bert grabbed a napkin from the steel dispenser and dabbed the powdered sugar from his lips. "When'a we staht?" he said.

"Whenever you're ready," said Sal Giordano.

"I'm ready now," the old man told him, and he slid his skinny haunches across the vinyl booth.

CHAPTER FORTY-TWO

IT HAD been many years since Arty Magnus gave someone a ride on the crosspiece of his bike, and doing so now pulled him back to the heartbreaking sensuality of the endless days of boyhood summers: the feel of a girl leaning fearlessly against his arm, the smell of her hair blowing in his face and tickling his nose, a smudge of dirt at the back of her knee, the sticky taste of a Creamsicle at the corners of her mouth.

"Debbi," he said, his long legs pumping, "this is great."

She swiveled as well as she could on the hard metal tubing and smiled at him. Her red hair and her green eyes looked so nice that Arty's breath caught. A woman you really liked looked prettier after you'd been to bed with her; a woman you didn't, did not. This was one of the ways a man knew if he might be falling in love.

They rode under rustling palms and leafless poincianas, skirted the cemetery, and dodged the skulking, furtive cats, the flat dogs sunning themselves next to the tires of parked cars. When they got to Joey Goldman's house, Arty regretfully put on the brakes. The bike slowed, leaned, and Debbi hopped off onto the sidewalk. Arty regarded her in her black tights and purple leotard.

"You left your scarf at my house," he said.

LAURENCE SHAMES

"I guess I'll have to come back for it sometime."

"Tonight?"

She bit her lower lip, looked up the gravel driveway at the airy house. "I don't know," she said. "I'm still a guest and all."

"Then wangle me a dinner invitation. I want to look at you."

She kissed him on the cheek and headed up the lawn. He turned his bike around and pointed it toward work.

He rode off slowly and with dignity; then, when he was safely out of sight, he popped a wheelie, cut some swooping slaloms, and reached as high as he could reach to knock wood against the over-hanging boughs of banyan trees and frangipani.

The sky above lower Manhattan was the swirly, smeary white of paint that needed mixing. Somewhere in the glary clouds, sleet was waiting to happen, but for now the air was dry, though sharp with the blue smells of ice and invisible winter lightning.

Bert d'Ambrosia, his dog nestled in his solar plexus, sat in the vast cabin of the Staten Island ferry, in the sullen company of the friend of a friend who was serving as his escort. The guy had a mousy chin and a twitch that pulled his left eye down like a windowshade; he didn't want to talk, seemed deeply put out at being asked to do someone a favor. So Bert looked through the dirty Plexiglas at the surging gray water of the habor. He'd spent the last three hours being driven from Mafia enclave to Mafia enclave around the boroughs of the city. He'd been to Benson-hurst, he'd been to Todt Hill. He'd been through tunnels, over bridges; now he was on a ship that stank of cheap hotdogs, thin burned coffee, and the caustic stuff they use to mop up floors when someone pukes. All this to go eight blocks from where he'd started. A helluva way to do business, he thought.

The boat neared the towering shore, and without a word the escort got up to go back to his car.

The ferry docked, the pilings groaned. Bert was driven in moody silence past Wall Street, up through Chinatown, into the shrinking precinct of Little Italy. They passed Umberto's Clam House, where Crazy Joey Gallo ended face down in the linguine. They passed Salvatore's Neapolitan, favored by Nino Carti for its air-dried braciole. Bert's heart was pounding. It had been a long time since the ancient muscle pumped like this around its bypassed valves. It wasn't fear that did it, it was the promise of action, the coming alive of memory. He looked around. Fire escapes. Big cheeses hung in storefronts in harnesses of rope. These things seemed suddenly uncanny, surreal. Bert licked his lips, ran a hand through his white hair with its glints of pink and bronze. He felt jumpy as a wire with its insulation freshly snipped.

His escort pulled up in front of an unmarked building with closed steel shutters and a metal door that was blank as a dead man's mind save for a peephole the size of a lentil. Bert stood close to his mousy companion as he approached the door and knocked. He knocked two times loud, two times soft, paused, then three times loud again.

After a moment the peephole slid open and a voice like a saw said, "Yeah?"

"Dis is Bert the Shirt," said the mousy man. "He's OK. Says he got business wit' the boss."

Some seconds passed. A cold wind poured down Broome Street, carrying sheets of filthy newspaper. The guy behind the peephole didn't like where Bert's right hand was. "Why the fuck you got your hand inside your coat?" he asked.

"I got my dog in heah," said Bert.

"Yeah? Lemme see."

Bert held up the chihuahua. The man inside saw drooping whiskers, legs hanging down scrawny as chicken wings.

Three, four locks clicked open quickly. The metal door fell back a quarter of the way. A huge hand grabbed Bert's arm, pulled him in. The door slammed shut and in the same instant Bert was twirled, face to the wall, to be frisked. It had been a long time since he'd been patted down; the feel of it was distant and naughty as the recollection of illicit sex. Don Giovanni whimpered softly at the invasion of his master's lap and tummy. The doorkeeper stepped away and said, "OK. I'll take ya back."

The big man led the way past the pool table where no one ever shot pool, toward the sitting areas under the skimpy lights at the rear. Beyond the doorman's meaty shoulder, Bert saw mismatched chairs, cockeyed pictures of lounge acts. Then he saw four guys sitting at a green felt card table meant for six. He saw Aldo Messina in a topcoat. He saw a handsome punk and an ugly punk. And he saw Gino Delgatto, very much alive.

The four of them were deep in muffled conversation, huddled low, their heads turned in like the petals of a carnivorous plant converging on a bug. Bert had a few seconds to study Gino. His hair looked damp, like he'd just had a shower. He was freshly shaved, but his skin looked more yellow than pink. His clothes were clean but maybe they didn't fit exactly right. Something was wrong about his nose, though there weren't any marks.

The doorkeeper cleared his throat and everyone looked up. "The Twitch brought this guy in," he said. "Says he got business wit' youse."

Bert watched Gino. Gino's face crawled like there were worms beneath his skin.

Aldo Messina turned his doleful gaze on the visitor. "Bert d'Ambrosia, am I right?"

Bert gave the slightest of nods. He'd been active when Messina was a nobody. Messina remembered. That was good.

"So what's your business?" asked the boss.

Bert slowly raised the hand that wasn't holding the chihuahua and pointed a finger at Gino. "This guy," he said. "This guy's the business." He paused long enough to find out if anyone had anything to say about that, if anyone would flinch. No one did, and so the Shirt turned full face toward Gino. "Your father's been very worried about you. The way ya just disappeared and all."

Gino looked halfway up the old man's chest, couldn't seem to crank his eyes any higher. In a clenched monotone, he said, "Tell my father he don't have nothin' ta worry about. Everything's just fine."

Bert petted his dog. White hairs the length of eyelashes fluttered to the floor of the social club. "I'm glad ta hear it. I thought maybe there was a beef."

"There was a small misunderstanding," said Messina. "It's over. It's settled."

One of the punks, the handsome one with high hair,

cracked his knuckles and said, "Lotta things are gettin' settled."

"Shut up, Pretty Boy," Messina said.

Bert smiled at the guy who'd been scolded, hoped to egg him on. Then he said, "Mind if I sit down a minute?"

"Bert, we're kinda inna middle a somethin' heah," said Gino.

Bert nodded understandingly, then reached up and spread a hand across his chest. "I'm sorry, I'm not feelin' very well." He lowered himself into a chair.

Messina rubbed his slender hands together. The other punk, the ugly one with a crescent scar, said, "Ya wanna glass a water, somethin'?"

Bert squeezed out a yes and Bo went to the bar.

The old man made a dismissive gesture, like they should just forget about him and carry on. They didn't. Messina looked down at his cuticles. Gino kept his eyes on the felt trough at the edge of the table.

Bo brought Bert some water. The old man raised the glass and said "*Salud*. Ta gettin' everything settled."

Pretty Boy gave a speedy little laugh. "Settled like two birds wit' one—"

Messina shot him a look. "Take a walk," he said. "Now."

The handsome thug seemed unsurprised to be exiled from the group. He stood up jumpily, went to the pool table, started rolling the cue ball off the cushions.

Bert drank his water. "So gents," he said, "I'll go back ta Florida, I'll tell Vincente Gino's fine, everything is settled. 'Zat correct?"

Messina considered. Before he could speak, Gino blur-

272

ted out, "Wait a second. I don't want 'im in Key West right now."

Bert listened hard to Gino's tone. It was a whine, but a strong whine, the pushy whine of a person whose desperation gave him the right to ask for things. The old man said casually, almost jokingly, "Hey, Key West is where I live. Whatsa difference—?"

Gino talked right over him. "I don't want him talkin' ta my father. I don't want 'im seein' nobody."

"But Gino," said Bert, "the whole reason I'm heah—"

"Stay outa my face, old man," said Gino. He said it with his teeth together; the voice gurgled through his throat like lava through a crater. "You're a dried-up old pain innee ass, you're just makin' everything more complicated."

Don Giovanni whimpered. Pretty Boy manically rolled the cue ball. Then Bert said, "Wha', Gino? What am I makin' more complicated?"

The closest thing to an answer was a manic snort from Pretty Boy. A moment passed. Then Aldo Messina softly said, "Gino's right."

"First time for everything," Pretty Boy chimed in.

"Y'aren't going back to Florida just yet," the boss told Bert.

"But if everything's OK—"

"Bo here's gonna baby-sit ya a day or two."

"But I promised Vincente—"

Messina cut him off, unruffled and implacable. "Bert, the questions you're asking, they're unhealthy questions. Stop it, please."

Bert sat back, licked his dry lips, petted his feverish dog. He tried to lock onto Gino's eyes but they slid away like some wet thing in a swamp. The old man recoiled in his soul from what he saw in his friend's son's shallow face—an emptiness beyond shame and the particular hate reserved for a would-be savior by a person who knew that he could not be saved.

"Someone to see you," said Marge Fogarty, standing in the doorway of Arty's office at around three that afternoon.

"Who?"

"One of the men who was here the other day. The white one."

"Ah shit," said Arty. He had a new lover with whom he was smitten, he was having a marvelous day. Why spoil it sparring with Mark Sutton? "Tell him I'm not here."

"He says it's important."

"Of course he does. I'm out."

Marge shrugged, but as she turned to go she nearly walked into the stocky agent's rippled chest. "I distinctly asked you to wait outside," she scolded.

Sutton ignored her. "It *is* important," he said to Arty. "And you're in."

"You ever been sued for harassment?" Arty asked him.

At this the young cop could not suppress an impish smile. He took the question as a compliment. Three years with the Bureau, he knew how things worked: You wanted a lifetime as a street agent, you followed procedures, went by the book. You wanted to make a hot career, you took some chances, tested the limits. Instead of answering Arty's question, he said, "I have something I think you'd like to see."

Arty frowned. Marge Fogarty discreetly withdrew. Sutton approached the editor's desk, reached into the small briefcase he was carrying, and produced a glossy eight-by-ten of Debbi Martini and Bert d'Ambrosia.

"So?"

"Nice-looking young woman," said Sutton.

"A little tall for you," said Arty.

Sutton gave a quick wince, erased it by flexing muscles. "Apparently just right for you."

"Meaning?"

"We've been watching you. We've been watching her. It seems, to put it delicately, that the two of you have become an item."

"And what are you, the sex police?"

The agent crossed his arms, pushed up his biceps with his knuckles. "Mr. Magnus . . . May I call you Arty?"

The other man just leaned back in his chair and glared at him.

"Listen," the agent resumed. "I'm not your enemy. I'm trying to help you out. Your ladyfriend here—you know she's on probation on a drug charge?"

Arty tried not to look surprised. But he couldn't help glancing at the picture of Debbi, the wide and avid eyes, the smile so big it was almost goofy. Steeling himself, he said, "This is Key West, Sutton. Am I supposed to be scandalized?"

"Scandalized? No. But I thought you might be a little bit concerned."

Arty said nothing, struggled to hold his face together. A nasty glozing doubt had suddenly sprung up to mock him. Reluctant Arty. *Cautious* Arty. What did he really know about this woman he'd fallen into bed with? Only that she had a trusting, life-embracing gaze and an exhilarating way of shrugging. Only that she seemed the greatest thing that had happened to him in as long as he could remember.

"She was caught redhanded with cocaine," Sutton hammered on. "Not a little stash for personal use. A lot of cocaine."

"You're telling me she's a dealer?"

"I'm telling you she got off with a suspended sentence and probation. Part of the probation—no contact with felons. Like Gino. Like Vincente. Arty, listen to me. We tell what we know, we show the pictures, she goes away for two, three years. She won't be the same person when she gets out, believe me."

Arty sat. Something seemed to be pushing down on his shoulders, sapping the starch from his posture. He thought about thrall. The thrall of his pledges to Vincente, now the more visceral thrall of desire, of the joyful and reckless beginnings of love. He looked at the picture of Debbi, then said miserably to Sutton, "Just what the hell do you want from me?"

By way of reply, the agent reached into his briefcase again. He pulled out an infrared image of Arty and Vincente at the metal table on Joey's patio, placed it next to the other photo. Vincente had his finger raised in a Socratic gesture. Arty had his notebook on his lap.

"I think the pictures tell the story," said Mark Sutton. "You lied about why you go to that house, Mr. Magnus. You looked us in the eye and you lied. But OK, no hard feelings. Let's keep it practical. Over here, you've got the girl. Over here, the Godfather. You can protect one of them, Mr. Magnus. You can't protect both."

Arty splayed his hands out on his desk, let out a long slow breath. Behind him the droning air conditioner dribbled condensation onto the rotting floor.

"I'd like to know what you're hiding," said the agent. "Maybe you'd like to tell me what you and Delgatto talk about. Maybe you'd like to show me what's in that little notebook."

"And if I tell you it's got nothing to do with you?"

Sutton frowned down at the picture of Debbi Martini. "I think we both know that's not good enough," he said.

CHAPTER FORTY-THREE

"CERTAIN THINGS in life," the Godfather was saying, "they just ain't supposed ta happen."

He and Arty were sitting around the low metal table on Joey Goldman's patio. It was dusk. The still swimming pool gave off a sapphire glow; in the west, behind the aralia hedge, slabs of flat red cloud were squeezed between layers of green and yellow sky.

"A child dies," Vincente said. "Shouldn't happen. A beautiful woman gets a cancer in her breast. A rotten son of a bitch gets to de end of his life wit'out it ever catches up wit' 'im. A son turns against his father. These things make any sense to you, Ahty?"

The ghostwriter sat with his spiral notebook spread open on his lap. His cheap pen was in his hand. Now and then he broke through his own preoccupations long enough to scrawl a phrase, but his mind wandered. For the first time he thought he truly understood what Vincente meant when he spoke of being overstuffed with secrets.

"On'y way it makes any sense at all," the Godfather went on, "is if ya figure maybe there's some crazy balance, it's got nothin' ta do wit' good and bad, right and wrong, who deserves a break and who deserves a hot poker up de ass, it's just some crazy way that things, like, average out."

Slowly, stiffly, the old man reached forward toward his glass of wine. Arty watched him. He didn't look tired, exactly; he looked drained and jittery together, at that point of fatigue and strain where one has forgotten what it is to rest. His hand trembled slightly as he raised his glass; his lower lip pushed out to meet the rim as in an awkward unsure kiss. Then he said, "An' this is where God comes into it. Ya see what I'm sayin', Ahty?"

"No, Vincente, I don't think I do."

"If it's all just averaging out, random like . . . I mean, lemme ask ya this. Which d'ya think is worse: Ya don't b'lieve in God at all; or ya wanna b'lieve, ya try, but ya look around and y'end up sayin', Wait a second, what kinda cruel sick bastard could He be? I mean really, which is worse?"

For this Arty had no answer. The Godfather didn't seem to notice. He took a wheezing breath and reached under the lapel of his satin smoking jacket.

"OK," he went on. "So say it all comes down t'averaging out. So whaddya do? Ya do what ya can ta help the percentages, improve your odds. An' 'at's where this comes in."

He pulled his hand out of his jacket. It was holding the snubnosed .38.

Arty's mouth fell open. He'd never seen a gun in someone's hand so close to him. It looked obscene, disgusting. The barrel had a dull industrial sheen, the muzzle was dark as the bottom of a mine.

"Yeah, ya get yourself a gun," the Godfather resumed, absently gesturing with the weapon, "an' ya tell yourself you're helping your chances, improving your odds, it's less likely you're gonna be the one that gets fucked. But ya know what, Ahty? Y'ain't doin' nothin' about your odds. Nothin' ya do does nothin'. That's the joke. Innee end, things either work out or they don't."

He broke off, slowly waved the gun, put it softly on the metal table. Arty's eyes followed it down, and he was visited by an ugly thought. Perhaps Vincente really was just a criminal and nothing more, as mean and vulgar and unredeemed as Mark Sutton made him out to be. Could there be any virtue in standing up for such a man, any goodness or even any sense in sacrificing others on the crooked altar of promises made to him?

Vincente was looking off toward the west, at the fading clouds. His tunnel eyes were out of focus. After a time he said, "But where was I goin' wit' this?"

Arty put his notebook down, leaned far forward, his forearms on his knees. "Vincente, you OK?"

The old man didn't react right away. Then he put on a masked wry smile, scratched behind an ear. Was he OK? This was not a question he was often asked. Of course he was OK. He was the Boss, the elder, the one who knew. He had to be OK; why bother asking?

Why bother answering? Instead, he said, "Ah, I remember now. The gun. I'm showin' ya the gun because I was thinkin', this book we were doin', it woulda been nice ta leave the gun out of it, like, ya know, it didn't exist, wasn't part a the story. Like we could say Vincente Delgatto wasn't a punk, he was a man wit' some dignity, maybe he knew a couple things. But ya couldn't leave the gun out, Ahty, ya couldn't pretty it up like that—"

"The book we *were* doing, Vincente?"

The old man pulled up short. His mouth worked a

couple of seconds before sound came out. "Before things got all fucked up. Before it got too dangerous."

A yellow light came on just inside the house. Joey, carrying the enormous pasta bowl, appeared in the doorway and told them it was time for dinner. He saw his father's revolver glinting dully on the table and pretended he did not.

When he'd withdrawn, Arty said, "Vincente, you and me, we have a deal. You don't just break it off like that. The deal lives as long as we do, remember?"

The old man's eyes stung, he rolled his tangled brows down to hide them. Talking through that book, easing his mind—it was as close as he was ever going to come to salvation, but he wasn't going to get anybody killed for it. Bitterly, he said, "The deal lives unless it doesn't."

He put his hands on the arms of his chair, and began the arduous process of getting to his feet. Arty closed his notebook and wondered if he'd just been released from his pledges, wondered how he would know honor from treachery, gallantry from treason, beyond the strict bounds of his promise. Perversely, his gaze was pulled toward one last look at Vincente's thuggish weapon; somehow the Godfather had already stashed it. He must have been wicked quick when he was young, the writer thought.

Gino Delgatto, wearing borrowed clothes that didn't fit exactly right, drove his rented T-Bird south on Seven Mile Bridge, on his way to murder Arty Magnus.

The thought of Arty dead didn't trouble him in the least. In fact his own world would seem considerably less cluttered without this skinny brainy Jew outsider who had somehow wormed his way into his father's confidence, was taking money from the old man while seducing him onto a course that could only end in family humiliation and disaster. A book! A public gut-spilling! And meanwhile this nobody is skimming off his five grand every month and getting tighter with Vincente every day, getting to be real buddies, confidants. He had to go.

Still, Gino wished there was someone else to do the killing. He drove under the starry sky between the Atlantic and the Gulf, barreled past the muck-anchored pylons that carried power to Key West at the end of the line, and wished to hell that Pretty Boy and Bo had done the job. It would have been so neat that way; it would have been over with by now.

Who knew about this FBI connection? Who knew even now how far it went? So Messina had thrown it back on Gino. That was the deal—if you could call it a deal. He killed the writer, he was given absolution; he didn't kill the writer, he'd better not buy green bananas. If the writer was wired, if the Feds were watching him, that was Gino's problem; he would take the fall.

Gino chuckled over that one as he drove. Him take the fall? In a world of ratouts and gut-spillings, him be the only sucker that keeps his mouth shut? Not likely. Worse came to worse, the Feds nailed him murder one, he'd sing; he'd sing so loud they'd think Caruso had come back. The kind of information he could give them . . .

What kind of information *could* he give them? He was the Godfather's son, OK. But what did he know, what could he tell, that would give the prosecutors a bigger hard-on than a sure conviction on murder one?

Right offhand, Gino couldn't think of anything, and for a single awful moment he doubted he was as important as he liked to think he was. He banished the thought, watched a moonlit pelican fly next to the road. He wouldn't need to cut a deal. The killing would go just fine. To reassure himself, he reached a hand into the pocket that held the nine-millimeter pistol graciously lent by Charlie Ponte. It made him confident that the odds were heavily on his side.

CHAPTER FORTY-FOUR

IN THE cramped kitchen of a fourth-floor walkup on Sullivan Street, Bert the Shirt d'Ambrosia, his monogrammed cuffs rolled up past his elbows, was making meatballs, while his sniffly chihuahua lay on the cracked linoleum, content in its master's nearness and in the homey smells of meat and garlic and frying onions.

The old mobster, humming tunelessly, sculpted a hollow into the big raw mound of blended beef and pork and broke an egg in it. He kneaded the mixture through the fingers of both hands; it made squishy sounds as the egg yolk ran and bubbled. Then he split the gooey mass into two batches.

He went to the doorway and peeked through it into the living room. Bo, who believed that people should keep up with things, was sitting rapt in front of the evening news, frowning at earthquakes and warlords. He wasn't getting up anytime real soon.

Bert went back to the counter and reflected on how lucky he was in his jailer. Bo had been nothing but considerate, gentlemanly. He'd taken Bert uptown to the Stafford, let him gather up his things, even carried his bag for him. Downtown again, they'd walked Don Giovanni together, shopped for dinner like roommates, met Pretty Boy for a drink at a bar on Bleecker Street. The handsome thug moved from speedy to opinionated, in what seemed the early stages of a night of getting blotto, but Bo had remained a pleasant companion all the while.

He'd been so nice that the Shirt felt almost bad as he dumped the rest of the flaxseed into Bo's half of the meatball mixture and worked in the oily pellets with his fingers. The arthritic chihuahua roused itself at the familiar smell and did a jointless little pirouette next to the garbage can.

The ceiling fan turned slowly above Joey and Sandra's dining room table; the blades sliced through the steam that wafted up from the giant bowl of fusilli and shrimp and the tails of langostinos.

Arty held out a chair for Debbi. He smelled her hair as she settled in, but his mind was not at peace.

When everyone was seated, Vincente, regal in his smoking jacket, raised his glass and said, "*Salud.*" Five arms stretched across the table; glasses clinked.

Heaping bowls of pasta were handed round. Arty thought about the first time he'd eaten here. Out of nervousness, he'd had three helpings of linguine, and everyone had offered an opinion on his appetite and his physique, talked about him like he wasn't there—or as if he'd always been there.

Now salad was making its way around the table. The ghostwriter, his insides stuffed with secrets, felt no appetite. He tonged a few leaves onto his side plate. Joey said to him, "Take more. There's avocado at the bottom. You like avocado."

Debbi shot a quick wry look at Arty; this was just the

kind of thing the two of them would smile about together. Arty felt her glance but was too knotted up to return it. "How do you know I like avocado?" he said to Joey.

"Come on," the other man said. "I don't know what you like by now? I don't see? It's like family already. Family, ya know who likes avocado, who hates onions, who peppers make 'im burp. Ya just know."

So Arty dug out some avocado.

There was a silence which then phased into a rumble as the air got ready to carry sound. Vincente said softly, "Family changes. It changes. I didn't used ta think it did, I thought it was the only thing that stayed the same. I was wrong—what else is new? The feelings change, the boundaries, like, they ain't so solid like I thought. People leave. People come in. It changes, yeah."

He blinked from underneath his awning brows. He looked through the steam that wafted from the pasta bowl, saw Joey and Sandra, Arty and Debbi. They were staring at him, and only when he saw them staring did he realize he'd spoken aloud. They looked worried, they looked sad for him. It didn't do for people to be sad at table, and Vincente tried to smile. To his surprise, a small smile came easily, he felt in some way unburdened. "It changes, yeah," he said again. "I ain't sayin' that's bad."

Bo the gentlemanly thug dabbed his thick lips on a napkin and patted his distended tummy. "Terrific meatballs, Bert," he said. "Howdya make 'em?"

The old mobster, his own small stomach pressing lightly against the bone buttons of his shirt, got up to clear the table that was squeezed into a shadowy alcove with a hissing radiator. "Ya gonna tell me why you're keepin' me heah?" he said.

"We been tru dat," said Bo. "Ya know I can't."

"Then I ain't givin' up my recipe." He ran dishes up his arm and headed for the kitchen. His dog followed stiffly behind, paws ticking on the floor.

"Ya puttin' up coffee?" Bo asked him.

Bert put the dishes in the sink. There was a clock on the wall; it said ten after nine. With the dog, it usually took about an hour for things to happen with the flaxseed. Of course, Bo was a lot bigger than the dog. Then again he'd had a lot more meatballs. Bert didn't know if it would make a difference either way. He didn't hurry on the coffee; eleven minutes were gone by the time the brown foam dribbled out the spout of the espresso pot.

Bo had moved to the living room by then. He was sitting in front of the television, but there was no sound on, only pictures. The Shirt handed him his coffee. Bo said, "So Bert, ya like it down in Florida?"

"Love it," said the old man absently. He'd settled into a blue vinyl chair from which he could see the kitchen clock.

"Ya drive New Yawk–Miami," Bo informed him, "the state a Florida is like one-third the ride. Lotta people don't realize 'at."

Bert reached down for his dog, put the brittle creature in his lap. "Big state," he said.

Bo slurped espresso, pictured the maps, the mileage charts in little boxes. "Big state," he agreed.

Bert smiled blandly, peeked into the kitchen. He figured that in forty-one minutes, give or take, things would start to rearrange themselves inside his captor's belly.

With some difficulty, Gino Delgatto, hunkered low and squinting over the steering wheel of his rented T-Bird, found the narrow and ill-marked entrance to Nassau Lane.

By the moon and the streetlamps he recognized the cottage that the Fabretti thugs had described. There were no lights on inside. He drove to the end of the short street, turned around in the cramped cul-de-sac. Stray cats fled from the panning headlights that lit up garbage cans, fallen coconuts, bundled cuttings of pruned shrubbery.

He parked across the street and one house up from Arty's place. He sat quietly a moment, summoning concentration like any workman with a job to do. He pulled on a pair of rubber gloves, thin and supple as condoms. He checked the pistol in his right-hand pocket, the small flashlight in his left. He got out of the car and walked past the close-together Christmas palms to his victim's door.

The screen was torn; a corner of it hung down and shook like a brittle leaf in the light breeze. The front door lock had not yet been repaired. Gino tried the knob; it turned easily.

He stepped inside, his right hand in his pocket, and closed the door behind him. He took out the little flashlight and looked around the living room. He saw the mismatched furniture with its loose strands of splintered ancient rattan. He saw the cheap table with its metal legs, the rough rug with its unraveling edges. "Place is a fuckin' dump," he murmured aloud. "Guy's a fuckin' nobody." He moved toward a low bench that held a telephone and an answering machine and casually yanked their wires out of the wall.

He poked his head into the narrow kitchen, saw two unwashed coffee mugs in the sink.

He slipped into the bedroom, let his light explore it like a doctor's shameless fingers. Drawers had been hastily slammed shut with sleeves and cuffs still poking out of them. The bed had not been made, the light quilt was ranged with hills and valleys. "A fuckin' nobody and a fuckin' slob," said Gino. He saw a rickety chair with a couple of T-shirts draped over its arms. He saw a pink scarf on the back of the chair.

He continued his circuit around the room, found a cheesy lamp, a stack of dog-eared paperbacks, then suddenly yanked his light back to the scarf. He stared at it. It gleamed a lewd and fleshy rose against the darkness all around it. No, he thought, it's impossible. Heavily, he walked around the bed. He picked up the scarf in his obscene gloved hand. He held it tight against his face and smelled it, then let it drop as though it carried some terrible contagion. "That fucking slut," he said. "That two-timing skinny-ass whore."

He scrunched his fat face into a mug of wronged trust. He started to pace but there was nowhere much to go. He moved back to the chair, picked up the guilty swatch of silk, and started tearing it to shreds. It was light cloth but it was hard to tear; Gino sweated as he ripped it. The fabric made a desolate rending sound as it was destroyed. Charged pink tatters fell from Gino's hand, he had to kick them off his pants leg.

At length, wet in his clothes and breathing hard, he sat in the dark in the bedroom chair to wait. Outside, breeze rustled the palm fronds, smells of jasmine and salted dust came through the open window. Gino's gun was in his lap, his gloved fingers stuck to it like gauze to a scab. Patiently, he waited for Arty Magnus, the nobody who had to go, and for that fucking tramp whose name he wouldn't say, if she happened to be with him.

CHAPTER FORTY-FIVE

"You like him, don't you?" Sandra said.

She and Debbi were working elbow to elbow in the kitchen, rinsing dishes, slipping them into the racks of the dishwasher. Water was running in the sink; the sound was companionable, intimate.

"I like him a lot," said Debbi.

"It shows."

Debbi flushed at this; her sunburned forehead got redder at the roots of her red hair. Like everyone with a secret, everyone with a new emotion, she wanted to probe it, tease herself with it, bring herself to the delicious cusp of going public.

Sandra put silverware into its basket. "Maybe the two of you wanna go for a ride or something. Look at the ocean, go downtown. You're welcome to the car."

Debbi looked down, her long lashes threw faint fan-shaped shadows on her cheeks. She could not hold back a cockeyed little smile. She knew she was close to spilling the beans as usual, but she couldn't help herself, it felt too good. "If we go for a ride," she said, "we'll go on Arty's bike."

"The two of you?" said Sandra. "Together?"

Debbi bit her lower lip and nodded.

Sandra dried her hands and turned off the water. In the sudden quiet, crickets and tree frogs could be heard.

"That's so nice," she said. "Romantic."

Debbi glanced up at the ceiling, gave a shrug that brought her shoulders almost to her ears, a shrug so big it was almost goofy. "Romantic," she said. "Yeah, it is."

"'Nother big state?" said Bo, the thug who liked geography. "Virginia. People don't realize. Plus ya got them fuckin' tolls in Richmond."

Bert nodded, stroked his dog, glanced through the kitchen doorway at the clock.

"But wait a second," Bo went on. "You flew up, didn't ya?"

Bert nodded again, plucked a short white dog hair from his trousers.

"It's abrupt, like, when ya fly," said Bo. His scarred face scrunched up in disapproval. "Da things ya miss."

Bert nodded a third time.

"So like all of a sudden, *boom*, you're in New Yawk. I mean like, for you, Bert, how's it feel, you're dropped all of a sudden in New Yawk again?"

Bert reached up, tugged the stringy flesh beneath his chin. He thought about the oriental guy in earmuffs shelling peas at what used to be Perretti's. He thought about working the phone with nobody to call. "Lemme put it dis way, Bo. Y'ever seen a car up on blocks?"

Bo didn't answer right away. He made a strange face, squirmed a little bit, reached down to straighten out his pants. Bert couldn't tell if he was thinking hard or if he was uncomfortable, if maybe his tubes were starting to shift and gurgle.

*

Arty and Debbi walked across the lawn in front of Joey Goldman's house. The moment seemed to call for holding hands, but Arty's arms hung limp at his sides, and the blandness in his posture sent a small dart of disappointment through Debbi. Had her new lover already lost the habit of aimless affection? Was he in fact no more romantic than other men she'd known?

When they reached the place where the writer's old fat-tire bike leaned against a palm, Debbi thought it would be wonderful if he took her in his arms. He did not. He only dropped his spiral notebook in the basket, then steadied the bicycle for her to climb aboard. Saddened and suddenly uncertain, she did.

They crunched along the gravel driveway, headed for the beach. The bicycle's wide tires made soft sucking sounds as the treads rolled off the asphalt. Wind tossed the enormous pendant fronds of the royal palms; they billowed up like lifted skirts. Debbi shifted her thin behind on the crosspiece of the frame, leaned back against Arty as he pedaled, but no longer felt quite safe with her flank against his chest.

At County Beach, they left the road and swerved onto a narrow zigzag path that wound through shrubs and sand and picnic tables. A gibbous moon hung high above the Florida Straits, it threw a jagged beam that rose and fell with the ripples in the water and tracked them as they rode. By an ancient slatted bench, Arty stopped the bike and said, "We have to talk."

They sat, neither one at ease enough to settle back. Arty said, "I don't know where to start."

Debbi said nothing. She didn't know how to help him start and she didn't like what she imagined was coming.

Would it be the nocommitment speech? The old-girl-friend-in-the-wings routine?

"I'm writing a book with Vincente," Arty blurted. "I'm not supposed to tell anyone. I haven't told anyone. But it seems like everyone's found out. Those FBI guys—that's why they're hassling me."

Debbi's eyebrows pulled together. This was not what she expected the talk to be about, and it was a lot to take in all at once. "I don't think I understand—"

"My notebook," Arty said. "They want my notebook. They seem to think it's full of things they can use against him."

"Is it?"

Arty threw his hands up, let them slap down against his thighs. "Who knows what they can use these days? He's on record that there's an organization, they make their own rules, and he's the head of it. Smart prosecutor, that might be enough to jail him till he dies."

"But they can't make you—"

Arty looked out at the water. It was placid, gorgeous. But life could turn impossible in beautiful places too. "Debbi," he said. "Debbi. They're threatening me. They're threatening you, if I don't cooperate. I don't know how much longer I can stall. This thing with your probation—"

She yanked in a quick breath, bit her lower lip, pulled her eyes away. Shame and frustration scraped at her insides. She thought about how hard it was to change a life, how tough to escape the old neighborhood. The neighborhood—she used to think it was made of buildings and street signs and fire hydrants; now she understood it was really built of old mistakes, old humiliations, everything that marked you, if only in your own mind, everything that shrank your world and held you back. "Arty, I guess I should have told you. There's been so little time—"

"It doesn't have to matter," Arty said, hoping to his soul he meant it. "It's just that—"

"I want to tell you about it," Debbi said.

"I've got no right to ask."

She reached up, grabbed her red hair in her fists. "These secrets! These fucking secrets, Arty. They're really not worth going crazy over. . . . Listen, I have a long sad history of picking Mr. Wrong. Maybe a shrink could tell me why I did it, maybe it's just the guys I met. Ya know, neighborhood guys. A year or so ago I dated a guy named Mikey. Seemed nice at first. They all do, right? Well it turns out he's a lunatic, a cokehead, a major dealer. A couple of months, I do the typical stupid thing, I try to look the other way. Then finally I've had enough, I go over to his place to break it off, and that's the day he's busted. He's away for five years. Me, no record, never done anything worse than playing hookey, I get probation. Lady judge. She says to me, 'Miss Martini, I think you're innocent. I could let you off, but I don't think I'd be doing you a favor. Probation'll give you a reason to think a little harder.' "

"So you fall in with Gino," Arty could not help saying.

Debbi sighed. "Stupid. I know. But it's not like he said, 'Hi, I'm Mafia, wanna go out?' You don't know at first. By the time ya find out, you're a little bit involved—"

Arty touched her hand. "You don't have to go on with this."

She looked down at the place where they were touching. Loss washed over her like clammy water, she felt it far more intensely than before he'd reached for her, when they'd been separate, guarded. "You don't wanna see me anymore," she said. It was not a question.

"I didn't say that."

She looked off at the water. There were no waves, but small ripples collapsed on the shore and made a soft boiling sound against the rocky sand. "Arty, don't do anything against Vincente because of me. Promise. I couldn't live with that. I made mistakes, I'll pay for them."

"But—"

She shushed him with a long finger placed against his lips. "Maybe you should take me home now."

He looked at her. Her face was soft, the big eyes chastened, the mouth pouting with the knowing irony of someone watching a chance go by, a dream become a perfect absence. He looked at her, and for an instant he imagined that what he felt was merely pity; it was his own loss masquerading as compassion. Then he understood with throat-closing clarity that her chance to change her life was his own best chance as well, her winning-through his own best stretch toward the high victory called happiness. He took her face in his hands and kissed her. Her surprised mouth was not ready to be kissed, the pout ripened to passion only slowly. "Home with me?"

She didn't answer for a moment, then nodded a yes against his neck. Buoyant on the wing of second chances, they headed toward the cottage where Gino waited, his pistol in his lap.

CHAPTER FORTY-SIX

"YEA, I think about dat sometimes," said Bo the philo-sophic thug. "In a vague kinda way, I mean. Gettin' old. Feelin' useless. Like ya can't do duh things ya useta do, everything's an effort. Mus' be a bitch. What the fuck can ya do about it?"

"Ain't nothin' ya can do about it," said Bert the Shirt. His half-blind shedding dog was in his lap, twitching in and out of sleep. The silent television threw random splats of color around the room.

Bo squirmed, plucked at his trousers, seemed to be trying to rearrange his guts, get his tubing at a different angle. "Like Pretty Boy," he said. "My partner. He don't think about it. He don't think about nothin'. Sometimes I think he's better off. 'Course, he's all fucked up wit' drugs."

Bert nodded.

Bo winced, just slightly; the spasm made the scarred side of his face hike up like a rising curtain. His pants squeaked as he shifted on the vinyl couch, then he said with delicacy, "You'll be OK a coupla minutes, Bert? I gotta go ta duh bat'room."

Certain things the old man could do as well as ever, maybe better. He kept his voice gruff and natural, his long face perfectly composed. "Sure," he said. "I'll do the dishes."

Bo rose, a little gingerly. Bert got up with him and headed for the kitchen.

He put his dog down on the counter, went to the sink, turned on the water as hard as it would go. He counted to ten, then turned and peeked down the narrow hall, saw that the bathroom door was firmly closed.

He left the water running, picked up his dog. He tiptoed to the living room window that gave onto the fire escape. He opened it wide, used his arms to help lift his legs as he stepped stiffly over the sill.

Out on the rusty landing, he tucked the chihuahua under his arm as though it were a football, then launched himself down the skinny metal stairs. He didn't so much run as fly, as in a dream of spiraling downward, giving in with an ecstatic trust to gravity, pivoting with ease around the frigid railings. The skyline wheeled around him as he spun, and in the freezing air the old man felt light, fearless, giddy. He was closer to eighty than to seventy and he was taking it on the lam.

Arty Magnus locked his bike to a Christmas palm, then kept a hand on Debbi's back as they walked through the moonlight to his cottage. He ached for a vacation from the hazards and the clamor of the world, a visit to a small safe universe of making love. They kissed once in front of the torn screen door, then he led her over the scuffed uneven threshold.

"I can't see a thing," she whispered when the door had shut behind them, blotting out the moonlight. The darkness seemed to call for whispering; it was an intimate, caressing darkness, but if it was sanctuary it was also peril. There were edges to walk into, rugs and wires to trip on.

"Don't have to see," Arty whispered back. "I've had this dump so long, I know which floorboards squeak."

He dropped his notebook on the ratty unseen table, then led his new lover through the bedroom doorway. He found the mattress with his knee, leaned down with the slow precision of a blind man, and grabbed the box of wooden matches he kept on his bedside table. He struck one. It flared to life with a rasp, a hiss, an acrid whiff of phosphorus. He reached the match toward a plain white candle glued with wax to a saucer, and that was when they saw the gun pointing at them from the far side of the bed.

They saw the gun before they saw the person holding it; it hovered gray, glinting, disconnected, as rude and stripped of context as a dildo. Next they saw the thick and hairy hand smeared inside its glove, and only after that the damp and slovenly bulk of Gino Delgatto sprawling in the chair.

The assassin clicked on his flashlight, drilled the beam at Arty's face. "Hello, Romeo," he said. He shifted the beacon toward Debbi, thrust it at her loins, her breasts, slashed at her face with the light as though it were a razor. "Hello, you fuckin' whore. Either a you makes a sound, you're dead."

Bert d'Ambrosia, in a monogrammed blue shirt without even a sweater over it, puffed and jogged to the corner of Sullivan and Bleecker, then turned west toward the bar where he hoped Pretty Boy would still be drinking, would by now be drunk. He found the place then paused for breath on the freezing sidewalk; wreaths of steam rose from his head. He petted his dog and went inside.

The tavern was crowded, smoky, dizzying after the blast of cold. The jukebox blared, laughter erupted here and there. Bert nestled the chihuahua against his wizened tummy, tried to shield it from the beery crush of bodies. Squinting against the smoke, he found Pretty Boy sitting near the far end of the bar, exactly where he'd been several hours before. But certain things had changed. Alcohol had conquered pills, and now the handsome thug's posture was hulking, his nervous mouth slack and surly. His high hair seemed to be deflating, whorls of it hung greasily over his forehead.

Bert approached his blind side and was right under his chin before he spoke. "Pretty Boy."

The thug looked at him stupidly. Recognition came on slowly, like an old tube radio warming up. He remembered Bert. They'd even had a drink together. But hadn't that been a different day? "Fuck you doin' heah?"

"Bo sent me. We're goin' back ta Florida."

In front of Pretty Boy was a glass with something brown in it. He took a swallow and said, "Wha'?"

"Word came from Messina. Bo's gettin' the car. Gino's business down there, it didn't go right."

Synapses were slowly coming alive in Pretty Boy. Vindication helped them wake up. "Send a boy ta do a man's job," he said. "We shoulda just did the fuckin' thing ourselves."

"Dat's what Bo says too," ventured Bert the Shirt.

"Yeah?" gloated Pretty Boy. "So now Bo says I was right?"

"Yeah. All along. Messina says so too."

"Fuckin' A." The gratified thug went back to his drink.

"Yeah, Bo tol' me all about it. No reason not to now. I said you were right. Thing like dat, ya don't trust it to somebody else."

Pretty Boy drained his drink, gestured with the empty glass. "I said dat from the start."

"Somethin' 'at important."

"Thing is, it didn't have to be that big a deal, we did it my way from the start."

Bert nodded sagely. "De other way, they made it too complicated, people goin' back and fort'."

"Fuckin' A." Pretty Boy lowered his voice a notch, breathed liquor mist in Bert's face. "My way, I tol' 'em, I said first chance we ice the fuckin' writer, and 'at's the end of it. We don't wait. We don't send fuckin' Gino. Am I right?"

Bert the Shirt summoned up a lifetime's practice in the poker face, the voice revealing nothing. "Yeah," he said. "You're right. . . . Listen, Bo's comin' wit' the car. Ya wanna take a leak or somethin' before we staht?"

This struck Pretty Boy as a good idea. He double-checked that his glass was really empty, then woozily slid down from his barstool and lumbered toward the men's room. Bert held his dog like a football and lowered his head like a fullback. He was on the street again in fifteen seconds.

CHAPTER FORTY-SEVEN

"You don't go off on your own like that," Ben Hawkins said. "It's not the way it's done."

Mark Sutton looked down at his plate and sulked. He thought he'd done a pretty good day's work, deserved a pat on the back and not a scolding. "Ben," he insisted, "I'm telling you, the guy is this close to turning."

"So what? Who is he, the underboss? He's a journalist, Mark. A civilian. What's he gonna have?"

"We'll never know unless we work him, will we?"

Hawkins didn't answer. The two men were finishing a late dinner in the dim and dreary restaurant at the Gulf-side Inn. The senior agent went back to trimming gristle from his steak.

But then Mark Sutton, giving in suddenly to a slow-brewed exasperation, pushed the remains of his own meal away from him and clattered down his silverware. "Dammit Ben, I'm trying to get something done down here, and you—I always heard you're like a legendary agent, but you just sit there; everything I do, you're negative, you shrug it off—"

The unflappable Hawkins looked at him mildly, knife and fork in hand. "Mark," he said, "I shrug it off because a shrug is what it's worth. The Bureau—listen. Half the time, probably less, you're on a case that's really a case.

The other half you're covering butt for someone. We're covering Manheim's butt. That's all we're doing. As soon as Carbone got killed, Delgatto became a sideshow. Face it, Mark. You're getting your bowels in an uproar over a goddam sideshow."

"I think you're wrong."

"I know you do. Which is why we're getting to hate each other's guts. But lemme tell you something. You got a hard-on for a great career, but you're exactly the kind of guy that burns out. You know which guys burn out? The guys who can't tell the real cases from the bullshit."

Sutton rocked his bullish neck. "Look, I got time and trouble invested in this guy. I believe that one more squeeze, a little more pressure on the girlfriend thing, we're gonna get something from him. I wanna get in his face again. You don't want me going off alone, come with me. You still think there's nothing there, I'll back off. Fair enough?"

Hawkins chewed a final piece of steak and thought it over. He nodded yes, then gestured for the waitress. The hyperactive Sutton was already halfway out of his chair when Hawkins thwarted him yet again by asking not for the check but for a cup of coffee and a slice of Key lime pie.

On freezing Bleecker Street, Bert the Shirt slid his skinny haunches across the cold upholstery of a yellow cab. "Go toward the Holland Tunnel," he told the driver.

The taxi roared away, the old man hugged his dog. Now and then he swiveled around with an ancient paranoia about being followed. But who would figure he was heading for the tunnel, and not the airport like he'd come? The cab slipped unharassed through the narrow streets of the Village, past jazz clubs, step-down restaurants, transvestite hookers in fake fur on the corners.

On Varick Street, two blocks above the tunnel, Bert spotted a pay phone under a defunct streetlight. "Stop here," he said. "Wait for me a minute."

The old man left the cab door open so he could look in on his dog. He picked up the icy handset and held it to his ear. Steam came off him as he dialed a number in Key West.

Joey Goldman picked up on the second ring. "Hello?"

"Joey? Bert. I need your father, he around?"

"Bert, where are ya? What's goin'—"

"Joey, please, I ain't got time. Put Vincente on."

The line went silent. Bert shifted his feet, the cold came up through his shoes. Traffic poured by, taillights leaving red streamers in the misty air. After a moment, Vincente's voice said, "Bert."

"Vincente. I can't talk long. I've seen Gino. He's alive, Vincente."

The Godfather sat in Joey's study. Moonlight smeared itself like butter across the glass block wall. He heard the words and instantly began to cry. It was an odd thin sort of crying. No sound went with it, and the feeling behind it was raw but distant, less an emotion than a memory of something that could be recalled but not recaptured.

"But Vincente, listen," Bert went on, "somethin' ain't right. I found 'im at Messina's club. They were tryin' much too hard ta look like friends. Then Gino turns around and says he don't want me goin' home, seein' you, talkin' t'anybody for a while. They kidnap me, like—"

304

"So how're you callin'?" Vincente cut in.

"I got away. I'll tell ya about it sometime. But inna meantime . . . Vincente, listen. Unless I have this very wrong—I hope I'm wrong, believe me—but how it looks . . . I think they made him take a contract on your buddy Ahty."

The line went silent. The Godfather held the phone a few inches from his face and didn't so much think as open old passageways to the flow of remorseless and untamed logic that would lead his colleague Aldo Messina to use one irritant to destroy another. Of course that's what he would do.

"Vincente, you there?"

He answered only with a wheezing breath.

"He's on his way, Vincente. For all I know, the job is done. I'm sorry."

Bert the Shirt, his lungs smarting, the phone like dry ice against his face, waited a moment, understood that no reply was coming, and hung up.

In Key West, the Godfather absently put down the handset; then, with trembling fingers, he riffled through Joey's desk drawers until he found a phone book. He looked up Arty Magnus's number; he dialed. The signal went as far as the ripped-out wires, then bounced back and rang and rang, it was hellish in the bland futility of its ringing. He shouted for his son Joey, told him to get the El Dorado ready.

On Varick Street, Bert climbed stiffly back into his cab. He picked up his dog, hugged it, and shivered. Then he looked at the cabbie's license mounted on the dashboard. The guy's first name was Pavel and his last name was mostly z's and w's.

"Pavel, ya feel like drivin' a Florida?"

Strange things happened in America. Pavel knew that from TV. "You are gangster maybe?"

"Thousand dollars, Pavel. Half up front."

"You vait vun minute pleass," the cabbie said. "I call vife."

"Ya know what I hate?" said Gino, punctuating the words with tilts and thrusts of his pistol. "I hate when a fuckin' outsider tries ta worm his way someplace he don't belong. Like a fuckin' smart-ass Jew in a Sicilian family. I mean, where the fuck da you come off? Gettin' buddy-buddy wit' my father. Skimmin' off money. Diggin' up secrets, stuff ya got no right ta know. You're a fuckin' worm, a bloodsucker. I hate that."

Arty stood there, pinned like a bug in Gino's flashlight beam. He didn't answer; there was nothing to say. He looked across the width of the bed and wondered if he would have a chance to make a move, to fight, before Gino killed him, or if he would go down passive and pathetic, without so much as a gesture of resistance.

"An' ya know what else I hate?" said the murderer. He jerked the light toward Debbi, seemed to want to ram it through her flesh. "I hate the kinda weak-ass woman who if her pussy's empty fifteen minutes, if she don't have a man t'usher her around, pay for things, she's in a fuckin' panic, she'll spread her legs for anything in pants. Even a Jew bloodsucker. Fuckin' tramp. I hate that."

Debbi said nothing. Her breath came in short quick puffs; Arty felt the heat of rage and terror pulsing off her flank.

Gino rose, he made a lot of noise as he unfolded his damp bulk from the chair. "The t'ree of us," he said, "we're goin' for a ride now. Someplace nice and quiet. The slut drives. I sit inna back. Ya don't do exactly like I tell ya, I splatter brains, I promise."

CHAPTER FORTY-EIGHT

JOEY WAS two blocks away when he saw the car shoot out of Nassau Lane and head up Fleming Street, pointing out of town. He couldn't see beyond the moonstruck windows, couldn't see how many people were inside. But he could tell it was a T-Bird, and he knew his brother's taste in cars.

He hit the gas, and the eight thick pistons of the El Dorado clattered in their bloated cylinders. His father braced himself with a thin yellowish hand against the dashboard. The old man still had his smoking jacket on, his face was gray and hollow under the flicking street-lamps.

At White Street the T-Bird ran a yellow light; Joey ran the red, tires squealing as the Caddy leaned fatly into the turn. He headed for the bridge that arched over Garrison Bight and led on to the highway. A rusty pickup truck pulled out of the bar at the marina, got between Joey and his quarry, and crawled. When it was time to make the left onto U.S. 1, the T-Bird slipped through on the arrow and the El Dorado sat there two cars back.

The Godfather watched the other car recede, his face like that of a dying man watching his own breath leave his body.

*

Calmly, unhurriedly, Mark Sutton and Ben Hawkins approached the empty cottage.

They saw Arty Magnus's bicycle chained to the Christmas palm. They saw the ripped screen on the front door. Mark Sutton knocked. When there was no reply, he tried the knob. It turned without resistance. He hesitated just a moment, then he entered. Ben Hawkins, weighing his misgivings, followed him into the living room.

The agents heard nothing, saw nothing save for the soft gleam of the single candle that still burned on the bedside table. An abashing thought assailed Mark Sutton: What if no one answered the door because Arty and Debbi were in the sack?

"Mr. Magnus?" he sang out, a little sheepishly.

He was answered by a hollow silence. Emboldened, he took out a flashlight and moved toward the bedroom. He found sleeves and cuffs poking out of drawers. He found the shredded pink tatters of what seemed to have been a woman's scarf. Ben Hawkins knelt to examine the ripped-apart fabric; there was mayhem in it, and he realized all at once that this sideshow might yet be a violent sideshow. By reflex, he felt quickly for his pistol in its shoulder holster. Then, suddenly intent, he took out his own beacon, combed the walls and floors and furniture with it. He went back to the living room, raked the light along the baseboards, found the yanked-out wires of the telephone.

Mark Sutton's beam discovered the moisture-fattened spiral notebook on the ratty table. "I have a feeling someone's coming back for that," he said.

"Maybe," said Ben Hawkins.

"I say we wait and see."

For the first time since they'd come to Florida, the senior agent didn't disagree.

Joey roared off at the green, wove in and out among the mopeds, the drunks who spilled forth from roadside taverns, the high Jeeps with their booming speakers. He scanned ahead, couldn't find the T-Bird. To the left, moonlight glinted on the Gulf of Mexico; to the right, the trashy neon of the Key West strip assaulted the eye.

Joey humped and veered, and at the east end of the island, just before the Cow Key Channel, he again picked up the Thunderbird, maybe a hundred fifty close-packed yards ahead. He urged more speed out of the Caddy's bellowing engine, trying desperately to catch his brother before the road narrowed, went two-lane, at Boca Chica. He cut onto the dusty shoulder to pass an ancient van; the huge tires shied on the gravel, Vincente bounced against the door.

When they passed the lane drop there were still half a dozen cars between them.

The honkytonk had been left behind now; both sides of the road were flat and dim. Slices of Gulf and ocean shimmered among plains of limestone spoil and creeping mangrove. Spectral pelicans swooped and dipped in moonlight. Joey kept sneaking into the oncoming lane like a voyeur creeping closer to a window, was thwarted in his attempts to pass by glaring headlights and screaming horns.

Three cars up, someone slowed to let an RV pull into the single line of traffic.

Joey braked, cursed, hammered on the steering wheel. Vincente, ashen, kept his veiny hand on the dashboard.

The Caddy passed one car, then another. The camper, big and square as a train, still loomed up ahead.

Moonlight poured down, the landscape grew ever sparser. Then Joey saw a little cloud of grayish dust, perhaps a quarter mile up ahead. The dust swirled and drifted at the margin of the roadway, pulsed and billowed like a genie.

"I think someone just turned off there, Pop. I'm not sure."

They neared the place. Vincente said nothing.

"What should I do, Pop?"

The Godfather looked at him with exhausted eyes, imploring eyes. "Your neighborhood, Joey. I need ya ta decide."

His younger son swallowed hard, braked hard, cut the wheel sharply to the right. The tires screeched, the car slid broadside, then was pointing through the cloud of limestone dust at an unpaved unmarked road that fell down from the hump of highway and snaked off through the mangroves.

Ben Hawkins unholstered his gun, positioned himself just to the right of Arty Magnus's bedroom doorway, and settled in to wait. The bedside candle still burned, soft breezes pushed its flame this way and that, shadows rolled around the walls with every flicker.

Mark Sutton staked out the kitchen. He put his pistol on the counter, leaned back and flexed his triceps. Now and then bugs rattled against the screen, time went very

311

slowly. He crossed and uncrossed his ankles and at some point he knew he was going to slip across the living room and borrow Arty Magnus's notebook from the ratty metal table. He knew he shouldn't do it, it was privileged property, a journalist's personal notes. He teased himself another minute; then he held his breath and, stealthily as any thief, he glided through the dark and grabbed the stained and moisture-thickened book.

Ben Hawkins saw him sneak past, understood what he was up to, and said mildly, "I don't think you want to do that, Mark."

Sutton ignored him. Back in the kitchen, he switched on his flashlight and felt a rude excitement, the arousal of a boy with a pocketful of filthy pictures. He riffled through the damp and wavy pages of Arty Magnus's scrawl, at first reading only the headings, which struck him as peculiar. History of Sicily. Courage to Judge. Gardening in Queens. He had no doubt that these puzzling phrases were somehow coded, that beneath them, in the all but illegible squiggles and loops of Arty's writing, would be all sorts of implicating hints: names of criminals, dates of crimes, places where the bodies were buried.

Straining his eyes around the thin beam of the flashlight, Sutton struggled to read, decipher, memorize. Time flew now, the young agent was wholly caught up in his work. He knew that somewhere beyond the old man's musings and complaints and gropings after sense, bound up in the tangled knots of the ghostwriter's scribble, were the forbidden secrets whose discovery would establish him as a rising star, a man with a brilliant future.

CHAPTER FORTY-NINE

THE UNMARKED road soon became a mangrove tunnel.

Tangled boughs arched overhead; rubbery vines clutched at them and dangled down. Frogs croaked. Mosquitoes buzzed. Lizards clung to rocks and stumps, puffing out their ruby throats. The only sign of human presence was here and there a bleached-out beer can, a shattered soda bottle.

The beam of Joey's headlights was swallowed up by foliage and moths. He drove on slowly, the car rocked over chunks of pitted limestone and through fetid puddles that stank of sulfur.

The ground grew softer, spongy, as he drove, phased without boundary into inches-deep sea. Water squished from porous rock as from sodden moss. He looped around an encroaching web of mangrove roots, and when he straightened out again his headlights found the red gleam of a car's reflectors a hundred yards ahead. He tried to go faster; his wheels spun in the muck, he felt the chassis sinking. He eased off, cruised forward slowly as a docking ship.

They reached the dark car. It was a Thunderbird. There was no one in it. Vincente was out the door before Joey could speak, clambering through the rooty seeping swamp in his soft and slick-soled loafers.

Mangrove leaves drank up the moonlight, but here and there waves of brightness poured through like milk. In the gleaming patches there was water coated with pollen, tiny crabs nipping sideways over stones. Joey trailed his father as the old man pressed on through the marl. Wetness covered his shoe tops; the canopy of foliage cracked open to show a starry sky.

By its pallid light, Vincente Delgatto, himself still unseen and unheard from fifty feet away, saw his firstborn son standing calfdeep in slimy water, holding a moonlit gun on Debbi Martini and Arty Magnus. The tableau suggested a macabre wedding. In the silvery glow, Debbi looked like a bride, her skin lucent through her tear-streaked makeup; close at her side, Arty, his hands clenching and unclenching, had the posture of a nervous groom. Before them, Gino stood like a devil's priest who would bind them together for eternity.

The Godfather trudged on, dragging his feet through the sucking morass. The heavy air around him moved and pulsed as it got ready to carry sound. In a voice that was low and ancient and commanding, he said, "Gino, put the gun away."

His son's head snapped around like that of a boxer who's been jabbed; his eyes searched for the voice in the broken moonlight. Then he said, "Stay the fuck outa this, Pop. Don't come any closer."

Vincente kept coming. Each step through the slime took all his strength; one of his shoes was pulled off in the mud; he continued on without it. "Put it down, I said."

Gino licked his lips. Mosquitoes were flying in his ears, his eyes, he swatted at them with a gloved hand.

314

"Mind your fuckin' business, Pop. These people gotta die."

The Godfather moved forward. Crabs scampered in front of him, toads leaped on floating leaves. He was twenty feet away. "They ain't done nothin' wrong," he said.

Gino laughed. It was a bitter mocking laugh, diabolical, forsaken. "You still think that's how it works, old man?"

Vincente dragged himself on. Hot blood pounded in his head, green streamers streaked behind his eyes. "Yeah, Gino, I do."

"You're wrong as shit," said his firstborn, waving blindly at mosquitoes.

"Gino," said his father. "Please." He trudged inexorably forward. Joey appeared at his shoulder. Arty and Debbi looked stiff and frail as glass in the cool white moonlight.

"Right, wrong—you're fuckin' nuts, old man."

"Don't hurt them, Gino. There's no reason."

"Pop, you just don't fuckin' get it, do you?"

No one saw Vincente reach into his smoking jacket. Wicked quick, his .38 was in his hand. "Put the gun away, Gino."

Pale light glinted on Vincente's weapon. It took a moment for Gino to believe that he was seeing it. His tone turned wheedling, whiny, as full of despair as cruelty. "Pop, I can't."

"Drop it, Gino," Vincente said.

His son turned away from him, faced back toward his victims. His pistol was raised, his thick finger wrapped around the trigger. His voice was thin, metallic, his throat engorged with blood. "The way it stacks up, Pop, it's either them or me."

"Gino."

This time there was no answer. The Godfather saw his son's arm tighten the way it does in the heartbeat before a person shoots.

"Then it's you, Gino," he whispered.

He did not aim. He shot. The gun's report silenced the world. Bugs ceased buzzing, frogs held their baffled breath. The bullet smashed through Gino's ribs, punctured his heart, exited through a small hole in his side.

For a moment the dead man hung suspended. His expression was bewildered, the eyes affronted, blaming, like the eyes of a caught fish. Stiff-legged, he tumbled forward with a splash. Warm water covered him halfway up his thick torso and he instantly began to sink, undiscoverable, into the muck among the mangrove roots.

Starlight rained down. The swamp noises started in again. For a long moment no one moved. Then Joey Goldman went toward his slain half-brother, touched his subsiding form with a mad mix of hate and grief and love and horror. Debbi's shoulders hitched and trembled, though she made no sound. Arty stared at Vincente. The old man looked very thin and brittle in the moonlight, his long gray face still and archaic as a statue. The hand that held the gun hung limp, as if forgotten, disowned, at his side.

Then Arty saw it start to move. It moved slowly, in a lazy, looping, arcing motion that was bringing the muzzle around to the Godfather's ear.

The ghostwriter yanked his feet out of the marl,

strained and slogged and lunged to Vincente's side, threw himself against the old man's lifted arm. The gun deafeningly discharged as the two of them went tumbling to the oozing ground.

CHAPTER FIFTY

THEY LAY there together in the muck, salt in their eyes, thunder in their ears, their brains subsumed by a weirdly serene curiosity as to where the bullet had struck. They waited for pain, kept a vigil for injury. Feeling no seep of blood, aware of no wounds opening their flesh to the shallow sea, they slowly pulled themselves out of the mire and stood exhausted in their sodden clothes.

Meanwhile a strange lucidity, the lucidity of disaster, came over Joey Goldman.

He picked up his father's .38, threw it as far as he could throw into the ocean. Then he moved to the Thunderbird, climbed in, drove it chassis deep into the water, wiped the steering wheel and door handles with his handkerchief. The car would be found, he knew, and he knew it didn't matter. Gino had never rented a car in his own name in his life. It was a point of pride with him. Let that be my brother's epitaph, the surviving son reflected bitterly: He never thought he had to pay, and he was always right except for once.

The ride back to Key West was a despondent one, a funeral. No one spoke until they'd left the highway and were on the sleepy streets of Old Town. Then Joey said, "Pop, what you did, you had no choice, we all know that. Arty and Debbi, you saved them."

The Godfather said nothing, sat there blank as death. Streetlamps flicked sporadic light across his ashen face, it was like a sheet was being raised and lowered over him.

On Nassau Lane, Joey stopped. Arty and Debbi slipped out of the Caddy. No one said a word to anybody.

Inside the dark cottage, Ben Hawkins and Mark Sutton heard the vehicle's sudden approach, the opening and closing of doors. They heard the car drive off; then, in the deepened silence, they heard footsteps moving up the path. They struck their marksman's posture, held their pistols in front of them, left hands bracing right wrists.

Depleted, numb, Arty Magnus pushed open his front door, gestured Debbi in ahead of him. They were just across the threshold when Mark Sutton screamed out, "Freeze!"

Arty had thought he was all out of adrenaline, that his burned-out nerves could no longer carry messages of panic. Still, by the kind of ancient stamina that makes a chased deer resilient beyond all reason, he jerked alert again, his hands shot up, his heart hammered.

Ben Hawkins switched on a light, hid his disappointment at finding no kidnapper, no invader, only a terrified and ravaged couple. He appraised them. Debbi Martini's red hair was wild, stalled rivulets of mascara stained her cheeks, her legs were caked with gray muck. Arty Magnus's shorts and shirt were damp and gritty, his neck was streaked with slime. "You look like you've had a rough night," the agent said.

Arty dropped his hands. "It's no business of yours. What the hell are you doing here?"

Mark Sutton had lowered his gun and was leaning

against the kitchen doorway. "This is a crime scene," he said. "We have a right to be here."

"What's the crime?" said Arty.

Sutton gestured vaguely toward the yanked-out phone wires. Then Ben Hawkins produced a tatter of pink silk. "Who did this, Miss Martini? Looks like someone who's pretty mad at you."

Debbi pursed her lips. "Maybe I caught it in the fan," she said.

Hawkins frowned. Mark Sutton flexed his muscles against the doorframe.

"Listen," the younger agent said, "someone was here tonight. Someone pulled your phone. You come back looking like you've been through a war. Just what the hell went on?"

Arty and Debbi, side by side, kept silent.

"There's only one person you could be protecting," said Ben Hawkins.

"Only you can't protect him," said Mark Sutton. "You're in too deep for that. You, Magnus, you've done nothing but lie to us. You work for Delgatto; you're his flunky. Under RICO, you're an associate, an associate who lies. And you, Miss Martini, you're in dutch up to your eyeballs. You have a cup of coffee with a criminal, you go to jail. Ever seen a women's jail, Miss Martini? Ever seen the guards?"

Sutton hammered away, and suddenly Arty felt hugely tired, worn down, weary almost past the bounds of caring. Why—by what rule and at what grim cost—was he so stubbornly intent on shielding Vincente? Who *was* Vincente, this old man whose very existence seemed such an affront to all things lawful and legitimate? Who was this Godfather who had filled Arty with his story, who had become a sort of formidable roommate in his skin? Arty was a law-abiding person and he'd just been witness to a killing. He knew where the subsiding body was, could lead these legitimate men to it. And maybe then—

His musings, and Sutton's tirade, were ended by a stark emphatic gesture from Debbi. She fired out a skinny arm, pointed a long red fingernail at the ratty metal table. "Your notebook, Arty. It isn't there. These sneaks took it. I'll bet you anything they took it."

Arty looked at the bare place on the tabletop; then he looked at Sutton. The young agent tried to hold his face together, but beneath the skin it crawled like soil shot through with slugs. Arty moved toward the kitchen. Sutton blocked the doorway with his squat hard body.

"Get out of my way, please. I live here."

Sutton shot an imploring glance at Hawkins; Hawkins had no help to give. The muscular agent suddenly looked absurdly young, unripe, a swollen child with a badge. Sulkily, he stepped aside at last. Arty saw the stained and moisture-fattened notebook on the counter and could not repress a small and cockeyed smile.

"Well," he said. "Well."

Mark Sutton, as if afraid of being cornered, had moved to the middle of the living room. He turned on Arty and said, "Don't think that changes anything. You're still—"

"I think it changes everything," said Arty. "Your fingerprints all over a journalist's private files? It won't look good in the papers, Sutton. First Amendment violation. Harassment. Entry on extremely shaky grounds. They don't like that kind of news in Washington."

Sutton squeezed the back of the settee. "You dare to threaten—"

"You bet I do. Isn't that the way you guys do business? Threats. Leverage. Who's got what on who?"

Sutton's jaw worked but he could find no words. He looked at Hawkins, but the man's dusky face offered him no solace.

"Listen, friend," said Arty. "You say you can make trouble for us. I know I can make trouble for you. You don't, I won't."

Sutton bit his lip, tightened down his muscles. Outside, crickets rasped, breeze made the foliage sizzle. Debbi and Arty locked eyes, the stare was an embrace.

"Take the deal, Mark," Ben Hawkins said at last, and it almost seemed that there was a note of vindication in his voice. "This gets out, trust me, your great career goes right in the shithouse."

CHAPTER FIFTY-ONE

A FEW weeks later, Arty and Debbi, in shorts and T-shirts and grimy sneakers, were silently working in the crammed lush garden in back of Arty's cottage.

It was early March. For human beings, the weather was barely changed from a month before, but for plants it was a different era. Winter things were dying back under the rough kiss of the higher sun. Tender flowers bowed their heads, kitchen herbs turned woody and ran to seed. It was time to trim, to prune, to strip away the things whose time had passed and to open up the light to the oleanders, the allamanda, the thick-skinned beauties that flourished in the steaming orgy of subtropical summer.

But Debbi didn't like to prune. It hurt her to snip off stems that still had green on them, to sever twigs in which the sap still ran. She looked over at Arty, on his hands and knees in a bed of leggy moribund impatiens. It didn't seem to bother him to uproot the dying plants, though she knew how much he loved them. Why didn't it? It had to do, she supposed, with an acceptance of things being lost, a faith that other things, as good or better, would grow up in their place.

She resolved to be more stalwart in her trimming. Still, as if with a mind of their own, her shears kept sliding toward the merest edges of the plants, kept trying to spare a few more leaves. With a secret consternation she looked down at the paltry pile of her cuttings.

Then the air rumbled behind her. Wizened arms came down around her shoulders; spotted ungloved hands wrapped over hers on the handles of the shears, guided the blades down along the helpless stem. Vincente said, "A good gardener can't afford to be so tenderhearted."

She looked over her shoulder at the old man. The sun was behind him, it glared bright yellow at the edge of his unraveling straw hat. He wore his old thick gardening trousers, his rumpled blue work shirt was dampened here and there with sweat, his red bandanna was loosely tied around his neck.

Together, they clipped the branch whose time was over. Then the Godfather whispered, "Debbi, maybe you'd like some iced tea, something. I'd like a little time alone wit' Ahty."

She nodded, shook bits of twig and leaf from her red hair, and headed for the cottage.

Vincente walked slowly to the flower bed, dropped to his knees in the dirt next to his friend. Without a word he started pulling up spent flowers, shaking the rich imported soil off their frizzy roots. "Look the way the sun bleaches 'em out," he said, holding up a yellow stem. "Most things, sun makes 'em darker green. I'll never understand it."

Arty just nodded, gave a little smile, threw another exhausted plant on the pile. Since Gino's death, Vincente had hardly come out of his room at Joey's house, had hardly eaten, hardly spoken. Even now his eyes were distant, glazed, his voice thick and sluggish from disuse;

Arty didn't want to push him, wanted to let him return at his own pace to the world of living people.

The Godfather plucked a tortured flower and said, "I'm goin' back ta New Yawk soon, Ahty. That's why I came over, ta tell ya that. I just tol' Bert, now I'm tellin' you."

"How's he doing?" Arty asked.

"Much better," said Vincente. "Gettin' some weight back on." He shook his head. "Pneumonia at his age. Two weeks inna hospital, drivin' everybody crazy sneakin' in the dog. The kinda friend he is, it humbles me, it's the way people oughta be."

Arty churned dirt with long bare fingers. Sunshine burned his neck and sweat trickled down inside his shirt. "New York," he said after a moment. "You really wanna go back?"

The old man took a breath before he answered. "Wit' Messina indicted onna Carbone thing, it's like chaos up there. I feel I got an obligation."

The ghostwriter nodded, wiped a hand on his shorts so he could scratch his neck. He looked sideways at the old man and said, "Vincente, what about our book?"

The Godfather swallowed. His Adam's apple looked painfully large and hard as bone as it rode up and down inside his stringy neck. He started to say something, then just shook his head. He looked away a moment, tried again. "It's no good, Ahty. It's too dangerous."

"Messina's going away," the younger man said. "Who else knows? Who would care?"

Vincente clawed lightly, slowly, at the sunbaked dirt. "Nah," he said, "it isn't really that. It's that . . . Ahty, when we stahted this thing, you and me, I thought I knew somethin', I had somethin' ta say, somethin' worth passin' along. The way it's ended up—" He broke off, absently sculpted a hole in the ground.

Arty kept his hands busy as well, didn't confront the dark tunnels of the Godfather's eyes. "Vincente," he said, "listen. I'm a washout when it comes to writing books, but a couple things I understand. You don't write a book to tell what you know; you write a book to find out what you know."

The old man cocked his head, gazed out hard from under the frayed brim of his straw hat. His lips worked, the hollows of his cheeks pulsed in and out. "I'm gonna miss talkin' wit' you, Ahty. Airin' things out. Gonna miss it." He ran the back of his hand across his forehead. "But now lemme ask you a question."

Arty just lifted an eyebrow.

"Debbi," said the Godfather.

"That isn't a question," the younger man said, a little nervously.

"Yeah, it is," Vincente said. "What's the story wit' the two a you?"

"Whaddya mean, Vincente?"

The Godfather scrabbled in the dirt, gathered up the fuzzy tendrils of a root. "Come on, Ahty. Ya think I don't see? Few weeks ago, Debbi was hardly at the house at all. She was here wit' you. Last weeks or so she's around a lot. Ya have a falling out? Someone havin' second thoughts?"

Arty looked away, shifted the position of his bony knees. "We're very different, Debbi and me."

"Dat's obvious. So what?"

"So—" He started but found he had nowhere to go.

The Godfather could not be lied to, and Arty knew that their differences weren't the point. The point was his old reluctance, which had lately risen up like a dormant disease, making him withdraw, making him jittery, glum, guilty in his desire to be lonely. ·

"Ahty, can I say somethin' ta you? Don't be a putz. You love this woman. You light up when she's around, you take joy in things, which, due respect, doesn't seem ta be what you're best at on your own. Ya let 'er get away, believe me, you're gonna kick your ass about it the resta your life."

Arty took a deep breath. The turned soil had a faintly minty smell, you had to be close to the ground to smell it. "You say that like someone who knows, Vincente."

"I know," the old man said. "I know."

"Tell me about it," said the ghostwriter.

The Godfather had been bent over too long now; the hinge at the bottom of his spine was starting to complain. Still kneeling, he slowly straightened at the waist, balled his fists above his scrawny buttocks as he strained to arch his back. Yellow sunshine poked through the parting strands of his old straw hat. He took the red bandanna from around his neck to mop his face. "Sometime," he said. "Sometime I'll tell ya."

"And about the fig tree," Arty said, "the one you piled the linoleum and tires on."

Vincente gave the echo of a smile from sixty years before.

"And about nightclubs in the forties," said the writer. "And Havana in the old days. And old cars—Stutzes, Packards. And about the code of honor back when it really was a code, a way to live. We still have a lot to talk about, Vincente."

The Godfather said nothing, just knelt there in the warm imported soil. His tangled brows rolled down like awnings, his black eyes slipped away as distant as the hopes and errors of desperate youth, and he listened to the rustling fronds that made an island sound, Latin, like maracas.

TROPICAL DEPRESSION

In LAURENCE SHAMES's stunning new novel, TROP-ICAL DEPRESSION, Murray Zemelman, a.k.a. "the bra king", wakes up one morning, pops a Prozac, and instead of doing himself in, leaves his trophy wife and boring lingerie business in New Jersey and heads out to Key West. There he meets up with Tommy Tarpon, a local Native American from an obscure tribe, and together they cook up a plan to build Key West's first legal gambling parlour on Tommy's tribal grounds – a tiny, alligator-infested island.

But other reptiles want in on the deal, including the local mafioso, and before you can say Bugsy Siegel, Murray and Tommy are fighting for their money and their lives in a battle of wits, writs and anti-depressants.

Now read on . . .

CHAPTER ONE

WHEN MURRAY ZEMELMAN, a.k.a. the Bra King, started up his car that morning, he had no clear idea whether he would go to work as usual, or sit there with the engine idling and the garage door tightly shut until he died. He was depressed, had been for several months. His mind had shriveled around its core of gloom like a drying apricot around its pit, and he saw no third alternative.

So he sat. He looked calmly through his windshield at the gardening tools put up for the winter, the rakes and saws hung exactingly on Peg-Board, his worthless second wife's golf bag suspended at a coquettish angle by its strap. The motor of his Lexus softly purred, nearly odorless exhaust turned bluish white in the chilly air. He breathed normally and told himself he wasn't choosing suicide, wasn't choosing anything. He was just sitting, numb, immobilized, gripped by an indifference so unruffled as to be easily mistaken for a state of grace.

Then, in a heartbeat, he was no longer indifferent. Anything but. Maybe it was just a final squirt of panic before the long oblivion. Maybe the Prozac, as dubious as vitamins in its effect these last few weeks, had suddenly kicked in.

Murray said aloud "Schmuck! Schmuck, you fuckin' nuts?"

He reached for his zapper, flashed it at the garage door's electric eye. The wooden panels stretched, then started rolling upward, but not quite fast enough for Murray in his newfound rage to live. He threw the gearshift into reverse and stomped on the accelerator. Tires screeched on cold cement, the trunk caught the bottom of the lifting door. Varnished cedar splintered; champagne-colored paint scraped off the car, snaggled boards clawed at its metal roof. The bent garage door rose almost to the top of its track, then jammed, the mechanism whirred and whined like a Mixmaster bogged in icing.

Murray Zemelman, gasping and sweating on his driveway, opened his window and sucked greedily at the freezing air with its smells of pine and snow. He coughed, gave a dry and showy retch, mopped his clammy forehead. A shudder made him squirm against the leather seat, and when the long spasm had passed, he felt mysteriously light, unburdened. New. He felt as though a pinching iron helmet had been taken from his head and a grainy gray diffusing film swept clean from his eyes. He blinked against the sidearm brightness of a January sunrise; in his refreshed vision, the glare became a glow that caressed objects and displayed them proudly, like a spotlight that was everywhere at once.

Amazed, Murray looked at his house, looked at it as if he'd never seen it before. It was a nice house, a grand house even—big stone chimney, portico with columns—and in his sudden clarity he was able to acknowledge, not with sorrow but ecstasy, that he hated it. Yes! He hated every goddamn tile and dimmer switch and shingle. This was not the house's fault, he understood; but nor was it his. He'd worked his whole life to have a house like this; he'd paid through the nose to own it. By God, he was *allowed* to hate it. To hate the plaid-pants town of Short Hills, New Jersey, where it stood. To hate the dopey high-end gewgaws that cluttered up the living room. To hate the stupidly chosen second wife curled in bland, smug, already-fading beauty on her own side of the giant bed.

He hated all of it, and in the wake of the nasty and forbidden joy of admitting that, came a realization as buoyant as the feeling of flying in a dream. He didn't have to be there.

He didn't have to be there; he didn't have to go to work; he didn't have to kill himself. He remembered with surprise and awe that the world was big, and for the first time in what seemed like forever, he had a fresh idea.

He wheeled out of his driveway, burned rubber around a sooty snowbank, and headed for the Parkway south.

He drove all day, he drove all night, giddy and relentless in his quest for warmth and ease and differentness.

At nine-thirty the next morning, he was draped across his steering wheel, dozing lightly in yellow sunshine cut into strips by the tendrils of a palm frond. His back ached, his jowls drooped, his hips and knees were locked in the shape of the seat, but he'd outdistanced I-95, barrelled to the final mile of U.S. 1. He'd made it to Key West.

By first light he'd found a real estate office called Paradise Properties. He'd parked his scratched-up Lexus at a bent meter and then contentedly passed out.

He was awakened now by a light tapping on his windshield.

He looked up to see a slightly built young man in blue-lensed sunglasses. The young man made his hands into a megaphone. "Looking for a place?"

"How'd ya know?" said Murray, rolling down the window.

"Jersey plates," the young man said, more softly. "Ya got a tie on. And, no offense, you're very pale." He held out a hand. "Joey Goldman. Come in when you're ready, we're putting up coffee."

Murray yawned, climbed out of the car, tried to stretch but nothing stretched. He saw yellow flowers, flowers on a living tree in January. He sucked air that smelled of salt and iodine, air the same temperature as his face. He smiled tentatively then dragged himself into the office.

Joey Goldman, at his desk now, regarded him. Joey had lived in Key West half a decade. He knew that almost everyone who came there, came there on vacation—and there was nothing duller in the world than a person on vacation. Some came to snorkel and drink. Others came to drink and fish. Some came to chase sex while drinking. Others just drank. But one visitor in a thousand, Joey had observed, probably more like one in ten thousand, was not a tourist but a refugee. Sometimes it was refugee as in fugitive. Sometimes it was refugee from a monster spouse or lover, or from a northern life that had finally hit the wall. Joey looked at the new arrival's houndlike bloodshot eyes, his kinky graying wild hair, his rumpled shirt and posture that somehow seemed exhausted and frenetic all at once. He decided that maybe the frazzled fellow was not there on vacation.

"So, Mr.—"

"Zemelman, Murray Zemelman."

"Some coffee, Mr. Zemelman?"

Murray nodded his thanks and an assistant brought over a cup for him.

Joey said, "What can I do for you?"

Murray held his java in both hands and gave a little slurp. "Place on the ocean."

"Onnee ocean," Joey said, "that'd have to be a condo. No rental houses onnee ocean."

"Condo's fine."

Joey cleared his throat. "What price range—"

"Someplace nice."

"You know the town?"

"Not well," said Murray. "I was here once, twelve, maybe fifteen years ago."

"Ah," said Joey.

"With my first wife," the Bra King volunteered.

"Ah. Well—"

"And yesterday I was thinking," Murray rambled. "I don't mean thinking like *trying* to think, I mean the thought just came to me, out of the blue, that maybe it was the last time I really had fun."

Joey riffled through his boxful of listings.

"The crazy things ya remember," Murray went on. "This old Spanish guy, big hairy birthmark on his cheek, like four feet tall. Had a big block of ice on a cart. Shaved it by hand, with a whaddycallit, a plane. Put it in a paper cone with mango syrup. Franny loved it. Cost fifteen cents."

Joey pulled out an index card. "You know where Smathers Beach is, Mr. Zemelman?"

Murray blinked himself back to the present. "By the airport, no?"

"Up that way," said Joey. "There's a condo there, the Paradiso."

" 'S'nice?"

"Very nice. Coupla former mayors live there. State senator lives there when he's not up at the capital."

Murray yawned.

"There's a penthouse available," Joey went on.

"Penthouse?" Murray said. "Like thirty stories up?"

"Like three stories up. We're not talkin' Miami. It's a little pricey—"

"On the ocean?"

"Across the road. We're not talkin' Boca. Three bedrooms. Three baths. Master suite has jacuzzi—"

"Okay," Murray said.

"Okay what?

"Okay I'll take it."

"You don't wanna see it first?" said Joey.

Murray shrugged dismissively and reached into a pocket for his checkbook. "Company check okay?"

"Fine," said Joey. "It's five thousand a month and they'll want a month's security."

"I'll take three months for now," said Murray, and he wrote a check for twenty grand.

Joey took it and examined it briefly, discreetly. The company name rang a bell. "Hey, wait a second," he said. "BeautyBreast, Inc. Murray Zemelman. I thought you looked familiar. The guy that does the ads, right? Late at night. Wit' the crown. The Bra King crown. Always wit' the women in their bras."

"*My* bras," Murray corrected softly.

"Dancin' with 'em," Joey remembered. "Bowling, playing volleyball—"

Murray nodded modestly.

"My favorite?" Joey said. "The opera one, the one where all these women in their bras got spears and shields, and you come down, what're you wearin', a bathrobe, somethin'?—"

"Toga," said the Bra King. "I didn't know they aired down here."

"Me, I'm from New Yawk," said Joey. "Everybody here, they're from somewhere else." He opened a desk drawer, pawed his way through many sets of keys. "The Bra King," he muttered, "whaddya know . . . Okay, this is them. The square key, it's for the downstairs lock. The round one's for the penthouse. There's three buildings, like in a **U** around the pool. You want West. Got it?"

Murray took the keys and nodded.

Joey shook his hand, stole a final look at him, almost spoke, but realized it would be indiscreet to ask if they touched his hair up for TV.

Tropical Depression

is now available in Macmillan

hardback priced £15.99

All Pan Books are available at your local bookshop or newsagent, or can be ordered direct from the publisher. Indicate the number of copies required and fill in the form below.

Send to: Macmillan General Books C.S.
                Book Service By Post
                PO Box 29, Douglas I-O-M
                IM99 1BQ

or phone: 01624 675137, quoting title, author and credit card number.

or fax: 01624 670923, quoting title, author, and credit card number.

or Internet: http://www.bookpost.co.uk

Please enclose a remittance* to the value of the cover price plus 75 pence per book for post and packing. Overseas customers please allow £1.00 per copy for post and packing.

*Payment may be made in sterling by UK personal cheque, Eurocheque, postal order, sterling draft or international money order, made payable to Book Service By Post.

Alternatively by Access/Visa/MasterCard

Card No.   ☐☐☐☐☐☐☐☐☐☐☐☐☐☐☐☐☐☐☐

Expiry Date ☐☐☐☐☐☐☐☐☐☐☐☐☐☐☐☐☐☐☐

Signature   _____

Applicable only in the UK and BFPO addresses.

While every effort is made to keep prices low, it is sometimes necessary to increase prices at short notice. Pan Books reserve the right to show on covers and charge new retail prices which may differ from those advertised in the text or elsewhere.

NAME AND ADDRESS IN BLOCK CAPITAL LETTERS PLEASE

Name _____

Address _____

_____

_____

_____

8/95

Please allow 28 days for delivery.
Please tick box if you do not wish to receive any additional information. ☐